GRAY LADY'S REVENGE

ANNIE REED

ROBERT JESCHONEK

BLASTOFF
BOOKS

GRAY LADY'S REVENGE

Published by Blastoff Books

PRAISE FOR GRAY LADY'S REVENGE

"Annie... and Bob? Writing together? Folks, this is epic!"
 – Dean Wesley Smith, Editor, *Pulphouse Fiction Magazine*

"By the brilliant hands of Robert Jeschonek and Annie Reed, *Gray Lady's Revenge* rejects any trace of the flattened scifi woman. Stature doesn't hold over the skill of this weathered, whirlwind protagonist, whose level of trust in her own ass-kicking ability never bows to the strident influences of intergalactic law enforcement or arrogant old flames, much less to towering, shrouded foes. Space frontierism is subverted in this sharp-staked story that makes way for sensitive and authentic relationships and tender sacrifice, while still never forgetting to leave room for brawling badassery throughout."
 – L. Daniel, Reviewer

"*Gray Lady's Revenge* sweeps readers into a captivating intergalactic odyssey led by the charismatic pair of Augusta Light and Mephistopheles Drake. At the core of this adventure is Augusta Light, a formidable female protagonist radiating strength, dynamism, and determination. Penned by Robert Jeschonek and Annie Reed, the novel intricately constructs a universe teeming with complexity, heartwarming bonds, and spirited exchanges. For any fan of science fiction, this novel will prove not only entertaining, but deeply thought provoking. "
 – Bill Baker, Reviewer

ALSO BY ANNIE REED

ALSO BY ROBERT JESCHONEK

CHAPTER 1

The fifth time the shipboard replicator refused to spit out the last part Augusta Light needed to finish repairs to the *Golden Void's* weapons control system, she was ready to resort to an old armor jock's trick:

Hit the thing with a hammer.

Hard.

She sat back on her heels in front of the open panel that concealed the guts of the ship's replicator and muttered a few choice curses under her breath. Replicator guts weren't reinforced steel, they were advanced circuitry and programming and all sorts of delicate things that a hammer would obliterate. So hitting the thing with a hammer to let off steam was out of the question. But she was *this close* to climbing into her armor, jetting out the airlock, and blasting away at the closest piece of space junk. If nothing else, it would make her feel better.

Except she couldn't do that either.

She needed to replace one of the space-tight seals on her armor. And she couldn't do *that* because the replicator refused to spit out anything that vaguely resembled a space-tight seal.

She ran a hand through her short-cropped gray hair. A controlled blast from a laser pistol into the guts of the replicator might do the trick. She grinned as she imagined the delicate wiring and circuitry charred and smoking as sparks flew from the open panel.

Gus Light, the famous Gray Lady of Armor Division 83 (retired), had never been known for her patience.

Most people thought she got the nickname Gray Lady from her hair. She'd gone gray early in life. She'd never done anything about it. She was a military armor jock, not a fashion model. She climbed into a few tons of steel on a regular basis. The armor was man shaped with a full steel helmet that clamped over her head. Who needed to change hair color when most of the time nobody even saw your face?

But her hair was only part of the reason for the nickname. She'd enlisted in the Armor Division of the Free Worlds Alliance military when she'd been barely eighteen. She'd not only been the youngest trainee, she'd been the only woman in her squad. She was short and stocky and female, and no one had taken her seriously, especially not her instructors. She'd decided the only way she'd survive as an armor jock was to become the biggest badass in the history of armor jocks.

The first thing she did was ditch the name Augusta.

She became Gus Light, a balls-to-the-wall fighter in and out of her armor. She took no shit from anyone, including her instructors if and when she didn't agree with them. She started to outshine most of the men in Armor Division, even those with twenty years or more in the service. Gus Light, the woman no one expected to last through training, was kicking ass.

Most of the time, anyway.

Of course, that didn't sit well with some of the men in her squad. One day she came back from a particularly disastrous training session her instructor had set up to try to teach her to work with her squad instead of trying to outshoot everyone only to find that her name on her locker had been scratched out. *Gray Lady* had been etched on the metal in its place.

"Bow to the lady, gents," someone had called out, and everyone laughed.

She'd hated the nickname. She'd hated how they'd meant it—that she'd never be one of them, a *real* armor jock, just a spoiled brat pretending to be a high and mighty lady. A showoff who'd get them all killed on the battlefield.

But she never let them see how she felt. She'd played along, even sketching a curtsey before she flipped them off. Then she'd redoubled her efforts, both in the training sessions and in the weight room. She studied battle tactics, read every book she could find on the use of armored infantry in modern warfare. She listened to her instructors and learned how to work *with* her squad. Practiced how to be the best individual armor jock but still be part of the team.

Throughout it all, the nickname stuck.

By the time she'd been awarded the first of many medals she'd earned for bravery on the battlefield in the face of overwhelming odds, nobody used the name to make fun of her anymore. Not that it mattered. She'd embraced the nickname. She *was* the Gray Lady. A hellion in battle. A berserker who didn't know the meaning of the word quit. A Viking warrior who dealt death and destruction to any enemy who dared cross her path.

A force to be reckoned with.

And now she couldn't fix a damn replicator?

"Son of a—"

The sound of a guitar interrupted the start of a very long, very inventive string of curses she planned to send the replicator's way.

The access panel for the replicator's guts was in one of the interior corridors on the *Golden Void*. If he wasn't needed on the bridge, the captain of the *Void*, Mephistopheles Drake, had a habit of strolling through the corridors strumming old cowboy tunes on his antique guitar.

When he wasn't engaged in other, more pleasurable pursuits with her.

"Did I just catch you swearing at *my* ship?" His grin told her he knew exactly what she was swearing at.

"*Your* damn ship deserves it."

She got to her feet, her knees protesting the movement. The *Void* maintained near-Earth gravity and it had a decent workout area in the cargo bay, but nothing beat planetside exercise. Or even a few days working out on a good-sized space station. They hadn't docked anywhere in almost a month, and Gus felt it in her muscles and joints. Space was supposed to be easier on old bones, not that Gus was all that old. But even in her sixties and a decade removed from active military service, she was still an armor jock who kept herself in shape. If she didn't get some exercise in soon, more than her knees were going to start giving her grief.

"And here I thought you could fix anything," he said.

She could. All armor jocks knew their way around whatever tools were needed to repair their armor on the fly. Most of them, Gus included, also knew how to fix essential systems on a ship—life support, navigation, propulsion—to keep themselves alive if their transport ship got into trouble.

Gus had taught herself more than just the essentials. She'd modified her armor, something the military strictly forbade, and fiddled with enough different ships' systems that she'd earned the respect of most ship mechanics and engineers. She'd never met a ship she couldn't fly single-handed or a security system she couldn't hack. The problem with the *Void* was that only half its systems were state of the art. The rest were anachronisms never meant for use outside a museum. Like the steering wheel Drake insisted on using for maneuvering in a planet's atmosphere, the joystick he steered the ship with in space, and all the knobs and dials and switches on the control panels instead of holo controls and touchscreens.

The *Void's* replicator was the bastard lovechild of high-tech meets Stone Age. If she didn't need a replicator to kick out the parts for the weapons control system and her armor's leaky seal, she really would be tempted to just hit it with a hammer or fry it with a laser blast.

She didn't bother to say any of that. She just stood glaring at him, hands on her hips.

Drake strummed another couple of chords, then slung

the guitar around on its strap until it was hanging upside down against his back.

"Anybody ever tell you that you're cute when you're angry?" he asked.

"Then I must look skudging adorable because—"

He interrupted her with a kiss.

His kiss tasted like cinnamon. Drake chewed gum like it was going out of style, and cinnamon was his favorite.

Before she could protest that he wasn't fighting fair, his arms circled her shoulders and drew her in close, and the light kiss turned serious. Her annoyance didn't stand a chance. She lost herself in the taste of cinnamon and the feel of strong muscles against her own.

Drake wore the persona of a laid-back cowboy who belonged in a long-ago era like she wore her armor, but he'd been a smuggler for a long time before she'd met him. Underneath that persona was a backbone made of steel. He had grit and determination and courage, and a whole lot of smarts. And it didn't hurt that he was more than easy on the eyes, what with his salt-and-pepper hair and beard and eyes that most always held a glint of good humor.

For some reason, he liked her, and she didn't make it easy. It wasn't just because they were the only two people on the ship. She'd had relationships like that in the past. Encounters that were mostly physical and more about passing the time or releasing tension than anything else. But with Drake it was different. There were feelings involved. There was gentle teasing and mind-blowing sex and long conversations that actually meant something.

And pillow fights.

She couldn't remember ever laughing as much as she had during their first pillow fight. That had been the first time they'd been together in his cabin, when she'd discovered that his guitar wasn't the only old-fashioned thing on the ship (besides all the knobs and dials and switches). He actually had a down comforter and feather pillows on his bed.

She'd teased him about the pillows to the point that he'd smacked her with one of them. She'd retaliated with the other—no one beat the Gray Lady in a fight, even one fought solely with pillows.

One of the pillows had eventually ripped, sending feathers floating everywhere like thick, fluffy snowflakes. They'd laughed until tears ran down their faces, and then they'd had mind-blowing sex that, for the first time, felt like it was something more than merely physical.

She could keep right on kissing him now, which would lead to more mind-blowing sex—maybe right there in the corridor, one of the joys of being the only two people on the ship—but they did actually have a mission: tracking down the weaselly bastard who'd tried to kill Gus not once, but twice. They couldn't get on with it—the mission, not the sex —until the weapons control board, not to mention her armor, was fixed. She couldn't fix either one as long as the replicator refused to replicate.

She pushed Drake away with a gentle hand on his chest. He stared at her mouth for a long moment with eyes that were dark and serious, then his laid-back grin took over his expression and he took a step back.

"We're going to have to replace that replicator," she said. "It's a piece of crap."

"It's an old piece of crap," he agreed, "that doesn't have your stamina." He winked at her. "Or your sex appeal."

"Thank God." She wondered just how many years he'd been alone on this ship, and then decided she didn't want to know.

"You've got to admit that we've been abusing the poor thing," he said.

She thought about saying *Not as much as you have,* then decided not to.

Besides, they *had* been abusing the replicator. The *Void,* not to mention Gus's armor, had taken a beating not that long ago. The replicator was rated for use on a cargo vessel, which was the *Void's* official purpose. All the hidden compartments in the walls and in between decks had been what the designers would have called after-market additions. So were some of the more serious weapons Drake had used to save both their skins. The replicator wasn't meant to be used to replace armor or hull plates or meters and meters of fried wiring and dozens of charred circuit boards.

If they were still in Alliance space, they could just dock at the nearest space station and buy a new replicator with a higher rating. But they weren't in Alliance space. They were in the Frontier where things like friendly space stations, much less well-stocked friendly space stations, were a rarity. Going into potentially hostile territory without a working weapons control panel or space-worthy armor was just asking for trouble. And continuing with their mission without Gus's armor, not to mention the *Void* at one hundred percent, was just plain suicide.

"The Frontier's your territory, space cowboy," she said. "Any idea where we can pick up something to give this poor old abused replicator a rest without getting blown out of the sky?"

His grin widened. "As a matter of fact..."

She cocked an eyebrow at him. He was going to draw this out. For fun? Or for something else?

Sometimes she thought she had him all figured out, and then she'd have to remind herself that Drake had been a smuggler for a long, long time. Not always a successful one, judging by how down on his luck he'd been when she'd first met him, but he'd been good enough to keep himself in one piece even out on the Frontier. Smugglers survived on wits and charm, and Drake could charm the pants off anyone. He'd certainly charmed the pants off her.

Although she liked to think that last bit had worked both ways.

"Spill," she said.

Instead of answering her immediately, he swung his guitar around and strummed the first few chords of "Back in the Saddle Again." She stifled a groan. That was his *I've got something up my sleeve* song.

"As a matter of fact, there's someone I know," he said, "not too far away from here. Stocks everything and anything a respectable smuggler might need to stay in business."

"Reasonable?"

"Fairly," he said.

"Friendly?" she asked.

His eyes twinkled. Actually twinkled. "Fairly," he said.

She would have punched him in the shoulder, but she didn't want to hurt the guitar. It really was an antique.

"Give me the coordinates," she said. "I'll program them in."

"Already did that," he said.

Son of a…

"You *knew* I wouldn't be able to fix the damn thing," she said. "Before you even came down here, you knew we'd need a new one."

"What can I say? The replicator came with the ship. Until you hired me and got me involved in that little dust-up?" He shrugged. "Didn't think I'd need to replace it."

Translation: Until she'd hired him and paid a pretty penny for his services, he couldn't afford to replace it.

Or more precisely—before she'd hired the *ship.*

She should have double-checked the replicator back then, but she'd been in a hurry and all she'd done was make sure the skudging thing still worked. She had a history with the *Golden Void* long before Drake had ever set eyes on the ship. It had gotten her and her squad out of a jam thirty years ago, and this time with Drake at the controls, it had saved her life again.

She still had a good feeling about the ship. Not about its replicator, which they'd overworked until it was nothing more than a piece of space junk, but that was just a part they could replace. She'd certainly replaced enough parts in her armor over the years, and that hadn't changed the fact that it was *her* armor, the same armor that had saved her life on the battlefield time and time again.

This time she did hit his shoulder, more of a shove than a punch. "Well, what are you waiting for?" she said. "Fire up those engines and let's go see this friend of yours."

He chuckled as he turned around to head off to the

bridge, still strumming that damn song. "I never said she was a friend."

Gus caught the *she*.

"More like an old girlfriend," he added over his shoulder.

Suddenly the "fairly friendly" made sense. Smugglers were con men too, and if he'd conned the wrong woman…

"She going to shoot at us?" Gus asked. "Need I remind you we don't have weapons control up and running?"

He didn't say anything, just kept strumming that dumb song.

"Drake?"

"Don't worry," he called before he disappeared toward the bridge. "She's gonna love you."

"What about you?" she called after him, but he was gone.

Fairly friendly could mean a whole galaxy of things. Like stay in your ship or I'll blow your brains out, or like…

"'Back in the Saddle,'" Gus muttered. Yeah, like that.

She kicked the replicator's open panel so she wouldn't punch the wall. He'd been playing that song the first time he'd invited her to join him for a drink of the good stuff.

It had been Drake's prelude to a good, solid flirt.

He was taking them both to see his ex. To ask her for a favor. Just what was he hoping to trade in return? Getting back in the saddle while he was still—metaphorically speaking—in hers?

"Dream on, space cowboy," she said as she aimed another kick at the poor abused replicator. "Dream on."

CHAPTER 2

A good cowboy never let on that he was nervous…yet that was exactly how Drake felt as the *Golden Void* drew closer to Chrysallix, a planetoid deep in the Obsidiac system. It didn't help that Chrysallix was familiar ground, and at least one familiar face awaited him there; if anything, all that just made it more nerve-wracking.

But he was determined to keep his case of nerves to himself, to hide it from Gus…even as his blood ran a little on the cold side, and his legs and fingers tightened and twitched with tension. At least he didn't have to worry about keeping it from her at the moment, since she was elsewhere, probably tending to her armor or still fighting with the replicator while he kept the *Void* on course. It was probably a good thing that he'd hidden the hammer he kept on board, or the replicator would be toast by now.

Damn, but she looked good when she was all riled up.

He liked to needle her sometimes just to get her good and riled up, because then things got *really* good.

What would she think of him if she realized just how nervous he was at the thought of setting foot on Chrysallix again?

As good as his relationship with Gus had gotten, as much as they'd shared, just the two of them alone on the *Void*, he still instinctively played certain cards close to his vest. He wanted her to think of him as strong, in control, and mysterious in all the best ways, not a sap who'd let himself be taken advantage of by a pretty face back in the day.

Hell, *he* didn't like to think of himself as a sap who'd been taken advantage of by a pretty face.

That, of course, could get tricky, as he was taking both of them to see that very face. A face that belonged to a woman named Rhapsody Harrison.

"Is she gonna shoot at us?" Gus had asked.

Good question.

He'd ignored her question because he really didn't know the answer. The way he'd left things with Rhapsody, it could go either way.

Reclining in his padded pilot seat on the *Void*'s bridge, he strummed random chords on his guitar and wondered what Rhapsody looked like these days. She'd been a stunner and a half—a tall, sultry blonde with flashing green eyes and proportions he'd considered beyond perfect...plus a hint of genetic modification or alien DNA that gave her features an exotic look and a trace of a golden glow. The day they'd met, her looks had left him tongue-tied. All his natural charm had deserted him. He'd found her utterly

14

irresistible; so had every male in the quadrant, and plenty of females and other-genders, too. Just thinking about her in her prime set his engines to revving.

Of course, Gus set his engines to revving pretty much every day. Gus was a dynamo. Rhapsody? She'd been a siren.

But a lot could have changed over the last six years, he knew, and the truth was, he might not get to see her at all. They hadn't parted as mortal enemies, but they hadn't been the best of friends at the end, either. It was very possible she might turn him away before he reached orbit.

Though *that* wasn't the possibility he was most nervous about, to be honest.

Drake played a run of notes on the guitar—part of a new number he'd been working on called "Have the Years Been Kind?" It wasn't one he'd be sharing with Gus, since it expressed his speculations about Rhapsody...but the song had a Western twang, and he liked it. Writing new material was something he'd recently returned to for the first time in ages; he'd been away from it forever, it seemed, but lately he'd been feeling alive and inspired again. He probably had Gus to thank for that. In fact, he had a heck of a love-song ditty just waiting to be played for her once he put a few finishing touches on it.

But first, it was time to call his old girlfriend.

After plucking a few more notes, he spoke to the *Void*'s resident AI, knowing his voice would carry over the nearest microphone pickups. "Ship. Hail Chrysallix Central and transmit the following message: 'Independent freighter *Golden Void* calling Rhapsody Harrison. Reply requested.'"

"Hailing now."

The AI's male voice was deep and resonant over the speaker. Gus had taken to referring to the AI by various names since her arrival, most recently settling on "Earl." Drake had no idea why, and Gus hadn't explained herself. For all he knew, Earl could have been an armor jock she'd served with. Or someone she'd released tension with, which was Gus's way of saying that armor jocks hadn't exactly been celibate between missions.

As a long moment passed with no response to his hail, Drake got up, set aside the guitar, and planted himself at the navigation station. With practiced ease, he brought up an image of the approaching planetoid on the nearest viewscreen with a series of knob twists, switch flips, and button pushes. The controls were antiquated—his personal preference—but functional. He would never willingly swap them out for cutting edge holographic or touchless, thought-directed interfaces. Gus, to her credit, had made the best of them and never suggested an upgrade...though Drake knew darn well that a persuasive argument could be made for such a change.

"Chrysallix Central responds as follows," said Earl, interrupting Drake's thoughts. "'Interrogative: Who is speaking, *Golden Void*? Provide identifying nomenclature and reason for approach.'"

Chrysallix Central. Identifying nomenclature. Pretty darn formal for Rhapsody. She hadn't been that formal six years ago. Sure, even back then she was well on her way to becoming the hottest thing on Chrysallix—and he wasn't talking sex appeal—not to mention the most powerful, but the place was still just a Frontier planetoid with no central government that he knew of and definitely no ties to the Free Worlds Alliance.

"Send the following, Ship. This is Captain Mephistopheles Drake speaking. Reason for approach: urgent equipment request...and reminiscing while sharing top-shelf hooch with the woman formerly known in certain circles as Madame Buttercup."

Drake grinned. Let's see what his old girlfriend made of *that.*

"Sending," said Earl.

"Madame *what* now?" Gus asked.

Of course, she would hear *that.* She just happened to be standing in the doorway of the bridge at the exact wrong moment. He'd never even heard her come in. The door to the bridge hadn't made its customary *whoosh.*

Had she fiddled with the door? Gus was one damn fine mechanic and systems engineer. He was pretty sure she'd tweaked the AI's programming to get it to respond in that deep, resonant, *male* voice. He wouldn't put it past her to futz with all the doors on the ship just so she could sneak up on him.

How long she'd been back there listening to him, Drake didn't know—but he felt like she'd caught him red-handed. "Think of it as a call sign," he said. Determined not to appear rattled, he turned and grinned at her. "From back in the day."

"Call sign, right." She did not look amused.

To an extent, that was all right with Drake. If Gus was a little jealous of an old girlfriend of his, he'd be flattered. It showed she cared...and that wasn't always apparent from her sometimes gruff demeanor. She was much mellower now than when they'd first met, no question, and not stingy about showing her affection or telling him how she felt—but sometimes, her mood darkened, and he couldn't quite read her intentions.

Maybe, at times like that, she closed up some because she was thinking about her son—Nicholas Freemantle, the governor of Shepard's Moon. She'd left him behind twice now, once decades ago when he'd been a newborn baby and she'd been forced to flee with what was left of her squad, and again just a few weeks ago after she and Drake had saved her son's bacon from a warlord intent on installing himself as the leader of Shepard's Moon, no matter how many people he had to kill to get there.

Not that Nicholas knew Gus was his mother. She'd never told him.

Drake couldn't imagine what that must be like for her, knowing her grown son was out there and would never know who she really was. Right before they'd left Shepard's Moon behind, she'd told him that she wasn't going to tell Nicholas she was his birth mother because it was best for her son and the life he'd made for himself. When she got quiet and her mood got dark, it was pretty clear the decision hadn't been the best for her.

Whatever the cause of her occasional gloom, he definitely sensed there were times when he shouldn't pry. She was entitled to keep her dark moods to herself; depending on how things went in the next few minutes, he might be having a few of his own.

This didn't feel like one of those moody times, though. This felt like a bit of good old-fashioned jealousy. And if a little show of jealousy on her part put some positive reinforcement in the bank for a rainy day, he didn't think it would be such a bad thing.

He'd just have to make sure there were no misunderstandings between them. He wouldn't *mind* seeing Rhapsody, but he hadn't come all the way to Chrysallix with the notion of scuttling his thing with Gus—which was, by far, the best, most gratifying romantic relationship he'd ever had. He and Gus could not have been more perfect for each other, and he had no intention of letting anything or anyone get in the way of that.

Not even a stunning sex bomb who'd already proved she could turn his life upside-down.

"Captain," said Earl. "Chrysallix Central requests immediate real-time channel."

Real time. Okay, let's get this show on the road.

Drake popped out of the nav station, straightened his blue-and-black plaid flannel shirt, and ran his hands over his salt-and-pepper hair and beard. He was gratified to see that his hands weren't trembling—much—but his heartbeat had kicked into overdrive.

Gus snorted. "Preening, are we? I can't wait to see this ex."

Way to blow his laid-back, cool-as-a-cucumber, talking-to-my-ex-doesn't-faze-me-one-bit, space cowboy vibe. If Rhapsody hadn't been waiting on the other end of the communication, he would have blown a razzberry in Gus's direction.

"Request granted," he told Earl, pleased with himself that his voice didn't betray his sudden case of the nerves.

Lowering himself into the pilot seat, he cleared his throat, waiting for the channel to open…very aware of Gus hovering somewhere behind him, though he chose not to turn to see if she was actually in range of the camera.

"Channel open," said Earl.

As the comm system emitted its familiar activation warble, Drake smiled at the multipurpose viewer directly ahead. *Be that charming, handsome rogue she'd first met*, he told himself. Don't let anyone know that his heart was still racing as he waited for the video feed of Rhapsody to appear, looking back at him for the first time in ages.

Except she didn't.

Instead of Rhapsody's stunningly gorgeous face, he saw the planetoid's seal—a circle encompassing two crossed laser rifles with a huge diamond between them—shimmering in gold against a black background, straight off the flag of Chrysallix.

Frowning, Drake waited, but the feed didn't change, and he got the message. To his disappointment, she was going deny him what he'd been both dreading and expecting: getting a look at Rhapsody Harrison in all her glory.

He tried not to slump in his chair. She could still see *him*, after all.

And he could still hear her voice, loud and clear. One-hundred percent pure Rhapsody came through over the bridge speakers, just as sultry and smoky as he remembered…so perfect, in fact, that he got a little thrill just at the sound of it.

"'Madame Buttercup,' *chér*?"

She still had the slightest touch of an accent—part Caribbean, part European, and part something entirely different. He'd never known if it was natural or an affectation or maybe an enhancement, not that it mattered. He'd always found her accent incredibly sexy, at least when spoken by her. On Gus, it would have been ridiculous.

"Now *that* is certainly a blast from the past." Her laugh, as before, was a throaty purr.

"Hello again, Rhap." He couldn't resist grinning, even as the lack of a video transmission from Chrysallix annoyed him. "Long time no see." *And getting longer by the minute.*

If she caught the dig, she ignored it. "So what is this about an *urgent equipment request?*" she asked. "Did your homemade *still* stop producing the good stuff again?"

Drake laughed. "Replicator trouble, actually. We can't generate the parts we need to keep this bucket of bolts flying."

There was a slight pause and an even slighter chill to her voice when she asked, "What do you mean, 'we'?"

Drake smiled ruefully. Naturally, she'd zeroed right in on that particular choice of words. As a rule, he remembered, not much got by her.

"My shipmate and I." Looking over his shoulder, he saw Gus standing just out of camera range and shot her a wink. "Name's Gus."

"Good for him." Was that a twinge of relief in Rhapsody's voice? "Must be one hell of a crewman if you let him onboard your precious *Golden Void.*"

"It's Gus as in *Augusta*, actually," said Drake. "Not a crew *man* at all."

"You have a dog? Pets make the best company, don't they? Especially females."

"Wrong again, Rhap. Augusta's all woman...and yes, she *is* one hell of a crewperson." *Among many other things,* he wanted to add, but thought better of it.

"Ah." Rhapsody sounded disappointed, and the pause was longer this time before she came back. "So it turns out *our* replicators have been glitching lately, too. We might not be able to provide the replacement parts you so urgently need, old friend."

Old friend. From *chér* to old friend in record time, even for her.

Of course, this could just be the start of haggling over price. An opening salvo, Rhapsody style.

"Sorry to hear that," he said, putting the slightest tinge of regret into his voice. Return salvo, space cowboy style: *I can always shop somewhere else. It's a big universe.*

"I mean, we are only too happy to help if we *can*, of course…but you know how it is on the Frontier. The supply chain can get a little sketchy, even for me."

All right! She was actually backtracking. Giving herself a little wiggle room. Score one for the home team. Drake did a mental fist-pump.

"How about I send you the specs?" he asked. "Then you can check around a little while we make landfall."

Again, Rhapsody paused. "I would hate for you to come all the way down here for nothing."

More negotiating tactics. She wanted to know how easily he could be put off. She should know better, but then again, it had been six years.

He chuckled. "You call talking about the old days over a bottle of the good stuff *nothin'*? Because I sure don't see it that way."

"Well…"

The line went silent again…so long that Drake worried he might have gone too far and she'd hung up on him. The thought of it made him feel let down, though it shouldn't have; whatever they'd shared together, it was years gone and not coming back. He didn't *want* it back, either—but part of him didn't savor the thought of being rejected outright by her nonetheless.

It was a part he hoped Gus never picked up on. She might not appreciate that another woman had any kind of hold on his fragile male ego.

"Drake?" Finally, Rhapsody's voice returned to the call. "*Of course* you and Augusta are welcome on Chrysallix. I do indeed look forward to reminiscing...though you do not have to bring that bottle of good stuff with you."

"Why is that?"

"I quit drinking three years ago," she said. "I never touch that brew you are so fond of anymore."

"Well, congratulations," said Drake. "Good for you, Rhap."

"What about you, *chér*? Have you quit all *your* bad habits?" She said it with a mischievous twist at the end.

Drake knew all too well what habits she was referring to. "Depends who you talk to, I guess." He chuckled.

Rhapsody laughed along with him. He didn't have to see her face to know she had a twinkle in her eyes. Making Rhapsody laugh had been a favorite pastime of his.

"Okay, then," she said. "My people will send coordinates to our spaceport, and someone will be there to meet you when you land."

"Much obliged," said Drake.

"See you when you get here, Meph." Then almost as an afterthought. "See you *both*, I mean."

"See you then."

23

He was about to disconnect—he was getting tired of staring at the crossed laser rifles on his viewscreen—when Rhapsody said something else.

"Oh, and one more thing, *chér*. Do you still have that guitar of yours? The one you used to sing songs to me with?"

"Why? You want an encore?"

"I did not say *that*."

Without another word, she closed the channel, and the official seal of Chrysallix winked off the screen.

For the first time since the start of the call, Gus spoke. "*That* was your old girlfriend?"

Drake turned the pilot's chair to face her and shrugged. "Seemed like a good idea at the time."

"Was she as much of a sweetheart back then as she is now?"

"Pretty much, yeah. So far, she seems about the same from what I can tell."

"From that disembodied voice, you mean." Gus narrowed her eyes. "This ought to be an interesting visit."

"You might be right."

He wondered what she was getting at. As well as he'd gotten to know her since their shared struggle on Shepard's Moon, there were still times when he didn't have a clue what was going on in her head or what it might mean to him personally.

Gus crossed the bridge and checked the readouts on the nav console. "Looks like we're just an hour or so out. I'd better go get ready for our big face-to-face with her grace."

"Good, great," said Drake. "I'll confirm the two of us will be joining her."

"Don't bother," said Gus on her way out of the bridge. "She assumed I was an actual *dog*. No need to confirm you're bringing a guest if the guest is just a *pet*, right?"

Drake just sat there and watched the door slide shut behind her—again without its normal *whoosh*, he noted—and wondered how much trouble he was in already...and how much more there was to come by the time Rhapsody got done with him.

And Gus got done with her.

CHAPTER 3

Drake's ex-girlfriend had called her a pet. A pet! That had been one hell of an insulting assumption to make.

Young Gus, the one who'd set out to prove that she was just as good an armor jock, if not better, than the men in her squad, would have gone into take-no-prisoners mode at an insult like that. Oh, she wouldn't have blasted Rhapsody into billions of tiny pieces of space dust, but she would have made damn sure that *woman* never made another assumption like that again in her life. The Gray Lady who'd loathed the nickname wouldn't have let anyone compare her to a skudging *dog* and get away with it.

Gus liked to think she'd matured at least a little bit since then. Armor jocks had a reputation for relying on might to take down anyone who insulted them, but *smart* armor jocks used their brains as much as their armor's brawn.

Drake had corrected Rhapsody's assumption, but Gus had still given him shit before she'd stormed off the bridge.

She wanted him to think she was good and pissed, and not in a way that led to great sex. And if Drake was worried that she'd stormed off so she could throw a jealous little hissy fit in private? So much the better. That meant he'd be leaving her alone to give her time to calm down.

Gus didn't need to calm down. She wanted the alone time so she could think. There was something off about Rhapsody Harrison, and not just because the woman still had the ability to wrap Drake around her little finger.

Rhap, as Drake called her, oozed sex appeal, no question about that. It came through distinctly in the throaty purr of her voice, the little affectations she threw in here and there, like *chér*. So why would a woman who used an unspoken but clearly intended promise of sex not use one of the best tools available to show off her assets—video? Audio itself was fine, but audio and video together would be so much better.

Then there'd been that lag in communication when Drake had pressed for a face-to-face meeting. Rhap hadn't seemed too keen on the prospect of actually seeing her old boyfriend in person. She'd turned cold there for a moment, almost as coldly formal as that initial communication asking Drake to identify himself and his purpose. Did she have to clear their landing with someone else? From what little Drake had told Gus about Chrysallix, good old Rhap practically owned the place. So what gives?

Before Gus had snuck up on Drake on the bridge—she knew deleting the old-fashioned door-opening sounds from all the doors on the *Void* (except hers) would come in handy one day—she'd tried to find out what she could about Rhapsody from Earl. While Earl was able to spit out basic information about Chrysallix, there'd been not a single bit or byte of information in the ship's systems about Rhapsody. Earl didn't know anyone by that name. He couldn't even tell her if there'd ever been any information in the ship's computer about Drake's ex.

Gus couldn't imagine that Drake had been in a relationship with Rhapsody long enough for him to actually call it a relationship without mentioning the woman at least once while he'd been on board the *Void*. Hell, he'd probably written songs about her. But all that had been scrubbed from the computers.

That, if nothing else, told her how bad the breakup had been.

Now back in the relative privacy of the cargo bay, Gus accessed the ship's computer through the bay's terminal, the one she'd come to think of as hers. She wanted to double-check something, and she didn't want to use Earl to do it. She didn't think Drake would try to track her down to apologize, but just in case, she didn't want to get caught in a conversation about the kind of information she wanted from the ship's AI.

Drake wouldn't give it a second thought if he saw her working at the terminal. She used the cargo bay's terminal all the time when she was working on her armor. Her armor was stowed away in its usual spot in the bay, helmet off and powered down. The helmet was on the workbench next to Gus, an access panel on one side of the faceplate open. If Drake came in, he'd just think she was working on something she could fix while they were en route to Chrysallix.

Gus had no idea how long it had been since Drake had seen, much less talked to, Rhap. The way he'd preened on the bridge told her it had been a while...long enough for Drake to gloss over the bad times but not so long that memories of the good times had lost their hold on him.

Gus wanted to look at the dates of the entries in the *Void's* computer about Chrysallix. If it had been a couple of decades ago, she'd be dealing with a woman who'd screwed up Drake good and proper.

The initial entries in the computer had been made six years ago when the *Void* first made contact with Chrysallix. Drake had docked at the planetoid to offload some cargo. The computer files didn't say what he'd offloaded—not surprising; a smuggler wouldn't keep a record of exactly what he'd been smuggling—or whether Drake had loaded anything onto the ship.

She could have figured it out if she'd really wanted to simply by looking at fuel consumption records after he left. Her armor alone had added a couple of tons of weight to the *Void* when she'd first hired Drake to take her to Shepard's Moon, plus there'd been all the ordnance she took to go along with the armor. When she'd purchased fuel for the trip, she'd had to take all that extra weight into consideration. Even in space, propulsion calculations had to be accurate if you didn't want to find yourself floating in the literal middle of nowhere with an empty fuel tank and no place within reach to get any more.

Now what she started looking for was the date the *Void* had left Chrysallix. Just how long had it taken for Rhap to sink her claws into Drake anyway?

She didn't find just one date. She found a lot of them.

Gus frowned as she scanned the entries displayed on her terminal. Drake had come and gone a *lot* over a period of months. He was never gone for very long, and the *Void* had docked on the planetoid for longer and longer periods of time between trips.

"Son of a bitch," she muttered.

Drake had been smuggling *for* Rhapsody. That had to be it.

He had to have been making the trips for her. Short trips, all within the Obsidiac system. He didn't land the *Void* on any other planet or moon in the system or dock at any space station. As far as she could tell, there weren't any space stations anywhere in this sector of the Frontier. But he'd fly the *Void* to different coordinates within the system, hang out for a while—sometimes just a matter of hours—and then return to Chrysallix.

She was so intent on trying to dig up more information from the ship's computers that she nearly missed the chime on her chrono. She wanted to be back on the bridge when the ship made its final approach. She'd been unable to dig up any specs on the planetoid, and she wanted to see what they were getting into before they landed.

That was part of the problem with being exiled to the Frontier by the Alliance. They hadn't taken kindly to Gus using her armor—which she'd liberated (okay, stolen) from a military scrap heap because no matter what the brass said, her armor was *not* obsolete, thank you very much—to put down a rebellion. After her heroics on Shepard's Moon, hers and Drake's, to save her son and his people, the military had decided not to prosecute her on a variety of charges that would have put her away for life. In return, she —and her armor—could never set foot in Alliance space again. Gus could live with that, but the Alliance had also cut off her access to their vast computer network, not to mention access to all the money Gus had stashed in various banks throughout the Alliance. Goodbye to all the hard-earned money she'd earned during her career as an armor jock. At least she'd had the foresight to stash some of her funds in a few semi-reputable financial institutions in the Frontier or she'd be flat broke.

Without access to the Alliance's computer network, she had to rely on whatever information Drake had put in the ship's computer about the planetoid's infrastructure, not to mention its defensive systems. There'd been precious little, and now she knew that even that much was six years old. A lot could have changed in six years. Hell, six years ago she'd been happily drinking her way through her retirement in her favorite spacers' bar on Depak Station.

She wiped her search from the ship's computer, probably in much the same way that Drake had wiped all mention of Rhapsody, and headed toward the bridge. Before she left, she gave one last look at her armor. Without its helmet, it looked like an empty, useless shell. She felt its absence almost like it was a missing limb.

She was going to get it fixed, even if she had to put up with an ex-girlfriend who was a manipulative sexpot and a space cowboy whose raging hormones had even less sense than he did when it came to that particular ex-girlfriend.

She was almost to the bridge when a new thought struck her.

The dates on those computer entries about Drake's time on Chrysallix.

All of them had been six years ago.

His son had died *seven* years ago. His ex-wife had left

him soon after. The marriage hadn't been good, and the boy's death had been the final straw.

Drake had told her about his son, about his marriage. Some of the discussions had happened in the dark in his cabin when they lay wrapped in each other's arms beneath his old-fashioned comforter, mellow and happily worn out. He hadn't said in so many words, but she'd known anyway that he'd been devasted by the losses. Callum had been a good boy, a bright boy, a college kid barely out of his teens when he'd been killed in a stupid accident.

No wonder Rhapsody had been able to get her hooks in Drake. He'd been vulnerable. Not that he'd ever admit it, but she could remember how she'd felt after the double loss of her own son and his father the first time she'd been on Shepard's Moon.

She'd been deployed along with her squadron to protect the planet's peaceful inhabitants from a rebel uprising, all part of an effort to convince the planet to join the Alliance. The negotiations had gone on much longer than antici-pated, and the rebels, sensing that things might not be going their way, turned what had started out as a holding action into an all-out war. Her son's father—her squadron leader—had been killed the same night she gave birth to their son.

Gus had channeled her grief and rage into an all-out assault on the rebels. Along with what was left of her squadron, she'd wiped out each and every rebel within the planet's capitol city.

Then she'd been forced to flee the planet. She'd known that she was in no shape to be a mother to her son. It had broken her heart to leave him behind, but the woman who'd adopted him had given him a good home and the very best life, something he wouldn't have had as the military brat of a single mom subject to deployment on a moment's notice.

So yes, she understood how Drake must have felt when he'd first come to Chrysallix. Rhapsody had taken advantage of that.

Well, that was then, and this was now. And in the here and now, Drake wasn't alone. He had an armor jock watching his six. Hell, he had the Gray Lady watching his six.

If Rhapsody Harrison tried any of that shit with him now, she wasn't going to know what hit her.

CHAPTER 4

The spaceport on Chrysallix turned out to be on the edge of a bustling modern domed city. The city wasn't at all what Drake remembered from his days plying his trade in the Obsidiac system...and that alone made him curious and eager to explore.

To that end, he started plotting a course that would take the *Void* down fast, heading straight for the spaceport...but Gus asked him to extend their approach. She wanted to take a couple of slow orbits first.

"You've been here before," she said. "I haven't. I want to get a feel for the place."

She'd insisted on doing the same thing when they'd arrived at Shepard's Moon a few weeks back...only then they'd been preparing to go in with guns blazing to save the life of her son, and she'd been looking for enemy encampments. This was a very different situation—but Drake tended to trust her instincts and decided to oblige. What could it hurt? It wasn't like he was chomping at the bit to see Rhap again. It might even win him some brownie points with Gus on down the line.

"All righty, then." He worked the wheel and throttle, shifting into orbit instead of an immediate descent. "You let me know when that feel is enough, darlin', and I'll take her down."

"Thanks." She flashed him a smile, then resumed flipping switches to manipulate images on the viewing screens over the communications console. Each screen displayed a different shot of the surface below as picked up by the cameras mounted at various points on the hull of the *Void*.

Leaning back at the nav station, Drake tapped a rhythm on the arms of the chair. Most of his attention was focused on Gus instead of the screens. The way she worked the switches for the screens had a rhythm all its own, and his fingers couldn't help keeping time with her movements. If she noticed, she didn't say anything.

She was clearly more tense and distracted than usual, almost as if she were heading into battle. Did she get like this before she landed anywhere? Or was it just because she was about to meet his ex?

"So Gus," he said calmly. "What did you think of our call with Rhapsody?"

It hadn't been *their* call, it had been *his* call. Gus had stayed in the background, just out of camera range. But he wanted her to feel included, and hell, he valued her opinion. He'd be the first to admit that his opinions about Rhap weren't exactly impartial.

"Not much." Gus kept making adjustments to the comm

console controls. "It's too soon for me to tell much of anything about her."

"What's your gut feeling, though? Do you trust her?"

"I don't *know* her." Gus sounded a little annoyed. "How can I trust anyone I don't know?"

Well, *that* was certainly Gray Lady blunt. Here he'd thought *Rhap* had been blunt.

Sparks sure were gonna fly when those two met. Drake wondered if maybe he should try to convince Gus to take a few shots of the good stuff *before* they landed to take the edge off.

"So what do *you* think?" asked Gus as she continued to fiddle with the comm controls. "About Chrysallix, that is. You must know the place like the back of your hand, right?"

"Not so much anymore, actually." As Drake watched passing scenery on the various screens, he realized it wasn't as familiar as he'd expected. From what he could see, a lot had changed in six years.

The residential domes looked much the same as before, enclosing blocky apartment buildings interspersed with occasional parks and commercial development. The space-port was under the same kind of dome, only it looked like the dome and the port had been expanded over the years. It was certainly bigger and busier than he remembered, and he'd piloted the *Void* in and out of that port a lot.

Other manmade features weren't entirely familiar, though, like the network of tubes spiderwebbing the plane-toid's rocky surface. The tubular structures—which were much more extensive than he remembered—consisted of bits and pieces of decommissioned space stations that had been repurposed for surface use, mostly as tunnels for high-speed transport. The tubes linked many of the domes, as well as intersecting certain saucer-shaped structures that housed various industrial facilities and food production plants.

What caught his eye most forcefully, though, was something completely new to him—a huge, artificial structure towering high above every other building on the surface. It had not existed six years ago…and its purpose was clear.

"Nice weapons spire." Gus pointed at the structure's image on the central screen. "Was your ex always this well-armed?"

Even from the nav console, Drake could see the gun turrets, missile launchers, and arrays of laser cannons studding the skin of the massive tower. "Absolutely not," he said, impressed…and concerned. "Looks like they've beefed up their defenses since my last visit."

Gus got up, stepped over to the sensor console, and ran some quick scans of the object. "Can't identify that thing's composition. Some kind of metal that's new to our database." She turned a knob, flipped a switch, pulled a lever, and watched new information appear on a readout screen. "There's also a *massive* amount of energy emanating from the complex under it. Not quite sure what's generating that, though."

The last time Drake had been here, he hadn't exactly learned all the nuts and bolts of how Chrysallix generated the energy to power all the structures on the surface. He'd been too distracted by a certain tall, sultry blonde who'd kept him busy in a variety of pleasurable ways. Could be the tower was protecting the planetoid's primary energy source.

Or was it protecting something else? He knew firsthand that Rhap didn't always care where—or how—she got the goods she sold.

"Damn." He shook his head as the *Void*'s orbit carried them past the tower. "Looks like we've got a mystery on our hands...and a seriously *destructive* one, at that."

"Could mean trouble's in store," said Gus. "Seeing a weapons spire that big makes me think there's something at least as big and bad that they need to use it against."

Drake nodded thoughtfully, watching another stretch of domes unfold onscreen. "Could just be a necessary deterrent against threats in general. These folks are out here on the Frontier without an armor jock like you to watch their backs. Makes sense that this little world needs *something* to keep itself in one piece."

"Either way, it brings up a good question," said Gus. She turned away from the sensor console to look him in the eye. "Are you sure you want to go through with this little visit?"

"After coming all this way? Of course I do." Drake knew he might have answered a little too quickly, but he couldn't take it back. "We need a new replicator, and frankly, we need *friends* on the Frontier. If one of them happens to be armed to the teeth with ultra-powerful mystery tech, all the better."

She held his gaze for another long moment before she turned back to the console. "Maybe," she said, but she didn't sound convinced.

"I'm telling you, Rhap is a good friend to have. She can get *anything* if the price is right...including top of the line *armor upgrades*, I'm willing to bet." He smiled at her, trying for his most charming grin. "Wouldn't *that* alone be worth the price of admission?"

She shot him a look from the corner of her eye. "You trying to tell me my armor needs an upgrade?"

Uh-oh. Treading on dangerous territory, here. Gus drew a fine line between teasing and insults when it came to her armor.

"Talking top-of-the-line space-tight seals," he said, amping up his grin. "Maybe an extra laser or two."

Her expression was softening. Score one for the space cowboy.

"Long-range laser cannon," he said. "Piggyback surveillance drone." He didn't know if such a thing was possible for Gus's armor, but if somebody made it, Rhap would have one for sale.

"Now you're getting ridiculous," she said.

"You've never been to Chrysallix. Anything and every-thing a well-equipped armor jock could use to outfit her armor." He pointed at the screens. "Right down there."

"Not *everything* is about the *armor*, you know," said Gus.

"Now *that's* just crazy talk." He chuckled.

Gus grinned back. Finally. "You always know the way to a girl's heart, don't you, Broken String?"

He snorted. When they'd gone into battle on Shepard's Moon, he'd provided support with the *Void*. Broken String had been his callsign. Hers had been obvious: Gray Lady.

"I'd fight the whole *universe* single-handedly for that heart," he told her...and he meant every word. "Whatever keeps you *safe* is all that *matters* to me. Whatever makes you *feel* safest."

"Then you won't mind if I wear my armor to visit your ex?"

He couldn't help the hearty laugh that exploded out of him. Just the mental image of Gus in full armor marching out of the *Void* and towering over Rhap was too much.

"Yeah, *that* would go over well," he said once he managed to catch his breath. "Rhap ought to love that."

Gus's eyes danced with repressed good humor, but she shrugged, probably trying to maintain her *I'm-serious-here* demeanor. "Think she'll mind if I at least pack in a few *guns* of my own?"

Drake shook his head and grinned. This was the kind of banter that he loved. The back and forth with Gus that made sharing his ship—and everything else, including his heart—with this woman seem like the most natural thing in the universe.

"She'd probably be disappointed if you didn't," he said.

He came over to her then and gave her a solid kiss. She kissed him back thoroughly, as if to acknowledge the compromise they had reached. In spite of her concerns, they'd agreed to move forward with the visit as planned; however the chips fell from there, they would deal with it on the fly the best way they knew how—as a *team*.

When the kiss finally ended, she pulled back just enough to look him dead in the eyes. "Just so you know," she said, "to give you fair warning. If you start humming 'Back in the Saddle Again' when we land, I'm going to take one of those guns of mine and shoot something of yours that we're both rather attached to."

His eyes widened as he gauged whether she was serious. "Warning received," he said. "And don't you worry your head about me. I know what I'm doing. She's my *ex* for a reason."

Then, smiling, he leaned forward and planted a kiss on the tip of her nose.

Whatever happened on Chrysallix with Rhapsody and whoever else awaited them, they would face it *together*... and they would find a way to *succeed*.

CHAPTER 5

Rhapsody didn't meet them at the spaceport. Of course.

She sent a ground transport.

An unmanned transport.

"This usual?" Gus asked Drake.

He'd seemed to take the lack of a personal escort in stride, but she thought she'd caught the slightest hesitation in his stride once they hit the arrivals lounge only to discover Rhapsody wasn't there.

"Six years ago?" He shook his head. "Now?" He looked around at the shining metal and glass structure of the port's dome, a curious and eager glint in his eyes. "This place has grown, darlin'. Whatever's gone on here, seems it's been good for everybody."

Drake had an explorer's streak a mile wide in that heart of his. While Gus had been chafing at having to stay in the hospital on Shepard's Moon while she recovered from injuries she'd suffered when she and Drake had saved her son's bacon, Drake had been out with the locals chasing the last of the rebels from their strongholds and generally exploring the area.

He'd lived most of his life in space, earning just enough as a smuggler to keep himself and his ship more or less in one piece. When he hadn't been smuggling, he'd taken his time having a good look around to see what was out there. That was one of the reasons he'd spent so much time in the Frontier.

"New places to see," he'd told her, "new people to meet." And most of it uncivilized and more than a bit on the wild side.

While he'd occasionally dipped his toes into Alliance space, especially when he was tight for money and really needed a job, he didn't like to go too near the heart of the Alliance. That made sense to Gus. Smugglers tended to stay away from places where their every action was monitored by law enforcement. So did retired armor jocks who'd liberated their armor from the military's junk heap.

It was one of the things that made the two of them such a good team.

Gus would be the first to admit she was more than a little jaded when it came to exploring new places. She'd been deployed to so many different worlds when she'd been with the 83rd that the new had worn off. The only thing she'd looked around for back then was a place to get a good drink.

But Drake's excitement was contagious. If he wanted to explore Chrysallix, she'd do her best to relax and enjoy herself. She was a civilian now, after all. Until they tracked down Jorritz Tor and made him pay for trying to get her son killed, the most action she expected to see in the near future would be if someone made the mistake of trying to mess with Drake.

Someone like Rhapsody? That remained to be seen.

Except Gus couldn't shake the feeling that something was off here, and it wasn't just because she'd left her armor on the *Void*. She hadn't been joking about bringing guns along. The ones she'd concealed beneath her jacket would come in handy in a pinch, but they didn't have the kind of overwhelming firepower her armor did. There had to be a reason for that weapons spire. If the shit hit the proverbial fan, Gus didn't like the idea of relying on strangers for protection from whatever that spire was meant to defend against. Any civilization that existed beneath a dome could be wiped out simply by breaching that dome.

She tried not to think about that as the unmanned transport took them out of the spaceport's dome and into the city proper.

It was pretty obvious that the transport wasn't Rhapsody's private vehicle. It was comfortable enough, with a limited beverage station, padded seats, and wraparound windows to give passengers a clear view of the city. Small viewscreens embedded in the walls beneath the windows displayed the kind of quasi-informational garbage someone thought visitors to Chrysallix should know. Like which building they passed had been the first built in the city (an old blocky thing made mostly of metal with small windows that reminded Gus of a bunker more than anything else), the first government building (barely bigger than a single-family residence on most planets in the Alliance), and the shopping district—an expansive, crowded complex of shiny metal and glass buildings, flashy signage, loud music, and —by the look of things—about a zillion places to get rip-roaring drunk. Now that was something Gus thought space traders would actually want to know about.

She nudged Drake's shoulder. "You could probably make a pretty penny selling them some of your good stuff."

He snorted. "Darlin', my good stuff isn't for sale." He gave her a light kiss. "And I only share it with the people I care about."

She didn't mention that he'd offered to bring some of his good stuff along while he and Rhapsody reminisced about the good old days. Only Rhapsody had said she hadn't taken a drink for the last three years.

Curious that she'd mentioned how many years ago she'd given up drinking. What had happened three years ago to prompt the change? Even before she'd retired, Gus had done her own fair share of drinking when she was off duty. Most of the people she knew who made their living in space did, unless they had health issues that couldn't be fixed with enhancements or were part of some odd religious sect. Were enhancements that hard to come by in the Frontier? Drake had made it sound like Rhapsody could get her hands on whatever a spacer might want, and she didn't exactly strike Gus as the religious type.

So had she quit drinking because she didn't want to drink up the profits? Just how many of the businesses in the shopping district—not to mention all the other buildings they'd passed—did she own anyway? He'd said she was a big deal on Chrysallix. Exactly *how* big of a deal was she?

Chrysallix wasn't exactly a Frontier planet the way most people inside the Alliance thought of places in the Frontier

—a dusty and mostly barren world lorded over by someone with an iron fist, a very wealthy someone (by local standards) who wouldn't hesitate to use deadly force to get rid of anyone who opposed them. If the size of the spaceport, not to mention the city the transport was driving them through, was anything to go on, the population of Chrysallix could rival a lot of medium-sized countries on most Alliance worlds, and so could their tech.

Take the spaceport. Gus had expected that Drake would be docking the ship in a simple port with two or three terminals at most. Rhapsody's people had them dock at terminal *twenty-three*. More ships were docked in terminal twenty-three than Gus could count. Most of them looked like cargo ships, similar to the *Void*, although she'd spotted a few passenger yachts and smaller transports. The yachts were high-end models meant for long-range voyages, but the transports were short-range vehicles, which made her wonder where they came from and where they were headed. Chrysallix wasn't exactly within short-range distance of any other planets in the system.

At least she hadn't seen any military presence so far. Outside of the honking big weapons tower, that was. Just because Chrysallix wasn't part of the Alliance didn't mean it didn't have its own private military. If a planet had a military presence, they usually made themselves known in other ways.

Like military insignia in unobtrusive places. Guards posing as port security.

Or that honking big weapons spire.

That thing bothered her. Sure, the port was a bustling, busy place, lots of civilians milling around, just like in the shopping district. They'd passed a lot of other transports on the street—individual unmanned transports like the one they were in as well as larger, public transport vehicles. Chrysallix was a busy, bustling place. Given the way Drake was taking everything in, Gus would be willing to bet a lot of this stuff hadn't been here during his last visit. Building an ostentatious defense system was probably a pretty damn good way of telling anyone planning to take over the place that they should look for an easier target elsewhere.

But Gus hadn't even seen any civilian police on the drive through the city, and she'd been looking. It was a good bet the city and the port had some sort of surveillance system in place—video and audio feeds—but those only caught crimes in progress. Police presence, like the presence of the 83rd on some worlds, was more about deterrence than anything else.

Gus got her answer a few moments later when a drone dropped down from overhead and hovered next to the transport, keeping pace with them. Cameras studded the outside of the thing, along with small laser guns mounted on the framework beneath the drone's main body.

The drone focused its cameras to catch their faces through the transport's window. It reminded Gus of the drone Drake had hacked into on Shepard's Moon. The rebels had used the drone to try and discover her son's whereabouts inside the capitol building. Drake had used the Void's systems to hack into the drone's transmission so that they could see what it was seeing.

Gus didn't like drones. They were a necessary tool of battle—drones could be sent on missions that would be suicide for a human—but they were soulless machines. Her armor was different. When she climbed inside, it was like she and her armor became one being. A very deadly being that no one should make the mistake of crossing, but a living entity nonetheless.

"All firearms must be disabled before entering La Meilleure Towers," came a mechanical voice from somewhere within the transport. "Failure to comply will result in confiscation of your weapons. All confiscated weapons will be returned to you when you depart Chrysallix. Thank you for your cooperation."

Son of a bitch. The drone hadn't just taken videos of their faces, it had scanned the interior of the transport and found the guns she'd hidden beneath her jacket.

She didn't want to disable her guns. She already felt naked enough leaving her armor behind. But she didn't want to surrender her guns either. Disabled guns could be re-enabled, and thanks to her military training, Gus could do that almost faster than the eye could see.

"Well, that's certainly different," Drake said. Then to her surprise, he removed a gun from one of the pockets in his pants and expertly disabled its firing mechanism.

"What?" he said when he caught her staring at him. "You're not the only one who comes prepared."

"Thought you trusted her," she said. "That she'd be a good friend to have out here on the Frontier."

"She is, but that mystery we talked about?" He shook his head. "Always better to be ready for anything."

The transport slowed and pulled into a covered parking area.

The door didn't open.

"You have arrived at your destination," the disembodied mechanical voice said. "Hold out your weapons for inspection."

Gus wanted to tell the mechanical voice where to put that command, but she reminded herself she needed to play nice. For Drake's sake, if nothing else. But damn did she hate being told what to do by some automated piece of equipment. Maybe she could do a little exploring in the speech systems for the transport vehicles. Reprogram them to respond with Earl's voice. Or maybe Rhapsody's. Wouldn't that be a hoot and a half?

She and Drake held out their guns, neatly disabled, for the drone to get a good look at them.

A moment later the door to the transport opened with a slight hiss. Gus caught a whiff of some sort of spicy broiled meat accompanied by the rich aroma of coffee coming in from outside. Not bad for a Frontier world. Shepard's Moon had smelled like dust and sweat and pulverized perma-crete. Her stomach rumbled, reminding her that it had been a while since she'd eaten fresh meat.

Drake exited the transport and turned around. For a moment, Gus thought he was going to offer to help her get out of the transport, which meant she'd have to deck him. The Gray Lady didn't need help getting out of anything, much less a civilian transport, no matter how stiff her knees were.

A short walkway led to a set of opaque glass doors at the base of a fairly impressive high-rise building. When they didn't immediately walk toward the doors, arrows embedded in the walkway started flashing in progression, pointing the way.

More automated directions. Gus almost felt like she was

in the heart of the Alliance, what with all this tech. Rhapsody must be doing well for herself indeed.

Drake took her hand and squeezed it. "Ready?" he asked.

She wondered who he was asking—her or himself.

She squeezed his hand back. After all this buildup, she couldn't wait to see the woman behind the curtain.

"Let's go meet your ex, space cowboy," she said.

CHAPTER 6

"Mr. Drake? I am Simeon Ezekiel."

A tall, middle-aged man in the black business suit—which Drake could clearly see was high-end and bespoke—was waiting on the other side of the opaque glass doors at the base of the high-rise when they slid open. Trim, balding, and straight-backed, with a snobbish air and an accent right out of Great Britain back on Earth, he tipped his head slightly forward at the sight of them.

Drake didn't have to look at Gus to know she was suppressing a grin. From what she'd told him about her time in the military, Gus Light didn't take people who put on airs too seriously. The fact that she hadn't even covered a snort with a quiet cough told him that she was trying to be on her best behavior—for his benefit, not for hers.

"As the chief of staff of Suzerain Harrison," the man said, "I welcome you both to Chrysallix."

Drake frowned at the unfamiliar name. "Suzerain?"

"It means, in effect, 'leader,'" said Ezekiel. "Much more than a governor but not quite a president. Her actual title is *La Meilleure*, but Suzerain is more commonly used."

"No kidding." Drake grinned. "I guess ol' Rhap has really moved up in the world."

"If you'll come with me?"

Ezekiel started down a corridor that stretched out in front of them, waving for them to follow. The flooring was made of faux marble tiles—nobody, not even good ol', moved-up-in-the-world Rhap could afford real marble imported from Earth. Ezekiel's shoes clicked on the slick tiles. The boots Drake wore squeaked slightly. Gus's boots didn't make a sound as she walked. That was military training for you.

"I hope you've brought your appetites," Ezekiel said. "The Suzerain has prepared a bit of a snack to celebrate your arrival."

"That's right hospitable," said Drake. "And here we are without a present for her."

"That's fine," said Ezekiel. "She'd have been insulted if you'd brought one."

"Good to know that much hasn't changed," said Drake. "Generosity was one of her best qualities back in the day."

Ezekiel did not offer comment, just continued his march down the corridor.

As for Gus, Drake was sure she'd heard and processed every word, but she didn't comment, either. Maybe she felt secure enough in their relationship not to offer a quip—or perhaps she was saving her response for later. She was still letting him hold her hand, after all.

Before long the corridor opened up into a spacious

atrium. One wall of the atrium was composed almost entirely of windows divided by metallic girders, going up almost as high as the eye could see. Glass-enclosed elevators disappeared into the distance overhead, presumably leading to apartments or offices on the upper floors of the high-rise. All that glass provided a spectacular look at a city that was far different from the one Drake had left behind six short years ago.

When he said not much had changed, he certainly hadn't meant the city. Looking out at the busy street and the buildings beyond made Drake think he'd made a serious miscalculation and landed them on a planetoid that wasn't Chrysallix at all.

Except Rhap was here. That was one thing he was certain of. Well, that and Gus.

Drake expected Ezekiel to lead them to one of the elevators, but instead he stopped before another set of opaque glass doors on the other side of the atrium.

"Here we are." Stepping to one side, Ezekiel waved his hand over a white sensor bulb on the wall at waist level—and the doors slid open with the faintest hiss. "Enjoy your meal."

Drake realized the enticing scents of broiled meat and coffee he'd been smelling since getting out of the unmanned transport was stronger through that open doorway than anywhere else they'd been in the building so far.

Was this a restaurant? Exclusive, just for the building's residents? If it was, it had to be damn near top-notch. Rhap used to meet clients for a few drinks before she got down to business, but she said she didn't drink anymore. For all he knew, she could be doing business these days over a nice meal instead of shots of the good stuff.

Drake nodded at Rhap's chief of staff. "Thanks, Zeke," he said, and then he stepped through the open door, the cooking smell drawing him along like a tangible thing.

Gus let go of his hand before she followed him inside, staying close behind, waiting as always for the slightest sign that the visit was going pear-shaped. It was good to know she had his back, as always, no matter what happened.

It was exactly then that the larger-than-life voice of the one-and-only Rhapsody Harrison boomed from off to the far side of a room that was almost as expansive as the atrium. *"Cher!"*

Grinning, Drake spun, expecting to see the same old Rhapsody he'd known and loved years ago, more or less—a little older, of course, but mostly indistinguishable from the woman he remembered.

Boy, was he in for a surprise.

"Welcome, welcome!" she said with clear delight. "Welcome home, *chér*!"

For once, Drake was dumbstruck. She walked toward him with her arms spread wide, and he was frozen in place, utterly flummoxed. If not for that *voice*, that unmistakable, smoky voice, he might not even have *recognized* her on the spot.

To say she had changed would be a tremendous understatement. Rhapsody was *big* these days, not only in terms of power on Chrysallix, but *physically* much larger than before. Gone was the slender, sexy figure with the perfect proportions he'd so admired. In her place was a woman of significant girth, at least twice the size that she'd been when they were lovers.

She was draped in a vast, flowing caftan of wildly swirling colors that reached nearly to the floor, but it couldn't conceal her greatly expanded midsection and voluminous hips. Her arms were thick, her fingers and the sandaled toes peeking out beneath the caftan plump. As for her face, her familiar features were padded and stretched, her cheeks and neck puffy.

Her hair was the most familiar thing about her, still lustrous and blonde, though perhaps *too* blonde—a little too platinum for the color to be all natural. It didn't quite flow over her shoulders the way he remembered, either; instead, she had it teased and sprayed into a kind of feathery crest around her head...not at all the carefully careless mane he'd once loved to run his fingers through in intimate moments.

As she threw her arms around him in a bear hug, engulfing him in a cloud of too-sweet perfume, he almost felt sorry for her and sorry he'd come to see her. He wished he'd left her where she belonged, in the past, forever frozen in his memory as the ravishing beauty she had been. He was angry with himself for being curious enough to come to Chrysallix, indulging a nostalgic streak that had led only to a swell of regret.

But even as all this emotion stormed through him, he refused to let it show. Drake being the gentleman space cowboy he was, being anything less than gracious to the woman he'd shared part of his life with, regardless of their acrimonious breakup, just wasn't going to happen.

"So good to see you again, Rhap," he said, only slightly breathless from the vigorous hug. "Thanks for having us."

At his reminder of another person in the room, Rhap broke the hug and turned to face Gus, who'd been standing barely three feet away this whole time. "Welcome to you as well...*Augusta*, that is it?"

"Gus is fine." Smiling warmly, Gus extended a hand. "Good to meet you...Suzerain?"

Rhapsody shook the offered hand energetically. "My friends call me Rhapsody, and my *special* friends call me Rhap." She winked one bright green eye. "*You* can call me Rhap."

Her eyes hadn't changed.

That realization almost came as a shock. So much of the woman Drake had loved had changed, but her eyes still glinted with the same mischievous good humor he remembered from back then. His Rhap was still here, there was just *more* of her than he'd expected.

He resisted the urge to scrub a hand through his scruffy beard. He probably had more gray in his hair and his beard and a few more wrinkles around his eyes than the last time *she'd* seen *him*, and she'd still welcomed him with open arms.

Man up, he told himself. And while he was at it—*get over yourself.*

"All right, then," Gus said. She shook hands with his ex a moment more. "Good to meet you. Rhap."

"You too...Gray Lady."

Before Gus could say another word, Rhap broke the shake and hurtled off across the room, her caftan billowing around her.

Gus looked at Drake, and he read the question in her eyes, but his only answer was a shrug. How did Rhap know Gus was the Gray Lady? He was clueless to explain.

"Now who is hungry?" shouted Rhap as she burst through a swinging door on the far side of the room. "Dinner is on the way," she called from the other side of the door, "and you are gonna *love* it!"

Drake frowned. Rhap's cooking skills had never been stellar when the two of them had been an item; if anything, they had been the *opposite*. Reheated prepackaged meals had been her forte back then, though she'd also made decent scrambled eggs and spaghetti when the mood struck her. Yet Ezekiel had clearly said that she'd prepared the snack herself, implying some level of cooking quality beyond what Drake would expect.

Then again, nothing in Rhap's orbit was what he'd expected so far.

It was pretty clear they weren't in a restaurant. These were living quarters, and pretty damn expensive at that. Nothing at all like the flat where the two of them had lived in the old days. This place was big and immaculate, with an elegant décor rich in glass, ebony, and glossy white surfaces. Like the atrium, most of one wall was all windows looking out at the surrounding city under the dome. Other walls were hung with impressionistic paintings of natural beauty, framed black-and-white photos of smiling strangers, and various objets d'art placed in pleasing and symmetrical arrangements. One section of the interior wall nearest the door featured a display of artfully placed weapons, including an assortment of rifles, pistols, and swords ranging from the antique to the cutting edge.

Gus must have spotted the weapons. "Interesting," she

said under her breath. "You think those firearms are disabled too?"

He had no idea, but he wouldn't put it past Rhap—at least the Rhap he'd known years ago—to find a way around whatever local law she didn't like. Or enact laws that applied to everyone except her.

As for furniture, a large sectional sofa upholstered in what looked like white leather dominated one side of the room, flanked by two chairs with the same kind of upholstery, only in black. A low table of polished ebony crouched in front of the sofa like a sleek, deadly predator, and sculptures of other animals he didn't recognize—most of them with big teeth on prominent display—were scattered around that side of the room. Not exactly a relaxing place to sit and have a casual chat.

The other side of the space was filled by a long dining table that could have easily accommodated over a dozen people. Now only six ebony-framed chairs were grouped around the glass-topped table, three on each end with a large open space in the center.

The three place settings on the end of the table closest to where Drake and Gus stood all featured crystal glasses, china plates and bowls, and silverware with gem-encrusted handles. Crystal decanters and china coffee and dessert service pieces occupied a sideboard along the wall adjacent to the swinging door.

The place was fit for a Suzerain—though Drake was equally certain the Rhapsody of six years ago would not have been caught dead in it...even *if* she could have afforded it. The truth was, though she'd made a pretty penny supplying goods to various Frontier worlds back then—with the help of a certain smuggler cowboy who'd loved her—she had *never* been smart about saving her money and had never managed to hold onto it for very long.

But maybe that had all changed, too, in the intervening years.

Did this place even belong to her? For all he knew, it came with the title. It could just be someplace where the Suzeraine, whoever that happened to be, entertained visitors. Someplace where the political leader of Chrysallix did business, and all the ostentatious wealth on display was meant as a negotiating tool. Wealth implied power. Not a bad place to start negotiations. His Rhapsody had always been aces when it came to negotiating a deal.

Although he had to wonder—how much of *his* Rhapsody was even left?

As beautiful as this place was, it felt cold. One thing his Rhap had *never* been was cold.

But she had always been smart about looking out for herself. If she made herself at home in a space like this, it was because it was the best thing for *her*. He'd do well to keep that in mind.

Suddenly, she bustled back in through the swinging door, carrying a big silver pot with steam curling from inside it. "Dinner is served! I made *sancocho* for this special occasion—my signature dish!"

"Sancocho?" said Drake as he and Gus drew up to the dining table.

"Dominican beef stew, *chér*, with yuca, plantains, and all *kinds* of good stuff. My mama's recipe, actually...with a couple of my own special touches for good measure."

"You grow all that locally?" Gus asked.

Instead of answering Gus directly, Rhap said, "We are very resourceful. That is why Drake brought you here, yes?"

Even though Gus didn't overtly react, Drake could feel the tension between the two ratchet up a notch. He wasn't exactly sure why, but he wasn't going to let it get out of hand.

"Well, it smells heavenly," he told Rhap...and was surprised to realize he meant it. As hard as it seemed to believe, Rhapsody Harrison had whipped up a dish that smelled so good, it was making his stomach growl. How could it *not* be delicious?

And just like that the tension was gone, at least from Rhap's side. Rhap smiled at the both of them as she put the pot on a silver filigreed trivet on the sideboard along the wall.

"Pull up a chair, *mes amis*," she said before he disappeared through the swinging door again. "Better yet, pull up *two* of them."

Drake and Gus took seats across from each other—Gus facing the glass door to the apartment, as she preferred. They both knew, from hard-won experience, to avoid sitting with their backs to a door, but Gus mostly won when there was a toss-up. Drake was fine with that, as she was the better fighter...and did her fighting for the two of them in any event.

"Get your taste buds ready!" Rhap returned humming and swinging a ladle...and that was enough to trigger a shot of déjà vu in Drake. Was it the tune she hummed? The way she entered the room, though she was physically so much larger than he remembered? He didn't know.

Whatever it was, it took him back, at least a little, at least for a moment.

"Everyone who tries my sancocho tells me how much they love it," said Rhap as she ladled stew into Gus's china bowl. "And they all *swear* they are not just saying that because I am boss of the *planet*."

Gus smiled, and Drake was relieved to see it was a sincere smile that touched her eyes. She didn't give those out easily. Whatever Rhap had said that got under Gus's skin, she'd decided to let it go. For now.

"Well, you can count on us for an unbiased opinion," Gus said. "We'd never dream of trying to butter you up to get a better price on the equipment we need...right, Drake?"

"Absolutely." Drake chuckled and held up his stew bowl. "Funny thing is, this is still empty, and I can already tell that stew is the greatest thing I've ever tasted!"

"Flattery will get you everywhere."

Rhap's voice sounded like a sexy growl when she said it, a vocal flourish that Drake remembered well from the old days. People had compared it to the unique delivery of an ancient film star named Mae West, though he hadn't understood the reference and had never bothered to look it up. Rhap was Rhap, as far as he'd been concerned. He didn't need to compare her to any long-gone film star.

Or to her former self.

That thought came as kind of a shock. *This* was who Rhap was now. He needed to stop comparing her to who she'd been, or he'd drive himself crazy and derail his side of the negotiations and end up paying way too much for a new replicator for the *Void*.

"Thanks," he said as she rounded the table, took the bowl from his hands, and started to fill it from the pot on the sideboard. "We appreciate the home cooking, Rhap."

"I am *always* cooking," she told him with a trace of her trademark growl...and then she chuckled, shifting gears. "It has become an obsession over the past few years, actually... as you can tell." She did a little self-effacing shrug. "I have come to enjoy my own cooking a little *too* much."

"Nothing wrong with a hobby that makes other people happy," said Drake. "Cooking and music are cut from the same cloth that way, I'd say."

She stopped ladling soup and aimed a frosty glare in his direction. "Music? That is not your way of telling me that you have brought that *guitar* of yours with you, is it?"

"What makes you think I'd do that?" Drake grinned. Here was something else that hadn't changed about her— her reaction to the music he played, especially the original songs he wrote himself. "How could I ever be so *rude?*"

"I would not put it past you," she said, still glaring.

Gus frowned, looking worried. Rhap had mentioned his music earlier, on their shipboard call, and everyone had seemed to brush it off as some kind of in-joke—but perhaps she was starting to wonder if there was something more to Rhap's aversion than that, if perhaps Gus herself might have to intervene in some way.

She opened her mouth as if to say something...but she didn't get a word out. No one did.

An explosion from somewhere in the city rattled the wall of windows in the apartment, near enough and strong enough to set the crystal and china rattling violently on the table and the sideboard. Drake felt the vibrations through the soles of his boots.

BAWHOOOOOM!

"What the hell?" asked Drake.

Gus got to her feet. "What was that?"

Rhap just sighed. She dropped the ladle in the pot of sancocho, set Drake's soup bowl on the sideboard, and shook her head.

"Not again," she said disgustedly, as if remarking on something no more serious than a barking dog or backfiring vehicle on the street outside.

Drake and Gus followed her as she crossed the room to the window-wall, then crowded around as she gazed through the glass at the towering high-rises of the city.

"There." She pointed at a spot on the skyline where a plume of gray smoke curled up into the atmosphere under the dome. "Many blocks away from here, thank Heaven."

"Okay, Rhap. What's going on here?"

Drake couldn't keep the mix of annoyance and worry out of his voice...and with good reason. An explosion inside a dome was no small thing. The atmosphere on Chrysallix, if it could be called an atmosphere, was toxic. The domes let the population live without the need to wear environment suits whenever they went outside a building and kept them from needing to go through the time-consuming and potentially deadly process of cycling through a building's airlocks whenever they decided to go anywhere. Any small breach in the dome could kill everyone inside.

And on a purely personal note, he hadn't come here to

get involved in another conflict or to put himself and Gus in danger. Whatever had caused that explosion may have been "many blocks away," but it was still much too close for comfort.

He shared a look with Gus. She'd gone into warrior mode, her expression deadly serious, her mouth set in a thin, tight line.

"Shh." Rhap held an index finger against her lips, signifying the need for silence. "Wait for it."

"I'd feel better if I knew what I was waiting for," Gus said.

No sooner had she finished saying the same thing Drake had been thinking than another blast erupted—this one closer than the first.

KRAKOOOOOM!

A second smoky plume climbed upward, this time much closer than the first. The high-rises kept Drake from pinpointing the source, but it looked to be in the immediate neighborhood, just a few blocks away instead of many.

"We need to get to our ship." Gus said it firmly, in the tone of a direct order. "Whatever's happening out there, it's coming closer."

What she really meant was that she needed to get in her armor. Drake felt that was a more than reasonable reaction under the circumstances. He'd feel better with the safety of the *Void* and its shields wrapped around himself and Gray Lady in her armor watching his six than standing behind Rhap's glass window.

"There is no need," said Rhap. "Our defense grid will handle this latest activity."

"You call blowing holes in your city *activity*?" asked Drake.

"It is a frequent occurrence, these days," explained Rhap. "You get used to it."

"You do?" said Gus. "How long has this been going on, exactly?"

"Quite a while now," said Rhap. "It has become our number one nuisance."

Nuisance? *Nuisance?* Explosions were a nuisance?

"But what *is* it?" snapped Drake, frustrated by her evasiveness.

"Oh, you know. Automated security robo-drones on a mission to enforce the laws of Chrysallix."

Like the drone that had swooped down out of the sky and scanned them while they were in the transport? The one that had demanded they either turn over their weapons or disable them? Drake had a sudden and extremely disturbing idea of what might have happened if he and Gus had refused to comply.

"Sounds pretty extreme for law enforcement," said Gus. "Are you sure there isn't something else going on out there?"

It was a reasonable question. Rhap said the city's defense grid would take care of the *nuisance*, but weren't automated security drones *part* of the defense grid?

And if that was the case... did that mean the security drones weren't the activity—the *nuisance*—Rhap was talking about?

The look that Rhap shot Gus was unreadable. Drake had a bad feeling about this. Just what the skudge was going on here? Whatever it was, it was pretty clear Rhap wasn't about to share.

Gus jabbed a finger toward the window. "Those explosions are overkill, and you know it." She started for the door. "I don't know about you, but I'm not going to stand around while people need help." She turned toward Drake without breaking stride. "You coming?"

She didn't wait for him to answer, but she didn't have to. Where innocent civilians were concerned, he and Gus were on the same page.

"Point taken," Rhap said. "It does take time for emergency services to come to the rescue." She marched across the room and stopped in front of the wall of weapons. "Having said that, it might not be a great idea to leap into the mix empty-handed…just in case, you understand."

She grabbed one of the laser rifles off the wall, then grabbed a laser pistol to go with it. "Help yourselves to my personal arsenal!" she said with an expansive wave of the hand holding the pistol. "I assure you, none of these weapons has been disabled. One of the benefits of being *La Meilleure!*"

Of course she'd make sure the law against carrying fully functional firearms didn't apply to her. In her flowing caftan, she looked ridiculous armed to the teeth, but Drake had personal experience with just how deadly she could be with a pistol when she needed to be.

"Thanks," Gus said, "but I'll stick with my own." She had already drawn both her guns and re-enabled them before she hit the door right behind Rhap.

Drake did the same with his own gun…but he decided to grab a laser rifle from the wall on his way past for good measure. Rhap's guns didn't violate the law, she said. His and Gus's did. If push came to shove, they could throw down their own weapons and he could still defend them with Rhap's rifle.

At least until they got back to the *Void* and Gus got her armor. In a battle between drones and a determined armor jock, Drake would put his money on the Gray Lady every day of the week and twice on Sunday.

With that, the three of them bolted down the corridor, heading for the building's exit…

…even as another explosion rocked the neighborhood.

WHABOOOOM!

CHAPTER 7

Gus could count on the fingers of one hand the number of times she'd waded into battle without her armor.

The 83rd Armor Division was officially part of the Alliance's infantry. They were boots on the ground just like standard infantry, but that's where the similarities ended. Infantry soldiers didn't have a few tons of metal and a few hundred circuits that controlled the most advanced targeting systems the military could buy between them and the bad guys. Standard infantry ran into battle with body armor, a rifle, hand grenades, and a shit-ton of guts.

The few times Gus had to run into battle armed with only a laser pistol—or two, like today—she thought each and every infantry soldier deserved a medal just for getting the job done.

She could kick anyone's ass when she was inside her armor, soldier and armor acting in unison, turning and firing and chewing up the distance between her and her targets with long, bounding strides like it was the most natural thing in the world. There for a while during the journey to Shepard's Moon, she'd worried that she'd lost her edge. She'd been retired for nearly a decade, her armor safely locked away in storage, before she'd hired Drake and the *Void* to drop her in the middle of the war her son was fighting—and losing—against a rebel warlord determined to take over the planet no matter how many people he had to kill to do it.

Gus hadn't known it at the time, but the warlord was backed by Jorritz Tor, a former Alliance official who'd used his position and his influence to stockpile enough Alliance tech and military hardware, including a dark matter cannon, to virtually guarantee that any strongman he backed would have an easy victory. Only Gus and Drake had shown up just in time to spoil his plans.

Tor hadn't expected that his hand-picked warlord would end up facing a seasoned armor jock. Gus knew military strategy like the back of her hand, and more importantly, she knew when to throw that strategy out the window and act on pure instinct. The warlord had been an insane megalomanic, a narcissist who didn't think he could lose. Gus had shown him otherwise.

Thanks to an insane encounter of their own on the way to Shepard's Moon, and a rather unique survival strategy cooked up by Drake, Gus had reconnected with her armor like she'd never spent any time away. Her armor had felt like the second skin it had always been. Aiming and shooting had felt as natural as running and breathing.

Any second thoughts she'd had about whether she

could still do *her* job—still be the Gray Lady? She'd left those behind in the rings of a gas giant.

When she'd engaged the warlord's troops on Shepard's Moon, she didn't feel an ounce of regret about taking out the enemy. That enemy been trying to kill her *son*, but more than that, they'd been killing innocent people. Hell, they'd used bound and blindfolded civilians as human shields. Cowards like that got what they deserved.

Gus didn't have her armor now, she didn't even have body armor, but here she was, running into battle with Drake—and Rhapsody, of all people, her wildly printed caftan whipping around her and her immovable hairdo sticking out like some weird helmet. In another time and place, the vision of Rhapsody, armed to the teeth, running into battle with her caftan and sandaled feet, might have been comical. It wasn't now.

Only the battle was over by the time the three of them got there.

Gus had no idea what criminal the security drones had been hunting, but they'd inflicted as much indiscriminate damage on innocent civilians as the rebels on Shepard's Moon had done to her son's people. Laser cannons were good at that.

She had no trouble identifying the weapon the drones had used. She'd seen the kind of damage laser cannons had inflicted on other worlds. The cannon the drone had fired had expelled enough energy to chew through glass and steel and the support structures underneath the ground floor of another high-rise only a few blocks away from Rhapsody's building, heating everything until it seemed like the very air had exploded. From the look of the debris, this part of the building had housed an actual restaurant. If the drone had been hunting only one person, it hadn't cared who got in the way, or how many people it killed to take out its target.

At least the debris from the explosion hadn't breached the dome, and fire suppression systems in what was left of this part of the building had put out any remaining flames. Firing any kind of weapon inside a dome was idiocy, much less a laser cannon.

What kind of security force equipped robo-drones with *laser cannons?* Against unarmed civilians?

Cowards, that's who.

Whoever had programmed the drones was no different than the warlord on Shepard's Moon. Gus didn't care what crime might have set the drones off. Even murder didn't warrant a response like this. She'd been on worlds before, worlds the Alliance was trying to convince to join up, where murder was punished with summary execution. But even on those worlds, the execution only took out the murderer. No one obliterated half a block of innocent bystanders with an explosion just to make a statement about not breaking the law.

The drone was gone by the time they arrived on the scene, but the carnage left behind almost turned Gus's stomach. When she'd been safe inside her armor, she hadn't been forced to endure the stench of battle. Hadn't seen the broken bodies of civilians up close with her own eyes instead of through her armor's visor screens. Hadn't heard the screams and sobs of the injured, the wails of survivors as they knelt by what was left of their loved ones. She didn't have that luxury here.

And Rhapsody had called this a *nuisance?*

Just what kind of a cold-hearted—

The thought died as Gus caught sight of Rhapsody's face.

La Meilleure of Chrysallix was devastated. Her face had gone slack with shock. Tears ran unchecked down her cheeks. She held her weapons loosely by her side. She'd probably forgotten she was even holding them.

Rhapsody had never seen devastation like this up close, that much was clear. Nobody could fake a reaction like that. No, Rhap had stayed in her spacious marble and ebony sanctuary, learned to cook her elaborate meals, maybe had her chief of staff or other friends or political hangers-on join her to eat what she'd cooked, and deliberately ignored what was going on in the city she was supposed to be in charge of.

And she ate. And ate. And over-ate.

She'd admitted as much, which explained Drake's odd reaction when he first caught sight of her, not to mention the half-appalled glances he'd been shooting her way when she hadn't been looking. The woman he remembered was gone, and he'd had trouble coming to grips with who she was now. Then he'd relaxed and settled into the moment, only to have something jar him out again.

Gus understood Drake's reaction, to a certain extent. She'd left a baby behind on Shepard's Moon, and when she'd come back, he was not only a grown man, he was the leader of his people.

Only Gus had expected to see a grown man on Shepard's Moon. Drake hadn't expected to come face to face with a woman who ate as a way to cope with what her life had become.

Gus had seen stuff like that before. Mid-level military wonks who drank their way into early retirement because they couldn't stomach orders they'd been given—and carried out. Was that what Rhapsody had been doing? Eating her inability to cope with a situation she felt responsible for but didn't have the ability to control? She could have tried alcohol first, only she'd been strong-willed enough to make herself stop.

That would explain a lot.

There was someone else—or some*thing* else—that was the real power behind Rhapsody Harrison's throne. Anyone strong-willed enough to walk away from alcohol was strong-willed enough to deal with the drone attacks, only she hadn't. Because she *couldn't*.

Someone had Rhap on a short leash. Probably the same person who controlled the weapons spire that Drake had never seen before.

Gus knew she should cut the woman some slack, but she didn't have time for that. There'd been another explosion in the city just as they'd run out of Rhap's apartment. Who knew what kind of damage that attack had done?

Gus shoved her laser pistols in the waistband of her pants, out of sight beneath her jacket but in easy reach. Even though she wanted to shoot every skudging drone out of the sky, none were in sight, and she had other things to do.

Drake stood at the edge of the debris field, rooted to the spot, staring in horror at a small boy trying to rouse his mother. The boy still had a Happy Birthday! holographic crown on his head. One look at the boy's mother told Gus the woman wouldn't be wishing her son a happy birthday ever again.

Drake was probably suffering from flashbacks of his own son's death. He hadn't been there when his son had been killed. That wouldn't have stopped his imagination from providing him with excruciating, horrible visions of what must have happened to his boy Callum.

Gus needed Drake to snap out of it. They could both deal with the horror later. Right now, there were people who needed their help.

Like this little boy.

"Take care of him!" Gus shouted at Drake, pointing at the little boy.

She didn't stop to make sure he did what she asked. She knew he would.

She spotted a civilian wandering through the debris, a young man who looked like he'd been lucky enough to escape most of the blast with only a singed haircut and a nasty burn on one arm.

"You!" she said, shouting at him. "You know basic first aid?"

He nodded at her, quick jerks of his head.

"Good." She pointed at a middle-aged man sitting on the remains of a table. He still clutched the broken handle of a coffee mug, his eyes staring at nothing, while blood poured from a gash on his head. "Take care of him."

The civilian did as he was told.

"Emergency services will be here shortly," Rhapsody said. Her voice was flat and shocky, and her face was still pale. "We can go now. We should go now. They will take care of all of this."

Gus marched over to Rhap. She fought the urge to grab the taller woman by the front of her caftan and shake her. Hard. Rhap might outweigh Gus by nearly twice her body weight, but Gus was angry enough she didn't care.

"Haven't you been listening?" Gus said. "This wasn't the only explosion. Your 'emergency services' are going to be busy. People are dying here, and they will keep dying if we don't help."

"We have to leave," Rhap said, her voice still flat, those remarkable green eyes of hers refusing to focus on Gus. "You cannot be here. We should not have left...I should not have let you leave with your...."

Over the sobs and shouts and wails of the injured and dying, Gus heard a sound she was all too familiar with.

The whir of a drone's blades. From the pitch of the things, this drone was larger than the one that had scanned their unmanned transport.

Rhap's eyes weren't vacant now. "We must leave now! Your lives are in danger." Her gaze shifted to where Drake held the birthday boy in his arms, trying to comfort him. "You re-activated your pistols within the city. Only my weapons can be activated in the city. Only mine! I should not have let you... but you left so fast, we left so fast, and I forgot that you still had your weapons..."

Gus understood, all right.

That wasn't an emergency drone she was hearing. It was one of the skudging automated security drones. One of the drones who'd used a laser cannon to take out a restaurant filled with civilians, only this time it was coming for Gus and Drake. And it wouldn't care who it killed in its quest to punish them for breaking the law by re-enabling their own weapons.

Just disabling their weapons wasn't going to cut it this time. They'd already broken the law, and the drone had judged them guilty. It was coming to carry out its sentence.

Gus grabbed the laser rifle and pistol from Rhap's slackened grip. If Rhap's guns were the only ones that could be active within the city limits, fine. Gus threw her own laser pistols into the middle of the street, fairly certain she'd never see them again.

"Get rid of your gun!" she shouted at Drake. At least he'd had the good sense to grab one of Rhap's laser rifles off her wall. "And say your goodbyes to birthday boy. We've got work to do."

She took off at a run *toward* the sound of the approaching drone, Drake running after her.

"What are we doing?" he shouted when he caught up to her.

She grinned the kind of grim smile the members of her squadron had come to know well. The kind of smile that said the bad guys weren't going to know what hit them. The smile that said Gray Lady, the hero of the 83rd Armor Division, was headed their way to bring down a world of hurt on their heads.

"We're going to kill that skudging drone," she shouted back. "And *then* we're going to figure out who sent it and pay them a little visit."

CHAPTER 8

Heart hammering, adrenaline blazing through his bloodstream, Drake charged headlong with Gus toward the approaching drone, furious at what it had done to the innocent civilians and ready to do whatever it took to bring the thing down.

Not even for an instant did he question Gus's decision to fight back against it, not after witnessing the carnage it had unleashed on the devastated high-rise. He couldn't get the image of that little boy's dead mother out of his mind. The boy had clung to Drake *so hard*. He wasn't a baby or even a toddler. No, he was old enough that he was going to remember for the rest of his life the day the world had exploded around him, taking his mother away from him forever. On his birthday, no less.

That made Drake furious. No child should ever have to lose a parent that way.

He'd shoved the boy into Rhap's arms before he'd taken

off sprinting after Gus. For a short, stocky, muscular woman, Gus ran *fast* when her blood was boiling. That was fine with him. Even if it hadn't been coming to kill them, the choice to retaliate was a no-brainer; additional innocent lives had to be spared, even if going after that thing with a paltry rifle or two meant possible suicide.

Gus had no armor. Drake had no professional military training. Somehow, though, as they rushed toward the drone through city streets filled with panicked civilians all running the other way, Drake never hesitated or considered turning back. What they were about to do *had* to be done, at any cost.

If he hadn't been so angry, so *furious*, his first sight of the drone might have made him miss a step. This thing was *huge*, nearly the size of the torso on Gus's armor, and it was fast. No wonder unarmed civilians were terrified of the things.

Zooming forward on four propellers in their circular casings, the drone emitted a loud buzz like a massive, angry insect. A bright red light flashed on the nose of its oblong body like a malevolent eye—the sighting beam for the cylindrical laser cannon mounted on its belly. As long as the light kept flashing, Drake wasn't worried; until it stopped, the weapon hadn't locked on its target and wasn't ready to fire.

Drake knew that much from past encounters with similar, if somewhat smaller, devices on other Frontier worlds. For a smuggler like him, fighting security drones was an occupational hazard. He had always had more luck dodging them than destroying them, though, and he certainly wasn't an expert on obliterating them with the perfect shot to a vulnerable spot while running toward the things.

Dodge and hide, that had saved his ass more than once. But then again, the security drones he'd encountered in the past hadn't been programmed to obliterate his hiding places along with everyone else inside just to make sure he didn't get away.

This time around, he was more than willing to give it his best shot. "For birthday boy, you skudging piece of space junk!" he shouted as he jerked up the rifle he'd grabbed back at Rhap's place.

He quickly aimed over the sights at the end of the barrel, curled his index finger around the trigger, and pulled, hoping to strike that very red light on the drone's nose. Maybe, if he could damage the sighting mechanism, the cannon would be incapable of unleashing its destructive power with any degree of accuracy.

Unfortunately, his shot went just enough wide that the shot deflected off the metallic shell of the drone's nose instead of striking the sighting beam. Cursing, he pulled the trigger again, and another blast leaped from the barrel —this time, kicking the nose left and leaving the red light intact.

It didn't stay that way for long, though.

Gus cranked off a shot that punched straight into the light, blasting it apart and dousing it for good.

"That was for his mother," Gus muttered, a grim smile on her face.

As if enraged, the drone bobbed from side to side as it kept coming, throwing sparks from the shattered sighting bulb. Unflappable as always, even without her protective armor, Gus stopped in her tracks and fired a series of shots, targeting the drone's propellers.

"And for the meal I didn't get to eat," she said as two of the propellers exploded within a breath of each other, showering the street with flickering sparks.

The drone flopped from side to side like a crashing transport wallowing through the air.

Jaws clenched, Drake took the next shot, blowing up a third propeller.

The drone floundered on its last remaining propeller for a moment, as if expecting to miraculously regain its stability...then flipped over on its back and dropped hard to the pavement, trailing black smoke from burnt wiring and fried electronics.

But it wasn't dead yet. It just couldn't see them.

So it proceeded to blindly shoot its lasers. Glass exploded as beams struck the high-rises on both sides of the street and blew out the windows on passing vehicles. More screams filled the air, and from somewhere, a baby started wailing.

Skudge!

Drake had had enough of this thing.

Both of them cursing loudly, Drake and Gus proceeded to pound the drone with a fusillade of rounds that did just enough damage that it finally gave up the ghost and stopped shooting. The lasers withdrew into its fuselage and the laser cannon hung loose on its frame.

Gus wrinkled her nose at the smell coming off the dead drone. Drake felt like doing the same thing, but he needed all the breath he could get, stinky or not. He hadn't been in a battle like that in years, just him and a rifle against a piece of tech programmed to kill him, and his heart was pounding hard inside his chest.

For the moment, the threat was over. He could stand here and catch his breath, let his heart settle down, but only for a moment.

While that particular unit would not continue to rain down death and destruction on innocent bystanders any longer, Drake wasn't foolish enough to think it hadn't called home as soon as it had come under attack.

"Damn thing." Gus shouldered her borrowed rifle and let out a long breath. "Even with the odds in our favor, it put up *way* too much of a fight."

"Toughest one I've ever gone up against, that's for sure." Drake nudged the drone with the barrel of his rifle, worried it might burst back to life and lash out again with murderous fury.

"Not so tough if I'd had my skudging *armor* on," growled Gus.

Just then, Rhapsody approached, without the boy. Drake hoped she'd found someone reliable to leave him with.

Her gaze focused grimly on the downed drone at their feet. "There will be more where that came from. They are probably already en route."

Drake thought for a moment, then nodded as understanding dawned. Not only had they re-enabled their own weapons within the city, which had sent the drone after them in the first place, they'd killed it instead of peacefully letting it carry out its sentence and kill them.

"Two crimes for the price of one," he said. "They tagged us on the video feed from this one, and I'm guessing we're now Chrysallix's most wanted. Every security drone'll be gunning for us."

"I am afraid so, *chér*." Rhap looked around worriedly. "I will need to file an exception request with the system AI, but that will take a bit of time...and the outcome is not guaranteed. Perhaps it would be best if you both...at least for a while..."

She didn't have to say the rest. Regret was clear in those remarkable green eyes that he used to love to gaze into during their more intimate moments. Catching up on old times would have to wait.

"Make ourselves scarce?" asked Drake.

"Exactly," said Rhap.

"There's no need." Gus was scowling. She still held both the rifle and the pistol she'd taken from Rhap. "We've got plenty of ammo left. We took this one out just fine. We can take out as many as they throw at us."

Spoken like a true armor jock. Never give up, not when she had the advantage. But she didn't, not really.

He had to be careful here. He couldn't just take Rhap's side against Gus, not when it came to something Gus was very good at. Not unless he wanted to do some fancy smoothin' over later.

"That's true," Drake said. "But think about it this way. If we make ourselves scarce—" he held up his hands in a *just give me a minute* gesture when Gus opened her mouth to argue "—we could put the time to good use." Drake gave the dead drone another nudge with his rifle barrel. "We still need to figure out who sent this thing, don't we?"

Now it was Rhap's turn to protest. He couldn't win for losing.

"That is no mystery." Rhap actually sounded affronted. "They were dispatched by the Chrysallix defense grid, responding to violations of criminal law."

"Dispatched by whom?" asked Gus. "Even if the drones and defense grid are automated, there must still be some kind of human operational authority responsible for programming and maintaining them, right?"

Rhap frowned. "It is complicated, I am afraid," she said with a sigh. "A contractor organization set up the system, but our contract with them does not include *robust* support. They have not been in contact with us since the initial installation, in fact, even though we have filed numerous trouble tickets with their help desk."

"And who mans their help desk?" asked Gus. If the tone of her voice was any indication, she was about at the end of her patience.

"It is fully automated," said Rhap. "Though I suppose there must be *someone* organic in the mix at some level."

This was ridiculous. The Rhapsody he'd known would have never been as lackadaisical about something as impor-tant as a security contract. She'd told him she hadn't had a drink in the last three years. Just how many brain cells had she fried with alcohol in the three years before that? She'd been a shrewd, if somewhat manipulative, businesswoman. It was pretty clear she wasn't the same woman anymore, and not just because of the way she looked.

"So you don't *know* who sent the drone, is what you're telling us," said Drake. "The actual human operators or programmers are a mystery."

From the look on Rhap's face, he hadn't been entirely successful at keeping the frustration out of his voice.

"Correct." Rhap looked increasingly nervous with each passing moment. "But I am more than a little certain that they will send more of these things very soon in your direction."

"Then I guess we need to get back to the ship ASAP," said Gus. "And have a good, long look at *this* thing." Bending, she picked up the drone by one propellor strut and gave it a rough shake. It still gave no sign of impending reactivation. Chalk up one for the good guys. "If *you* don't know the skudge-hole behind it, maybe Drake and I can figure something out by rooting around in this thing's guts."

"That is...well..." Rhap scowled. "Perhaps you could avoid doing that."

"Why?" Gus narrowed her eyes suspiciously. "Is there something you're trying to hide?"

Rhap shook her head. "No, it is just...you see..."

"Worried about breaking another law?" asked Drake.

"More like breaking the warranty." Rhap sighed. "Battle damage is covered, but after-market tinkering is not."

Huh. Just when he thought the shrewd businesswoman had up and disappeared, here she was again. Worrying about costs. It was a little too late for that.

"Sounds like you signed a bad contract here, Rhap," said Drake. "This security outfit really has you over a barrel, don't they?"

"You do not know the half of it, *chér*."

It was a wonder she had a contract in the first place. The last time he'd been on Chrysallix, the planetoid didn't even have a central government. No central government, no real laws, and certainly no way to enforce them. Without any way to enforce a contract, what was the point of having one? It sounded like this security company—whoever or whatever was behind it—had basically installed itself as the real power on Chrysallix. Had Rhap agreed to the deal—and that's what it really was, contract or not; just a deal made with a mercenary instead of a smuggler—to keep herself as a figurehead? Or did she truly have no other choice? An *accept us or die* proposition. Drake wouldn't be surprised. Rhap had always been good about saving her own skin.

At least he could help her out. With Gus's help.

"Well, not to worry." Drake grinned. "Gus has a magic touch with tech. She'll get the information we need and put that thing back together good as new...but without all the overkill, if you catch my drift."

Rhap smiled back at him in a way that reminded him of the old days, at least a little. It was good to know the old Rhap was still in there, no matter how much she'd changed...and no matter what mess she'd gotten caught up in here on Chrysallix.

"You always know the right thing to do, Mephistopheles," she told him. "I had forgotten how much I missed having you by my side when the *skudge* hits the fan."

"Happy to be of help, ma'am." Drake nodded, but not too gallantly. He was well aware that Gus was watching and he had no intention of being too deferential to his ex in her presence. Hobbling his current relationship in any way was simply *not* on his to-do list.

"*We'll* be happy to help," Gus said. She put enough emphasis on that first word that Drake was sure it wasn't just for Rhap's benefit.

"Of course," Rhap said. "*We* will be most grateful to you as well. But if you insist on taking what is left of that thing with you, even if you are able to fix it, I must insist that you leave now." She shot a worried glance over Drake's shoulder in the direction the drone had come. "It is simply not safe for you to be here talking with me like this."

Gus didn't follow her gaze. She was looking in the direction of the spaceport at the edge of town where the *Golden Void* waited. The spaceport's dome was barely visible in the distance.

"Assuming we can make it to the ship before those damned drones swarm us," Gus said.

No kidding. That was a long way to go on foot while they were lugging the remains of a good-sized drone along with them. Gus had picked the thing up like it weighed next to nothing. She had muscles on muscles, but even Gus had her limits.

"That, I believe I can help with." Rhapsody pulled out a comm device, thumb-typed rapidly on its touch screen, and squeezed an action button on the side of the rectangular unit. "The defense grid may be too independent for its own good—or mine—but I can still call a *cab* when I need one."

The words had barely left her mouth when a sleek, silver vehicle—a hover-car floating on a cushion of pressurized air—zoomed up from a cross street and stopped in front of them.

"Your ride has arrived." Rhap bowed slightly, smiling. "It will take you directly to your ship at the spaceport."

As she said it, the door closest to them slid open.

"Thanks." Gus tossed the drone into the vehicle. "I'm guessing the spaceport's not exactly a safe harbor."

Rhap shook her head. "Sadly, no. Not until the exception is granted."

If it was granted. Drake hadn't forgotten that one big *if*.

Gus only nodded. "Let us know when the heat's off."

Rhap looked around furtively as if she'd heard the sound of an approaching drone. "I will be in touch. Safe travels to you both, if such a thing is possible."

Drake didn't want to think that this might be the last time he saw Rhap. He'd be back. So would Gus. They'd figure this mess out, then straighten it out the way only an armor jock and a space cowboy could. They were damn good at it.

They'd be back. But until then...

"Tell this thing not to spare the horses," said Drake as he got ready to follow Gus into the cab.

"What horses?" Rhap frowned with confusion.

He couldn't help grinning. She hadn't always understood his colorful expressions back in the day, either.

"Just tell it to pour on the speed," said Drake. "And you be careful yourself, y'hear?"

"I do not think that is possible any longer," Rhap told him. "But I appreciate the sentiment, *chér*."

The cab did indeed *not spare the horses*. It took off at top speed the instant the door shut behind Drake. He barely caught himself from faceplanting in what was left of the drone.

"Easy there, space cowboy," Gus said as she helped push him into his seat.

He couldn't help himself. He looked out the cab's back window at Rhap's diminishing form.

Gus followed his gaze. "Something's rotten here," she said. "And your ex is smack dab in the middle of it."

"Yeah," he said. "I know."

She put a gentle hand on his shoulder. "We gonna kick some ass?"

He turned around in his seat and looked at the armor jock sitting beside him. If he had to kick some ass, there was no one he'd rather have at his side. Or watching his back. Or hell—leading the charge.

"We are going to kick some *major* ass, darlin'," he said, a promise he punctuated with a kiss.

Just as soon as they figured out whose ass they needed to kick.

CHAPTER 9

For a few tense moments, Gus thought they might have to blast their way out of the spaceport. All those law enforcement types she'd missed in the port the first time around were now omnipresent, although not exactly what she expected.

They were all bots. Every single blasted one of them.

Apparently Rhapsody hadn't been kidding when she said everything about the defense grid was fully automated. Although Gus didn't quite buy the whole "trouble ticket" and "help desk" explanation Rhapsody'd thrown at them. It sounded too glib. Too pulled out of her ass. And way too far-fetched, even for a Frontier world. Yeah, sure, a security contractor wouldn't necessarily set up a fully manned shop on a Frontier world when an automated system would do, but there *had* to be a living being somewhere in the mix. Gus was going to find that person and wring their sorry neck.

The cab had dropped them off in front of their terminal, and it had been a long walk back to where the *Void* was docked. None of the bots had bothered them, even though Gus was still carrying what was left of the drone. It might have had something to do with the fact that Drake was still armed with Rhapsody's laser rifle, Gus had another one of Rhap's laser rifles slung on a strap over her back, and they'd clearly taken out one of the bots' automated siblings with just those weapons. If that was the case, these security bots had a self-preservation directive. Good to know.

The trouble didn't start until they requested clearance to depart the dome. They were put on standby for so long that even Drake started to lose patience.

"Just how broken is the weapons control console?" he asked.

"Not so much that we can't shoot a hole in the dome," she said.

The hit didn't have to be precise. Any old hole would blow the dome open enough for the *Void* to get through. Not that Gus *wanted* to blow a hole in the dome. They were trying to avoid hurting innocent civilians, not expose them to the toxic atmosphere of Chrysallix. The people who could get to their ships would be fine, and she was pretty sure the spaceport's dome could be sealed off from the city's dome, but that still left a lot of civilians in the space-port who'd be screwed if they didn't have environment suits they could pop on at a moment's notice.

Just when she started tinkering around on the weapons console, trying to find coordinates that she could be sure the ship's weapons could actually hit, an automated message came through the bridge's speakers:

"*Golden Void*, you are cleared for departure. *La Meilleure* sends her regards and best wishes for a safe and productive voyage."

Drake heaved an audible sigh of relief. "See, what'd I tell you? Good ol' Rhap, she came through."

Enough to get them clearance to leave but not enough to stay, Gus thought but didn't say.

Drake fiddled with the controls, flipping switches and twisting dials, and finally engaged the joystick he used while the *Void* was in space. He maneuvered the ship into the airlock, and as soon as the dome's outer doors started to open, he didn't spare one single horse. The ship shot sideways through the opening between the dome's doors with barely a hair's width to spare.

He whooped, one fist raised in the air, as the ship blasted into space.

Gus shook her head, but she was grinning wildly too. She understood his impulse to blow off a little steam. There had been times after a particular intense space battle when she'd done barrel rolls in her armor for the same reason. Not that her company commanders had ever let her get away with a stunt like that without subsequently chewing her ass out in front of the rest of her squad. It had been worth the ass-chewing, and the glint in their eyes even as they read her the riot act told her they understood perfectly why she'd done it. And that maybe in their time they'd done something just like it.

She stood up from the weapons console. "Need anything before I go take apart that nasty little thing in the cargo bay?"

And put it back together. Without all its parts. Drake

had promised Rhap that Gus could rebuild the drone to look like new, except for its overkill options, of course. She wasn't quite sure how she was going to do that since they'd shot three of its propellers to smithereens and left the pieces back on the street. *And* they hadn't managed to get the new replicator they'd gone to see Rhap for in the first place.

"Hold up a minute and I'll come with you."

Drake studied the screen at the nav station, flipped a few more switches, and then apparently satisfied with what he saw, tucked the joystick back in its cradle.

She peered over his shoulder.

He'd set a course that would take them away from Chrysallix, but not *too* far away. Just enough to be out of range of any of the weapons on that weapons spire.

"Meet with your approval, Gray Lady?" he asked.

He'd craned his head around and was giving her one of his impish smiles. When they'd first met, he'd been very protective of *his* ship, and most particularly his bridge. Far from welcoming her input, he'd been actively pissed off about it. Of course, she'd been impatient as hell back then and probably not the easiest person to live with. She still wanted to get back to hunting down Jorritz Tor. That was their real mission, after all. But she was willing to bide her time to take her revenge on the weaselly bastard. Let him think he'd gotten away clean before she swooped in and taught him otherwise.

So if they had to hang out around Chrysallix a little while, help Drake's ex get a particularly vicious contractor off her back, she could live with that.

She smiled back. "You're the captain, space cowboy," she said, and she rewarded him with a kiss.

They locked the bridge down on their way to the cargo bay. Chrysallix *was* a haven for smugglers—well-behaved smugglers who didn't carry active weapons around with them—but that didn't mean the space around the planetoid was free of pirates. Gus didn't expect that anyone would try to overwhelm the *Void* and board her, but it never hurt to be prepared. She still had Rhap's laser rifle slung around her back, although she'd replaced Rhap's laser pistol with one of her own from their own weapons stash. Likewise, Drake had replaced Rhap's rifle with a replica of an ancient sawed-off shotgun. The shotgun's load wouldn't punch holes in the *Void's* hull, but it would shred any would-be pirate's body parts into hamburger.

It also made a hell of a boom when Drake fired it. He'd demonstrated it for her once on Shepard's Moon after she got out of the hospital when she'd made fun of him for carrying it.

"All part of the package, darlin'," he'd said then.

True. The more she got to know him, the more it seemed like he was a refugee from a past that few people knew about anymore, much less remembered. The ancient shotgun went with his ancient guitar and the old-fashioned controls for the ship. Sometimes she wondered why he didn't just find a nice Frontier planet only a few steps up the evolutionary ladder from the Stone Age, settle down around a campfire, and become the cowboy he clearly was meant to be.

"So how come you asked me to wait for you?" Gus said when they got to the cargo bay.

The drone, or what was left of it, sat on her workbench next to her armor's helmet. Even with only one propeller, its targeting light shattered into so much useless electronics, and the laser cannon hanging by a single wire, the thing looked deadly vicious. Gus would rather smash the rest of it beneath her armor's heavy metal foot, but she'd make nice for Drake's sake. So that he could keep his promise. That's what you did for people you cared about, and she more than cared for Drake.

"I want to poke around in that thing's brain. You fix things your way," he said, and he pulled a hammer—a small one—from one pocket with a smirk, "and I fix things my way."

She was about to smack him in the shoulder over the hammer—her favorite tool that she hadn't been able to find in weeks—but then he pulled a small piece of electronics from a different pocket and wiggled it in front of her face.

She recognized it. A self-contained AI, not linked to the ship's systems—hell, probably not linked to anything. She'd seen systems engineers use the things to troubleshoot meltdowns when they suspected malicious code had been inserted in otherwise benign systems. The AI could be wiped or out-and-out destroyed if the malicious code tried to replicate itself within the AI.

The gadgets weren't cheap, and the best ones were classified. They'd proved invaluable to systems engineers she'd known back when she'd still been with the 83rd. Frontier worlds seemed to attract wannabe dictators like the warlord they'd defeated on Shepard's Moon. That particular warlord had tried to use might and weaponry to take the planet over. Smarter, more devious wannabes combined brute force with schemes to take over a planet's infrastructure, planting malicious code inside operating systems that allowed them to control everything: power, water, air, transportation…

Defense systems.

The defense systems on Chrysallix were fully automated.

While she was going to be digging through the drone's guts, Drake was going to use the self-contained AI to dig through the drone's operating system. And he was going to do it in a way that would keep them—and the ship— perfectly safe.

"Just when I think I have you pegged," she said, "you go and surprise me. Where the hell did you get that? And where have you been keeping it?"

From the looks of the gadget he was holding, it was a pretty high-end piece of tech.

"A smuggler never tells," he said, smiling widely now. "I gotta say, foolin' you feels pretty good."

She arched an eyebrow in mock annoyance. "Oh, it does now, does it?"

"You are *not* an easy person to get anything by."

"That's a relief," she said. "Here I thought I was finally going senile."

He scrubbed a hand through her short, gray hair. "Never." He pulled her into a hug and planted a kiss on the top of her head. "Now, what do you say about getting to work? The sooner we get some answers to who's been pulling Rhap's strings, the sooner we can bust out the good stuff while we figure out what to do about it."

"The good stuff, huh?" she said, looking up at him. The good stuff was usually the prelude to a far different kind of good stuff that they hadn't engaged in nearly enough lately. "Sounds like a plan, space cowboy."

Less than an hour later, while Gus was working on putting back together everything she'd taken apart and spread over her workbench, she caught sight of a micro etching in a piece of the drone's housing. She'd thought at first that the part was formed from an ultralight alloy commonly used in drones, where every ounce saved increased the drone's effectiveness. Basic physics: lighter drones flew better.

Only this wasn't the kind of ultralight alloy she was used to. She tried scraping it with one of her tools. Her tool didn't make a dent. She tried heating it. No go. The numerous laser hits from the rifles she and Drake had shot at the drone hadn't done any damage at all to this particular part of the housing.

So she used the tool she liked best.

She hit it with the hammer Drake had given her.

The metal head of the hammer split down the middle. The piece of housing didn't even dent.

"Son of a bitch!" She put her hands on her hips.

Then she aimed a high-resolution camera at the etching.

The next time she swore, it was far more heartfelt and had much more anger behind it.

Across the bay, Drake swore even louder and far more inventively.

They both sat up from their stations, and their gazes met and held. She saw the same anger in his expression that she felt in her heart.

She gave him a single nod, and he gave her a grim, mirthless smile in return.

They knew who'd programmed the drones. Who Rhapsody's mysterious contractor was. They knew who was holding Rhapsody and the people of Chrysallix hostage.

Now they just had to figure out a way to kill him without getting blown out of the sky by his weapons spire.

Without a working replicator and without her armor at one hundred percent, they had to figure out a way to kill Jorritz Tor.

CHAPTER 10

Simeon Ezekiel was waiting for Rhapsody by the time she got back to her apartment.

"Suzerain," he said, with a bow of his head that was deferential enough for protocol, should anyone be watching, but not nearly as obsequious as when he escorted strangers for an audience with *La Meilleure* of Chrysallix. In public areas, like the atrium in her building, it was safer to assume that someone—or some automated *thing*—was always watching.

He stood next to her door. The door had locked automatically when she had fled after Drake and his Gray Lady, making sure before they left that Drake took one of her own rifles with him. The door had been coded to allow Ezekiel to enter, but he would only use that when he escorted expected guests. Decorum must be maintained.

She wanted a drink. Every cell in her body cried out for

a drink, but one drink led to the next, led to the next. It was difficult to maintain decorum when one was drunk.

Even more difficult to take advantage of an opportunity that had presented itself unexpectedly when one's mind was befuddled with alcohol. No matter how much she wanted it.

She didn't nod back to Ezekiel when she passed her hand over the white sensor bulb that unlocked the door to her apartment and went inside. She knew without looking that he would follow her.

Once inside, she let herself relax, but only a little. As the Suzerain, *La Meilleure,* the damn leader of what had once been a paradise of a Frontier world, she was entitled to privacy. Ezekiel swept her apartment regularly for listening devices. For concealed cameras. For motion sensors and heat sensors and any other type of sensor that might be used to spy on her. The ones he'd found had been quickly and efficiently tricked into transmitting only what she wanted them to transmit.

Ezekiel was far more than a political functionary or a glorified butler. Ezekiel had been with her since Drake had exited her life the first time. She had used Ezekiel—as she used all men, if she was being honest with herself—only to discover that he had been using her in his own quest for power by ingratiating himself with the right kind of people. In an odd way, she could respect that. She understood people who used each other. The only man she had truly cared for had been Drake, and he had been the only man who had not tried to use her for his own advantage.

Drake had been unique. He still was. Ezekiel was a poor substitute, but he had his uses.

She would never permit herself to care for Ezekial. Mutual respect was what kept them together. That, and the promise of wealth and power.

Wealth they had. Power they had inadvertently given away. Never again.

"This plan of yours," Ezekiel said. "It's dangerous."

Yes, it was. Rhapsody would be the first to admit it, but desperate plans often were.

And she was desperate. She had avoided witnessing in person the carnage she knew the drones were inflicting on her city. She had stayed away from the fighting on purpose. She had weapons, but fear of retaliation kept her from using them. She had been shown, in graphic detail, how easy it would be for her to be replaced with a new *La Meilleure*. He had done it before in a different place, this one man she had been unable to manipulate.

She had lied to Drake and his Gray Lady. She knew exactly who the driving force was behind the automated security grid that had taken her city hostage, and no amount of help desk requests—not that she had lodged any—would change that situation. She could have told the Gray Lady who that person was, but she wanted Drake's paramour to discover the man's identity for herself. Knowledge earned was so more delicious than knowledge served up merely for the asking.

Especially this knowledge.

"*Chér,*" she said, cupping the side of Ezekiel's face with one gentle, sensuous hand. "Fate will not send us a gift like this more than once."

She looked into his eyes, saw the doubt there. She had no need to be the flamboyant woman she had been with

Drake and his new lady. That had been a ruse. An act. An old persona she had wrapped herself in because it would be what Drake expected her to be. But even more than Drake, Rhapsody was counting on the paramour, the famous Gray Lady of the Alliance, to do what needed to be done.

She could not manipulate Drake the way she had done in the past. She had seen the shock, the disappointment in his eyes when he had first laid his eyes on her. That had been a disappointment. True, their relationship had been based solely on sexual attraction, at least in the beginning. The person she had been then could wrap anyone in knots. Everyone had wanted her, only a special few could have her.

Everyone still did, except Drake. His heart belonged to his Gray Lady, whether he knew it or not. Her own physical changes were too much for him to accept. His loss.

But it would not be *her* loss.

She entered a code on a hidden keypad at the base of her weapons display. A portion of the wall slid upwards into the ceiling, revealing a series of holo-viewscreens and two old-fashioned keyboards. Drake had extoled the virtues of systems so ancient that no modern hacks existed, like the keyboards and the switches and dials on his ship.

One of the holoscreens displayed a slowly blinking red dot against a map of the Obsidiac system.

She plucked the dot from the holoscreen and rotated it until a number appeared over the dot.

The rifle the Gray Lady had taken from her on the street. The device that tagged the rifle as one *La Meilleure* was allowed to use was useful for doing many things. Like tracking its wearer.

Rhapsody Harrison smiled. Drake and the Gray Lady had not gone far. That meant they would be coming back. She had been sure that Drake would return. The man she had known years ago had a soft spot in his heart for innocents. She had hoped he still did, a hope that had been confirmed when he comforted the young boy on the street.

That had been hard-won knowledge. Rhapsody would have nightmares for years about the damage done to innocents. The nightmares would be the cost of freedom not only for herself and Ezekiel, but for the people who believed in the figurehead she had become. She considered it a small cost to pay if this plan worked.

And it would.

Because even more than Drake's kind heart, Rhapsody knew what motivated his Gray Lady.

Revenge.

They had a common enemy, Rhapsody and Augusta Light. Even in the Frontier, news traveled fast if you had the right connections, and Ezekiel did. Before Drake had docked his ship on Chrysallix, Rhapsody knew everything she needed to know about the Gray Lady.

She was a warrior no longer fettered by the laws of the Alliance. She and Drake were chasing the man she blamed for the death of her son's father. For nearly killing her son through the surrogate warlord on Shepard's Moon. She and Drake had put out feelers, quietly trying to track down this man.

The same man who had out-manipulated Rhapsody.

The man who had taken by force what his worthless contract did not authorize him to take.

The man whose drones were killing her people, whose

weapons on the dreadful tower he had erected were aimed at the very things that kept her people alive.

The spaceport.

The pods where they grew the food she and her people ate.

The vast power plant that kept the domes lit and the air filtration systems working. That ran the water generators and provided heat and made every moment of every day bearable. There would be no civilization of this magnitude on Chrysallix without the power the plant generated.

And Jorritz Tor's weapons threatened it all.

Ezekiel brought her a bowl of *sancocho*. The soup had cooled, but the aroma still made her stomach rumble. Her traitorous stomach. If this worked out the way she hoped, the way they'd both planned, perhaps she would take up something other than cooking to assuage what was left of her conscience.

"You trust him?" Ezekiel asked.

"Yes." She put the glowing red dot back on the holo-screen where it took its place among the stars. "I trust *her*. Revenge is a hard thing to overcome. So is loyalty. This is a woman who stole her armor from the military and lived to tell of it. She is a hero. She will be a hero for us."

"Will there be anything left when she's done?" he asked.

He had never seen an armor jock, as they called them-selves, in action. Rhapsody had, long ago when she had been a child and had learned how to make *sancocho* from her mother, may she rest in peace. His worries about the damage an armored warrior could inflict were not unfounded.

"We will still win," she said.

She put her soup bowl down and wrapped a hand around the collar of his suit jacket. So prim and proper, her Ezekiel when he was acting in character. Such an untamed man when he was not.

"And that is all that matters," she said as she drew him down towards her. He did not mind that she was twice the woman she had once been. She had never minded, no matter how Drake's rejection had momentarily made her feel. "That we win," she said.

"That we win," he echoed.

She erased any further worries he might have had with a kiss that was all unbridled passion. She might have given that kiss to Drake, if he had only asked.

If he had not replaced her.

His loss.

It would never be hers.

CHAPTER 11

"Are we there yet?" asked Gus from the doorway of the *Golden Void*'s bridge.

"Almost," Drake said from the navigation station. "We're about fifteen minutes out, darlin'."

Gus grunted unhappily. Drake had been aware of her increasing impatience for the past six hours—ever since they'd found the connections to Jorritz Tor in the remains of the killer drone. Her desire for retribution against the arms dealer for his attempted murder of her son had been amplified now that a solid lead to Tor's whereabouts had been found.

Drake could identify. Tor had suckered in Rhap, a woman who'd never been suckered in by anyone in her life, and that pissed Drake off something fierce...but he was trying his best to keep a lid on things and channel their need for revenge in a productive direction. If Tor was on Chrysallix, or at least could be drawn there by strikes against his local security apparatus, Drake and Gus needed to make the right moves before showing their hand.

One thing they'd agreed on was that they shouldn't lash out indiscriminately. With her armor and the *Void*'s weapons control system still in need of repair, they weren't ready for a full-scale battle. Leaving Chrysallix without the replicator they needed to make those repairs, they were nowhere near 100% fighting capacity...and going up against Tor's tech and personnel like that could be fatal, or futile at best.

Which was why, very soon after their autopsy of the drone, they'd zoomed away from Chrysallix toward a new destination. Fortunately, Drake knew of a Frontier outpost where they might be able to score the necessary spare parts for repairs and beef up their armory in the bargain, a sketchy hole-in-the-wall where a smuggler like him might be able to swing an off-the-radar deal.

Unfortunately, said outpost was also the kind of place where Drake, Gus, and the *Void* could end up blown to smithereens for no good reason...*just because.*

"You really think this is the smart play?" It wasn't the first time Gus had asked the question.

Drake couldn't blame her, but he did his best to put her mind at ease. "I do." Fearless and driven as she was, he knew she didn't want to risk missing out on revenge against their mutual enemy. "The Bluff is close, historically well-stocked, and the kind of place most folks stay away from."

"But they stay away for the same reason that could get us both killed," said Gus. "Those old friends of ours."

"This is true." Drake shrugged. "But what the hell? I'm feelin' lucky."

"You're sure about that?"

He looked back at her and grinned. "Long as I've got my good luck charm, I am...and there *you* are, so yeah. I'm feelin' *real* lucky."

Gus moved up behind him, put her hands on his shoulders, and massaged them. "All right then. I guess we roll the dice."

"If it means taking out that son of a bitch Tor, it'll be worth it." Relishing the feel of her strong fingers digging into his aching muscles, Drake flicked switches and punched a button on the nav console, adjusting the *Void*'s trajectory. All over again, he appreciated the great thing he had going with Augusta Light; Rhapsody, for all her positive attributes, had always been one to *receive* massages, not *provide* them.

"There it is." Drake pointed at the blinking red dot that represented their destination on the big nav screen. "The one and only Buddy's Bluff."

"You take me to the nicest places, don't you?" Gus gave his shoulders a sharper squeeze for emphasis.

"Only the best for you, Gray Lady." He twisted a knob, changing the feed on the main nav screen to a real-time visual of the view ahead. Instead of a blinking dot, a blue-green sphere set against a glittering starfield appeared on the display, a placid-looking planet complete with lacy white clouds and what looked like twin blue moons on opposite sides of the orbital plane.

But as the *Void* got closer, it quickly became abundantly clear that the two objects were not moons at all.

"And there *they* are." Drake smirked and shook his head. A little chill shot up his spine at the sight of those things—though in his last encounter with something similar, he and Gus had emerged intact. It was only natural, as deadly and capricious as their occupants could be, to feel apprehensive at the sight of them.

Those giant, shimmering dodecahedrons were the terror of the galaxy. The only thing worse than encountering one of them was meeting up with *two* of them.

Which was exactly why more people didn't come to Buddy's Bluff...and those who did, didn't always come back.

These two were at least glowing blue. For now. If they turned red? As the saying went, red and you're dead.

"What is it with you and *the Fluke*?" asked Gus. "I'm starting to think you've got a thing for those *skudge-suckers*."

"Comes with the territory, darlin'," he told her. "Hang around long enough out here on the Frontier and you're bound to cross paths with those things."

"Meeting them once was more than enough for me," said Gus. "I hate any enemy I don't have a chance of beating in a fair fight."

"Can't argue with you there."

Drake remembered, all too well, their last encounter with the Fluke, en route to Shepard's Moon to rescue Gus's son. The secretive, hyper-advanced beings had pursued the *Golden Void* through the rings of a gas giant, their dodecahedron Prowler ship blazing with the reddish glow that signified impending hostile action. Only by creating a random display of colored lights and carving a giant smiley face in the churning purple clouds of the gas giant's upper atmosphere had Drake and Gus managed to escape, somehow inspiring their pursuers to end the chase and respond with a smiley face of their own.

Gus had nicknamed the maneuver the Smiley Face Gambit.

The whole thing had made no practical sense, of course —but then, the Fluke's actions rarely did. Sometimes they bequeathed miraculous wonders unto those they encountered; other times, they exacted terrible punishments. Their reasons for doing so, however, were not known to outsiders. They never showed themselves in the flesh to those they met, and the only way they communicated was with the screams of their unfortunate victims and the colors displayed on their prowlers. The Fluke were the very essence of chance and fate, as likely to destroy as to heal.

And two of their vessels were slowly rotating in orbit around Buddy's Bluff dead ahead, their intentions unknown as always.

"Who the hell would build an outpost on a planet orbited by Fluke Prowlers?" asked Gus.

"Folks who don't want bothered by most everyone else," said Drake. "I mean, sure, they could be arbitrarily disintegrated without warning at any moment...but they're mostly left alone in the meantime."

"Still seems crazy to me." Gus blew out her breath and shook her head. "And how long did you say *they've* been here? The Fluke?"

"Long before Buddy built the outpost, which was twelve years ago," explained Drake. "The Fluke were here when he got here, and they haven't budged since."

"Buddy sounds like one nutty son of a bitch, setting up shop in the shadow of those lunatics."

"He was."

"Was?"

"Before the Fluke killed him in an inexplicable strike five years ago," said Drake. "His kid, Buddy Junior, runs the place now."

"Seriously?" Gus stopped kneading his shoulders. "Why the hell would Buddy bring his kid to a place like this? And why would Junior stay on the same planet when the same aliens who killed his father right up here where they can do it all over again?"

"Beats me." Drake shrugged. "There's no place like home, they say. Be it ever so deadly."

"Still." Gus stared intently at the image on the nav screen as she resumed the massage. "It makes you wonder, doesn't it? Who's crazier—the Fluke, those unpredictable assholes—or Buddy Junior, who just keeps on living in their shadow even after they murdered his dad?"

"*Us*, probably, for showing up here even though we know better."

Drake checked several nav readouts and adjusted the *Void*'s course again, perfecting the ship's approach to the planet. His goal was to bring her in as close as he could to Buddy Jr.'s trading post while staying as far as he could from either Fluke Prowler. As certain as he was that the alien observers could see and hear everything that happened on and around the Bluff, he had no desire to draw their attention to the *Void* unless he had to.

"That doesn't exactly fill me with confidence," Gus said. "You really think we can get what we need here? Assuming we aren't randomly reduced to our component atoms by the Fluke, that is."

"It's worth a shot," he said.

"And someplace else isn't worth a better shot?"

Drake magnified the real-time video and panned over to one of the Fluke ships. It seemed quiescent enough, unlikely to cause any harm...which, unfortunately, made it no less likely to suddenly change colors from blue to red and unleash any number of horrific measures on anything it decided was in its way.

"Not this close," he said. "Buddy always had a rep for carrying just about everything a smuggler could need...and luckily for us, his credit terms were always pretty generous."

They'd gone over all this already, but that had been before he'd told Gus about Buddy Senior's unfortunate demise. Something like that wouldn't scare her off, not his Gray Lady, but she was taking it into consideration. They couldn't kick Tor's slimy butt if they were dead.

"What about his kid?" Gus asked.

"No reason to believe Junior changed things up much."

But Gus had a point. They didn't have a lot of cash to spare. If Junior wanted payment in full up front, they'd be in a world of hurt. Gus had been cut off from most of her savings and Drake's coffers were largely depleted. Credit was something they'd need in spades on this particular shopping trip.

Tapping Rhapsody's wealth might have taken off some of the pressure, but they'd decided not to tip her off to the details of their mission against Tor...at least not yet. Given her current situation, being at the mercy of an ultra-high tech security apparatus and all, it wasn't a stretch to assume she was bugged or that her personal staff had been infiltrated by Tor sympathizers.

Drake had never done business with Buddy's kid. If Junior didn't have the same generous credit policy as his father? They would be risking the Fluke going all malevolent on their ass for nothing.

"Just remember one thing, space cowboy." Gus gave his shoulder a sharp enough pinch to make him twitch. "My armor will *never* serve as collateral."

"The thought never crossed my mind." Though desperate times might call for desperate measures, Drake would never put her prized armor at risk...just as he was sure that she would never gamble the fate of his own prized possession, the *Void*, if given the chance. It was all part of having a loving relationship—recognizing and respecting the importance of certain things to the person you valued more than anything or anyone in the universe. There were lines you simply didn't cross, not if you wanted to keep the love alive between you...and that was something Drake wanted more than anything.

Perhaps more, even, than he wanted to retain possession of his ship.

The view on the nav screen shifted as the *Void* drew closer to the planet and its orbiting Fluke Prowlers. Suddenly, the dodecahedron on the right—hanging at approximately two o'clock above the sphere of the Bluff—began to change, its blue glow pulsing brighter, then dimmer, then brighter again.

"Look," said Gus. "One of them's changing."

Drake held his breath. If the pulses were a precursor to a

shift from blue to red, the *Void* might never get the chance to touch down on Buddy's Bluff—at least not as an intact object with undamaged human passengers aboard.

"Now they're *both* doing it," said Gus.

She was right, and the sight made his heart pound faster. The other dodecahedron was indeed pulsing like the first, its blue glow brightening and dimming...brightening and dimming.

"Should we back off?" asked Gus.

Drake had been wondering the exact same thing, but he shook his head. "My gut says no. Anyway, it's not like they can't get us if they want to, even if we run as fast as possible for open space."

Gus grunted. "Want me to suit up, just in case?"

"With all due respect, darlin', even if your suit wasn't down one space-tight seal, not even you could fight off a Fluke Prowler single-handedly. No one could."

"Maybe," said Gus. "But I'd rather go down fightin', if it comes to that."

"I can appreciate that...but let's play out this string a little longer, okay?"

Watching as the planet and the Prowlers grew larger on the screen, Drake resisted the urge to change course. The *Void* continued to glide forward, threading the needle between the enormous alien craft.

As it did so, the glow of the Fluke ships pulsed faster and reached greater extremes. By the time the *Void* slipped between them and Drake flicked the screen to a split view of the port and starboard Prowlers, the pulsing had become more like a rapid flashing.

Sweat trickled down Drake's back and sides. He'd

known destruction by the Fluke was a possibility, but now that it seemed imminent, his nervous tension was almost unbearable.

"Earl," he said, addressing the ship's AI. "What can you tell me about recent Fluke attacks on Buddy's Bluff?"

"No overtly hostile actions for the past three months," Earl said calmly. "There have, however, been multiple incidents of benevolent intervention during that same period."

"Historically, what does that suggest?" asked Drake. "Based on the frequency of past incidents, are we more likely to face a hostile or benevolent action?"

"The odds are approximately even," said Earl. "There is a statistically equal chance of either outcome—though it is also true that the Fluke have been historically unpredictable in this and other venues, and no forecast should be considered entirely…"

"Look!" Gus squeezed his shoulders harder than ever. "The one at two o'clock went dark!"

Gaping at the screen, Drake saw the starboard Prowler had indeed darkened. Without its glow, it hung there as a pitch-black sphere, blotting out the stars and part of the Bluff behind it.

"The other one did the same," said Gus. "I wonder what the *skudge* that means?"

"'Hello?'" Drake shrugged. "Or maybe they're just trying to spook us."

"Hey, Earl," said Gus. "Is there any record of these two Fluke Prowlers going dark before?"

"Negative," said Earl. "There is no record of these particular Prowlers exhibiting that behavior."

"Maybe it's nothing," said Drake. "That Prowler we

encountered en route to Shepard's Moon went dark, too, remember? Just before it lit up with a smiley face like the one we carved in the planet's atmosphere?"

"I remember," said Gus. "Do you think *they* do, too? Maybe word got around, and they're going to do the same thing?"

Before Drake could answer, the starboard Prowler flared with blazing white light—then cycled through a series of colors, one after another, each lasting for just a few seconds. The port Prowler did the same, though its sequence of colors was out of synch with those flashing on the surface of the starboard dodecahedron.

"What the *skudge?*" Drake scowled at the split-screen view, wondering what exactly what was happening. Were the Fluke displaying more of their typical random behavior...or was a sinister outcome in the works?

Suddenly, the Prowlers stopped cycling through colors —and Drake swallowed hard. The port Prowler had landed on yellow...and the starboard ship landed on red.

"I guess we should've backed off, after all," he said. "A red Fluke Prowler never means anything good."

"Yeah," said Gus, "but nothing bad's happening yet."

Sure enough, a moment passed without rampant destruction. Neither Prowler lashed out at the *Void* or anything else.

Then the colors started cycling again.

"Maybe the colors of both Prowlers have to match," offered Gus. "No match, no catastrophe."

Again, the changes stopped, leaving one Prowler purple and the other green. The next time it happened, one was red, the other was bright blue.

What had Gus said about rolling the dice? Drake might be crazy, but that's what all the cycling reminded him of: dice rolling down a felt-covered table, numbers tumbling over each other before the dice came to a stop and one number came out on top.

Only in this game there were two dice, and at the end of the roll, the numbers had to match.

The *Void* continued on its merry way toward the surface of Buddy's Bluff, unhindered.

"That seems to be the game they're running, for whatever reason," said Drake. "As long as red doesn't come up on both ships, we're okay."

"So I guess we should wrap our business up fast then, huh?" said Gus.

Drake watched the latest color cycle land on red...and orange.

"I'd agree with that assessment, Gray Lady," he said. "Time to put the pedal to the metal."

With that, he accelerated their drop toward the surface as much as he could, racing the *Void* toward Buddy's trading post on the deceptively sunny and lush surface of that Fluke-endangered world.

They were taking a big gamble, he and Gus, but it would be worth it if it enabled them to take down Tor and save Rhapsody's Chrysallix in the bargain. The risk was huge, but so were the stakes.

Tor had tried to murder Gus's son, seized control of Chrysallix from Rhapsody, and committed countless other crimes in his quest for profit and power. Risking their own lives in the shadow of the implacable and inscrutable Fluke seemed sensible given the scope of Tor's own monstrous misdeeds. The Fluke, at least, seemed arbitrary in doling out their disasters and balanced them on a cosmic scale with occasional blessings. Tor, on the other hand, was wickedness personified—the worst of humanity's sins wrapped up in one package.

Drake and Gus, if they survived this latest brush with the Fluke, would be justified in glowing only red—no trace of benevolent blue—when they finally got that foul package in their sights.

CHAPTER 12

The *Golden Void* made it to the surface of Buddy's Bluff without both Fluke Prowlers turning red at the same time. Score one for the good guys.

Not that Gus felt like celebrating. Not yet.

The Alliance military avoided areas of space where the Fluke tended to show up just on principle, and here they were, basically thumbing their noses at two Fluke ships by invading their territory. If they hadn't needed a new replicator so bad, and if Drake hadn't assured her the Bluff was the best possible chance of getting one without going bust, she would have suggested—strongly—that they hightail it to the next smugglers' paradise on down the line. Just because one Fluke Prowler had seemed amused by the Smiley Face Gambit didn't mean either one of these two would find the same kind of thing funny enough to leave the *Void* and the people inside her alone.

She wouldn't celebrate until they left this planet and the

125

Fluke were nothing more than glowing dots in the *Void's* rearview sensors. She wouldn't *really* celebrate until she had Tor in her armor's sights and pulled the trigger.

Cold-blooded? No more than the slimy weasel deserved.

They stepped down the ship's gangway into what felt like a sauna. Buddy Junior's outpost on the Bluff was located only a mile or so from one of the planet's deep blue oceans, and the surrounding land was heavy with all sorts of growing things. From small flowers with fiery bursts of red and yellow petals that reminded Gus of the last colors they'd seen the Prowlers display, to dark green foliage with shiny, spade-shaped leaves the size of dinner plates, to dense stands of trees that towered a good forty feet into the humid air. The ground underfoot was almost spongy damp and covered with something that looked like fermented leaves mixed with rotted bark and furry bits of things that didn't bear a closer look.

The outpost wasn't big enough—and apparently didn't have enough off-world visitors—to maintain a designated landing area. Drake had set the *Void* down in a clearing a good half mile away from the closest buildings. They'd have to hike through the trees and underbrush, but Gus thought she'd spotted a narrow path that was only somewhat overgrown.

A slight breeze brought a little relief from the heat. All of two minutes in this place, and her face was already slick with sweat. She'd grown accustomed to the climate-controlled interior of the *Void*. Even the dry heat of Shepard's Moon hadn't hit her this hard. She'd been deployed to more than one jungle while she'd been with the 83rd, but that was a lot of years ago. She'd kept her body in shape since her forced retirement from the 83rd over a decade earlier, but she'd spent most of those years on a space station. If she wasn't careful, the humid heat was going to mess with her, and not in a good way. Drake counted on her to watch his six, and she damn well wasn't going to let him down.

With any luck, they wouldn't be on this disgusting planet too long. They'd meet with Junior, Drake would do his charming smuggler thing, and they'd leave with what they came for. The sooner, the better.

She breathed in deep. Fresh air was fresh air, even if it was going to stink to high heaven thanks to all that rotting gunk underfoot.

Only it didn't.

She took another deep breath.

Nothing.

Not a single damn thing.

Not the hot-metal singe of the *Void's* hull. Not the stench from the dead things beneath her feet. Not the scent of the red and yellow flowers or the musty smell of the ocean blowing in on the breeze.

Not even the familiar smell of Drake standing right next to her, a comforting part of him she hadn't even realized she'd grown used to until it was gone.

What the hell?

"This place should stink," she said. "And…"

"…nothing," Drake said, finishing for her.

"Fluke?" she asked. The Prowlers had been glowing blue when the *Void* had entered their space. Blue denoted benevolence by the Fluke, but who knew what the Fluke considered benevolent?

"Not exactly one of their better gifts, is it, darlin'," Drake said.

No, it wasn't. Smell was part of life. Stink had been part of life in the 83rd. Unavoidable when you crammed a bunch of armor jocks into a transport after a battle and before they could wash the sweat off their bodies. That stink had been comforting too. It meant they'd survived. Add the acrid smell of blood into the mix and it took comfort away. The stench of fresh blood meant someone had been hurt, maybe killed, and that smell got everybody real quiet real fast.

She wiped away the sweat running down her face with an impatient hand. They had things to do, and yeah, the lack of smell was odd, but it was small potatoes compared to their mission. If Junior was in an accommodating mood, maybe Drake could cajole some extra ammo along with the replicator. She needed something that would pierce through the nearly indestructible metal in the drones, if he had it. If he didn't, she needed something she could reprogram to do the same thing. Rhap's rifle and laser pistol hadn't been up to the job.

Tor had probably made sure that the weapons Rhapsody was allowed to keep didn't have the firepower to shoot his drones out of the sky. Any off-worlder who brought a weapon onto Chrysallix that could do the job wasn't allowed to take it into the city without disabling it. Nice set of laws Tor had going there.

The fact that Gus and Drake had been able to shoot up a drone was due to luck as much as skill. Gus knew where to hit an automated piece of shit like the drone to disable it. No one thought of shooting out the blades or taking out its targeting eye. Most people went for the easy shot—right to the body. Most people did that with her armor, but that wasn't where her armor was vulnerable. The guerillas on Shepard's Moon had peppered her armor with projectiles and enough laser fire to power an entire city. It wasn't until their bastard of a leader had thrown more than a dozen missiles at her that debris from the explosions wrenched her armor's shoulder launchers from their mounts and ripped through the joints in her armor.

Gus and Drake weren't most people. Gus had over thirty years of military training and battle experience behind her, and Drake... well, he was the most resourceful, smartest, and bravest civilian she'd ever met. Once they realized they couldn't take the drone down with a shot to its body, they'd concentrated on its vulnerable spots.

But you couldn't always count on hitting a vulnerable spot.

Now that they'd taken one of the drones down, Gus would be willing to bet that Tor's people were re-engineering the things to eliminate as many vulnerable spots as possible. That's what she would do. Hell, that's what she'd *done* her entire military career. Every damn time somebody got a shot past her armor's defenses, Gus had upgraded her armor to keep somebody else from taking her armor out with the same kind of lucky shot.

The drones would be harder to kill now. She and Drake needed an edge. Some kind of weapon that could punch through the metal that Tor had etched his initials in. Metal that had broken her hammer. Metal that the guerillas he'd backed on Shepard's Moon had been mining for years and clearly selling to Tor in exchange for munitions and military hardware that were obsolete in the Alliance but more than enough firepower to take over a backwards planet like Shepard's Moon. She hoped Junior had something in his vast stock of "everything a smuggler could ever want" that would smash that crap to smithereens.

"You ever do business with Junior?" she asked Drake.

He had taken the lead, which was fine with Gus. He was the smuggler, she was there to cover his six. She'd brought the rifle that she'd taken from Rhapsody and she had her own laser pistol shoved in the waistband of her pants. She would have felt better wearing her armor. She didn't need a space-tight seal here, but an armor jock marching into a remote outpost might seem like a hostile move to the two Fluke Prowlers standing sentinel.

Drake had told her that smugglers wouldn't go to a place like this unarmed. He had his shotgun and a second laser pistol for backup.

"Nope," Drake said.

"Not while you were doing business for Rhapsody?"

He turned his head and gave her a sharp look.

She shrugged. "I wanted to know what I was getting into, so I asked the computer."

"And what did *Earl* tell you?"

He was more than a little annoyed like he'd been when she'd first invaded his bridge because she'd been impatient with how long it was taking them to get to Shepard's Moon. Since then he'd basically told her that his casa was her casa. Apparently that didn't extend to doing a little digging into his relationship with his ex.

But things had gotten real serious, real fast. Lives were on the line, and the time for subtlety—and sensitive topics —was over.

"*Earl* didn't tell me squat," she said. "The *computer* never heard of good ol' Rhap, the woman who *doesn't* like your songs, may I remind you."

Drake grunted in acknowledgment of the fact that Gus had never told him to quit playing his old cowboy songs on his old guitar.

"The computer did tell me how many trips you made from Chrysallix to other points in the system," she said. "Short-term trips, just like a smuggler would make for a preferred customer. Am I right?"

"You are," he said, but he still sounded pissed off.

"Look, cowboy, we both have our pasts. Rhap's part of yours. The extent of me caring about that extends only as far as me kicking her sorry ass if she tries to mess with you again." She raised an eyebrow and gave him a look. "Or if you go singing 'Back in the Saddle' to her anytime soon." She paused, then added, "Metaphorically speaking."

That made him snort out a laugh. "Point taken."

"So now that we're traipsing through a jungle that *doesn't* stink on a way to meeting some idiot who's crazy enough to live beneath the ever-watchful eyes of the Fluke —or whatever it is they have—catch me up on what you're thinking. Because *I'm* thinking we ought to hit up Junior for as much information as we can about what people are using for advanced weaponry out here on the Frontier. And who else has been doing business with Tor to their everlasting regret."

"And you want to know if he might be willing to part with any of that."

She shrugged. "We didn't exactly know what we were getting into on Chrysallix." Not even after they'd seen the weapons tower. The explosions in the city had still come as a shock, as had Rhapsody's callous initial response.

"For a price, darlin'," Drake said. "The saying went that on the Bluff, everything's available for the right price."

"Ain't that the truth."

A man's amplified voice came out of the trees in front of them.

Even as she flinched at the unexpected sound, Gus brought up the rifle in one smooth move. Drake followed a moment later with his own shotgun.

The trail had taken a shallow curve to the right to avoid a thick clump of tree trunks, only half of them belonging to still living trees. The rest looked rotted through, and it was amazing the things were still standing.

Only the trees weren't real trees. The trees were holographic camouflage for a lookout post.

Stupid, stupid! Gus had been so involved in her conversation with Drake that she hadn't been monitoring the trail for any electronic signals. The Bluff looked like such a backwards smugglers' outpost that she'd let herself get lulled into thinking that the normal precautions most people took when strangers landed wouldn't apply here since not a whole lot of strangers got past the Fluke ships.

She certainly hadn't smelled anything out of the ordinary, like the stink of sweaty men stationed out in the jungle for hours on end, but then again, she hadn't smelled anything at all.

Thanks a lot, Fluke.

"Now, now," the man said, "there's no need for that."

The whine of laser pistols being powered on came from both sides of the trail, and a red dot appeared in the middle of Drake's back. She didn't have to glance down to know that more red dots had sprouted on her chest and probably on her head.

Most laser pistols were programmed not to make a sound until they were fired. That told Gus that these pistols were meant to intimidate visitors, not to kill them where they stood.

"I think I'll hang onto my rifle, if it's all the same to you," she said, keeping her rifle aimed right in the middle of that fake stand of trees.

Incredibly, the unseen man laughed. "You always were a hotshot, Light. Or are you going by Gus? Or maybe it's still Gray Lady?"

Okay, so whoever it was, they'd done their research.

Unless...

Did that voice sound familiar somehow? Hard to tell with it amplified like that.

"You clearly know me, friend," she said. "How about you come on out and introduce yourself?"

"Can't wait to meet you," Drake said. "As soon as you get those lasers off our ass. Otherwise Gus here might be tempted to shoot you just for spite."

"It'll be the last shot she takes," the voice said.

"Not a bad way to go," she said. "Although Junior might be a little annoyed if you shoot a couple of customers."

"There is that," the man agreed.

Nobody moved for what seemed like forever. Gus evened out her breathing, getting herself ready to move and shoot. She was a trained armor jock, but she was no slouch with a rifle either. She'd been the best there was in her squad at the 83rd. She'd proved that yet again taking down that skudging drone.

She had no doubt that she'd take out more than a few of these assholes before one of them managed to shoot her. If they did. If she didn't die knocking Drake down to make sure he survived.

Not that she wanted to die. Not without taking Tor down first.

The red dots winked out.

Half a heartbeat later the holographic trees winked out of sight and a tall, gray-haired, gray-bearded man stepped onto the path in front of them. He had a long puckered scar on one side of his face that ran from just below his receding hairline down to follow the angle of his jaw. He'd developed jowls beneath that jawline since the last time Gus had seen him, but he was still as skinny as ever.

He held his hands out to the side in a *we're all friends here* gesture belied by the laser pistol he still held loosely in his right hand. Gus knew he could bring that pistol up in a nanosecond and hit whatever he aimed at.

He'd been the only one who had managed—once—to outshoot her on the practice range when they'd trained together.

She'd also found out after the fact that he'd been the one who'd given her the nickname Gray Lady.

He still had that same half smile the scar had given him. "How've you been, Gus?" he asked.

She didn't lower her rifle.

"Just fine," she said. "Earl."

CHAPTER 13

"Earl?" Drake looked with keen interest at the man with the scarred face...then swung his gaze over to Gus. *"The* Earl?" *The one you named the* Void's *AI after?* Drake didn't have to ask the question to know she'd received it loud and clear.

Gus shrugged behind the rifle sights. "Maybe."

Earl's perpetual half-smile opened into a full one as he looked from Gus to Drake and back again. "Well now! What've you been *tellin'* this fella about me, Light? Propogatin' the legend of my greatness, I suppose?"

"Sure, why not?" Slowly, Gus lowered the gun. "If it makes you feel good, you old war horse."

Drake followed suit, lowering his shotgun, but like Earl —*Earl!*—he kept ahold of it by his side.

Nobody besides Earl had stepped out onto the path. All those laser sights must have come from automated sentries. That would be new since the last time he'd snuck the *Void* past those skudging Fluke Prowlers to do a little business with Buddy Senior. Buddy Senior hadn't put much stock in anything automated that he didn't have to.

Earl was new too, and that was worrisome.

Though everybody's guns were down, Drake could feel the tension in the thick, tropical air…and it mystified him. Gus and Earl talked like old comrades; he'd even called her by her nickname, "Gray Lady," suggesting he'd known her quite well indeed. At the same time, there was a dark edge to their exchange—a hint of rivalry or friction from back in the day.

Not to mention, she'd not been quick to lower the rifle, and *that* suggested a dangerous subtext between them. If they were old friends, wouldn't she drop the gun immediately, perhaps even rush to embrace him with the kind of affection that burns brightest between those who've fought side by side and perhaps even saved each other's lives? Gus had told him how important her squadron had been to her. Hell, she'd left her *son* behind to save her squad from being court marshalled.

It was clear to Drake that there was more going on here than met the eye…as if he and Gus needed *more* complications on top of those they already faced. Weren't the Fluke Prowlers, the disrepair of the *Void* and Gus's armor, the hunt for Tor, and the desperate situation on Chrysallix trouble enough?

"Now how 'bout we finish those introductions?" Earl bobbed his head in Drake's direction. "Who's *this* scrawny drink a' water, Gus? I *know* he ain't no *armor jock*…so what is he, then?"

Gus stepped forward to stand next to Drake. "Business

associate," she said without hesitation. "Earl, meet Mephistopheles Drake."

Earl's scar puckered when he scowled. "What the skudge kinda name is *Miphistiphenes?*"

"It's Mephistopheles," snapped Drake. "But you can call me Mr. Drake."

He knew a power play when he heard it, but it still rankled. Just like Gus describing him as a "business associate." He figured it was part of a power play of her own, but it was going to take a minute for him to let that one go.

"*Mr.* Drake, is it?" Earl chuckled. "You do know *I'm* an armor jock, don't you, big stuff?"

"You *were*," said Gus. "And what're you doing *these* days, Earl?"

"What're *you* doing, Light?" asked Earl. "I heard you went on the run after stealin' some armor."

"Old news, old man…and you didn't answer my question. What *are* you doing, Earl? Running security on a planet that most folks are too scared to land on?"

"It's a high-stress gig, what with *those* skudge-bags always hanging around." He jabbed his laser pistol in the air, indicating one, then the other Fluke Prowler that hung in orbit like small moons. "Which, by the way, thanks a *ton* for setting them off. Some crazed Fluke action is *just* what we need right now."

"Who knows what sets those things off?" As Drake looked up, one Prowler turned bright violet, and the other changed to a shade of hot pink. "They're about as random as it gets."

"Tell that to Buddy Junior." Earl glared up at the

Prowlers, his bony hand clenched around the butt of his pistol. "And Buddy *Senior*, for that matter."

"What're you talking about, Earl?" asked Gus.

"I'm talkin' about *patterns*," said Earl. "Spend enough time around somethin' that makes no sense, you might realize it makes sense after all." He winked one bloodshot brown eye. "Or maybe you just finally get as *crazy* as the somethin' you've been watchin'."

With that, he lurched around and started off down the loamy path out of the jungle, gesturing for Drake and Gus to follow…giggling as he went.

Drake hung back just enough that he could still mumble to Gus out of Earl's earshot. "Anything I need to know about this guy?" he asked. "Other than the obvious, that is."

"He was a hell of an armor jock when we served together," said Gus. "A real force to be reckoned with. Also a complete and utter asshole."

"Seems about right."

"But not corrupt, at least back then," continued Gus. "Though how he is now, I couldn't say."

"Looks like he's been through some skudge," said Drake. "Judging from the scar."

"We all did," she said. "That scar's not new."

Drake shot her a look. "Wounded in battle?"

"The way he walks?" She gestured at where Earl was still lurching along the path in front of them. "He's lucky he's still got a leg that's mostly his. Had to hang up the armor after that."

And he resented the hell out of it. She didn't need to say that. Resentment oozed out of the man's every pore. The way they reacted to each other made a little more sense to Drake now. Though he still didn't know why she'd named the ship's damn AI after this jerk.

She frowned and sighed. "I'd say we need to hope for the best...and watch our asses in the meantime. I'm pretty sure he didn't end up on this godforsaken Fluke-ball in the depths of the damn Frontier for good behavior."

"Unlike us." Drake elbowed her lightly in the ribs. "Am I right, Gray Lady?"

When she looked over at him, her smile was tempered with an unexpected reticence, the slightest of winces around the eyes. "Right you are, Broken String."

Drake was puzzled. If he'd struck a nerve, he damn well couldn't figure out how...and he couldn't ask about it, either, at least not yet.

They'd arrived at their destination.

The jungle of trees and undergrowth had been beaten back—barely—to give way to a flat area with only the barest signs of civilization. If anyone could call the building in front of them *civilization*.

"Here we are, gang." Earl flung his arms wide, taking in the blocky black building before them. "Welcome to the galaxy-famous Fluke Off Trading Post!"

"Good to be here," said Drake.

The exterior of the place was pretty much as Drake remembered from his past visits—a squat, sprawling bunker that looked as if it had risen from the dark peat of the jungle floor itself. There were no external signs to mark its function, and the windows were little more than slits. Openings had been minimized to maximize the chance of survival in case the Fluke decided to unleash their monstrous might...though it was true there wasn't much anyone could actually do to protect against such outbursts. Any shielding was more for the psychological benefit of those within, making them feel the slightest bit safer and therefore possibly more inclined to be in a buying mood.

"Right this way." Earl strolled up to a recessed door, pulled a handle, and swung it open. Whatever security measures were in place to limit egress—and there *must* have been some, given the contents of the place—they were invisible to the outsiders in the group. "Buddy has been waiting to meet you."

Of course he has. Drake figured their approach had been monitored every step of the way, starting with the moment they entered the system. As much protection as the Fluke's presence provided, Buddy Jr. had to be at least as security minded as Buddy Sr. had been, or he would not have stayed in business as long as he had.

"Just remember, don't touch the merchandise without permission," said Earl as he ushered them inside. "And all transactions are strictly cash only, so get your wallets ready."

"Cash only, huh?" Drake didn't like the sound of that one bit. He and Gus had been counting on generous credit terms to get what they needed.

"You heard right," said Earl. "The days of easy credit ended when Buddy Senior bit the dust."

Drake managed not to shoot a look at Gus, and as far as he could tell, she wasn't lettin' on that their cash situation was a bit on the poor side. Number one rule of negotiation: never let anyone see you sweat. Metaphorically speakin', as

Gus would say. The damn jungle they'd just traipsed through made sweating unavoidable.

As soon as they entered the place, the skudging temperature and humidity dropped…and the ambient light brightened. It was like stepping into another world, one where sleek, gleaming metal and glass replaced dark emerald vegetation and black ground cover, reflecting and amplifying the output of incandescent light sources strategically mounted on ceiling tracks and alcoves.

Smell, however, did not return.

All that flashy, minimalist décor served to frame an assortment of objects arranged on glass pedestals, tables, and shelves. Each object, though artfully arranged, possessed significant destructive capabilities—all the way from a massive, shoulder-mounted laser cannon to a missile to a drone that made Tor's units from Chrysallix look like children's toys, down to an assortment of laser pistols that could be concealed in the palm of one hand and concussion grenades like the ones Gus had modified on Shepard's Moon to emit debilitating blasts of light and sound. The objects turned slowly on their displays, glinting with reflected light, looking more like luxury items than implements of destruction…not that Drake and Gus could afford to buy any of it given their cash-poor condition.

It was a far cry from Buddy Sr.'s original layout, which had put him in mind of a junk shop more than an art gallery. Drake remembered tripping over guns and grenades in the musty bunker, holding up ammo cartridges to read the specs in the dim light from bare bulbs strung overhead on sagging wires. There had been cats everywhere, he recalled, and music blasting, and hookah smoke hanging in a hazy layer just shy of the ceiling. There had also been a surly teen roaming the floor, tinkering recklessly with functional weapons, wolfing down junk food, and interrupting negotiations with obnoxious pubescent commentary.

The place hadn't been crawling with buyers back then, not like outposts that didn't have Fluke Prowlers hanging in low orbit overhead, but there'd been enough customers picking through all that junk to give rise to some spirited negotiations when more than one customer wanted the same piece of hardware. This time, the three of them— Drake, Gus, and the *skudge*-hole Earl—were the only ones on what was clearly a showroom floor.

Or not.

Now, in a place that was nothing like the one from his memory, Drake saw that very teen walking toward him, six years older and immeasurably more mature. He had red hair like his father, the same sharp nose and bright green eyes—but was otherwise a world apart from his dad and his younger self alike. Though he could not have been older than his early twenties, he was impossibly tall and slim, his bearing poised and professional, his dark business suit impeccably tailored.

He looked nothing like Buddy Sr., who had been known throughout the quadrant for his tubby frame, slovenly habits, floral shirts, and ever-present tumblers of alcoholic spirits.

It didn't escape Drake that Junior and Rhap had both changed drastically since he'd left this part of the Fronter behind, each going in the opposite direction. Six years hadn't seemed all that long to him, but it had been long enough for this kid to turn into a man.

"Mr. Drake!" Junior's smooth bass voice had no trace of his teenage self's braying croak. "So pleased you could join us here at the Bluff."

Mr. Drake. The kid hadn't just changed on the outside. Drake would need to remember that.

He marched over and shook Junior's hand, smiling. Time to get this ball rollin'.

"Good to be here, Buddy. Long time no see."

"I go by Bruce now, actually," said Junior. "In honor of my father, who gave me that name at birth."

"Bruce it is." Drake gave his hand one more vigorous shake, then released it. "And this is my partner, Augusta Light." Turning, he extended a hand in Gus's direction.

She walked over to join them and reached for a shake of her own. "You can call me Gus."

"Or *Gray Lady*," offered Earl, who had stayed back by the door.

Two men had joined him. Both were armed, but their laser pistols were still on their belts, and they had their arms crossed over their chests. Unlike Earl whose well-worn shirt and pants and muck-encrusted boots made it clear he spent most of his time in the jungle, these men were dressed all in black, their uniforms as upscale as Bruce's suit.

Store security.

Back in the day, Buddy Senior's security had run more toward the Earl end of the spectrum. Upscale security told Drake that Bruce must be doin' right fine by himself, Fluke or no Fluke.

Or else he was just puttin' on a show.

At the mention of Gus's nickname, Bruce's eyes flickered with recognition. Whatever Earl had told him about her, he remembered it well…and seemingly approved. "It is an honor to have you visit my establishment, Gus. Your legendary reputation precedes you."

"Thank you, Bruce." Gus finished the handshake and gestured at the room around them. "Quite a place you've got here."

Bruce made a gracious half-bow. "Thank you for saying that. We've worked hard to make our showroom as aesthetically pleasing as it is economically rewarding."

"Until the Flukers get a random hair up their asses sideways and decide to wipe it off the map." Earl snorted. "Asses or whatever they have instead of 'em, that is."

"We do exist in the valley of the shadow of imminent annihilation," said Bruce. "But when you think about it, how much different is that from living anywhere else in the universe, hmm?"

"Well said." Even as Drake smiled, he wondered what had happened to change the spotty, snarky teen into this erudite sophisticate. He'd stayed behind after Buddy Senior's death to run the outpost…so how had he gotten so cultured? Some kind of correspondence course or mental enhancement, perhaps? Had he used some of his dad's fortune to bring in a private tutor? The change in his demeanor was so dramatic, there *had* to be some kind of explanation other than simple maturity and self-directed learning.

Perhaps, thought Drake, it had been brought on by the

Fluke themselves—a classic case of them mysteriously bestowing a benevolent gift instead of a ruinous curse.

"Speaking of the Fluke..." Bruce rolled his eyes ceiling-ward, suggesting the alien observers hanging overhead. "They seem a bit—*agitated*—today. We've seen this kind of activity from them before, but I regret to say I'm unable to predict the outcome of the current round."

"They've done it before?" asked Gus. "The rapid color changes?"

"Their idea of fun and games," growled Earl. "Like shooting craps, only *they're* not the big losers when they finally throw snake eyes."

Drake narrowed his eyes, considering the analogy. "So when they both land on red, it's the equivalent of snake eyes? Is that what you're saying?"

"Exactly, Mephisto." Earl's scar crinkled as he sneered. "They keep rollin' till they hit double-red, at which point all holy Hell breaks loose...or else they just land on double-blue and make somethin' nice happen...or *their* idea of nice, which doesn't always match up with ours, the sadistic twits."

"Then they go dormant for a period of time," Bruce said. "They choose a color and stick with it. Although we've never been able to accurately predict the length of their inactive phases."

Drake nodded thoughtfully. The last time he'd been to The Bluff, the Fluke had ignored the *Void*. He'd congratulated himself on his stealthiness, but maybe he'd just arrived during the Flukes' nap time.

"So these particular Flukes aren't quite as random as their kind usually are, I guess?" he asked.

"That's about the long and short of it," said Earl.

"Huh." Drake reached into his shirt pocket and drew out a foil-wrapped stick of cinnamon chewing gum. "Sounds like a real pain."

"It is not exactly helpful." Bruce's tone suggested his words were an understatement. "Nor have our limited efforts at resolving the situation met with any success whatsoever."

"That's one way of puttin' it," said Earl.

"We just seem to make things worse," said Bruce. "Though with the Fluke, it's hard to tell."

"I can identify." Drake unwrapped the gum and folded it into his mouth. "We recently had our own run-in with those bastards."

"And lived to tell about it?" Bruce raised his eyebrows. "I'm impressed, Mr. Drake."

Earl swaggered over and leaned a little too close to Drake. "What happened? Did you come within a hundred light-years of those things and race away before they could get a bead on you?"

"More like a hundred meters," said Gus. "And we got them to communicate symbolically before letting us off without a scratch."

Earl's brow knotted with evident unhappiness. "You must be skudgin' me," he said without breaking eye contact with Drake.

Though Drake was tense, ready to fight Earl if necessary, he calmly shook his head. He had gotten the vaguest smidgen of an idea and wanted to shop it to his host without violent distractions. Perhaps, if he was lucky, there might be a way around the cash-only terms at the Fluke Off

Trading Post.

"Gus and I had an understanding with the Fluke," he said. "We worked things out and lived to tell the tale. I wonder if we might be able to do the same for *your* Fluke?"

"Don't you think other folks have tried?" Earl leaned even closer, the very definition of getting up in Drake's face. "Where did it get *them*, do you think?"

"All the more reason to consider a new approach." Drake kept chewing the gum, the repetitive motion of his jaws taking off some of the stress he was feeling. "Just like this new and improved showroom. Where would your business be if you hadn't tried something different?"

"There was *nothin'* wrong with the way Buddy Senior ran it before," snapped Earl.

So good ol' Earl, the skudge-hole, had been cooling his heels on The Bluff for quite some time. Drake filed that information away as maybe coming in handy.

"I didn't say there was, did I?" asked Drake, keeping his tone mild, not without a bit of effort. "But you can't tell me the place hasn't leveled up since then. I'll bet your numbers are better, too."

Earl didn't answer. As much of a big mouth as he was, he didn't seem to have completely forgotten that Bruce was his boss, and the current showroom was Bruce's baby.

"Those Prowlers have been in orbit a long time, Mr. Drake," said Bruce. "Maybe longer than any of us have been alive. In all that time, they've straight-up *annihilated* a lot of people—maybe lots more than we can imagine. Do you *really* want to take a crack at dealing with them?"

Chewing the gum slowly, Drake looked over at Gus. If

147

she was going to object to the proposal he was getting at, she didn't give a sign of it.

That was the problem with coming up with something like the Smiley Face Gambit. Even Gus seemed to expect him to have more tricks like that up his sleeve. That kind of faith was pretty damn humbling.

And say she did agree to go along with whatever crazy plan he came up with, did he have the right to ask her to? Putting his own life at risk was one thing, but throwing hers into the mix was quite another. As much as he loved her, he couldn't bear the thought of being responsible for her death.

But the potential reward was worth the risk. If only he and Gus could stage the right kind of random mayhem, similar in spirit to the Smiley Face Gambit, perhaps they could get through to the Fluke and walk away with the whole pot on the table. Maybe, in one fell swoop, they could set the stage for the rescue of Rhapsody, the liberation of Chrysallix, and the downfall of Tor.

Drake's heart pounded at the thought of it. He'd played plenty of hands of cards in his day, but never had the stakes been *this* skudgin' high. Never had a bluff been this risky, such a desperate measure for such an urgent mission.

And, fittingly, it was happening on Buddy's Bluff.

"Sure," he told Bruce. "I'm willing to take a crack at it."

Bruce's eyes narrowed with suspicion. "And what do *you* get out of it if you succeed?"

"Hold on a sec." Drake reached into his shirt pocket and pulled out a folded slip of paper. "I've got our wish list right here. You do have replicators and space-tight seals for armor in stock, don't you?"

CHAPTER 14

"What do you mean, you don't have a plan?" Gus asked.

They were back in the cargo bay on the *Void*. Drake had insisted to Bruce that before they could put their latest *let's outwit the Fluke* plan in motion, they needed a few things off the ship. That had seemed to mollify Bruce, who'd taken the handwritten shopping list, spent a few moments perusing it, and said he should be able to accommodate their needs.

When Earl had started to accompany them, Drake had given the man an icy smile and told him that while he wouldn't mind taking a turn on the dance floor with a battle-scared *former* armor jock, Gus was more to his likin'.

Gus had snickered, Earl had flushed a deep red, and the two security guards had hidden their laughter behind sudden coughing fits. Even one corner of Bruce's mouth had twitched. But the insult had worked. Earl had stayed behind.

She'd figured Drake just wanted some alone time with her to work out the details of his plan. There were no chunks of ice she could shoot to hell anywhere near the outpost, and none at all in orbit. She doubted shooting up the permafrost at the planet's poles would be seen by the Fluke as anything other than a hugely aggressive move, with double-red snake eyes the inevitable result.

The first thing Drake had done once they boarded the ship and the outer door slid shut behind them—silently, of course, thanks to Gus's tinkering—was to kiss the stuffing out of her.

Okay. Unexpected but damn nice.

And damn suspicious.

"Cough it up, space cowboy," she said once she got her breath back. "We're kinda operating on borrowed time here."

His gaze flicked away from her face. "First how about you tell me why you named the AI after that skudging *asshole*."

She laughed. "That's what's bothering you?"

When he glanced back at her, she saw something in those expressive eyes of his she never thought she'd see. Jealousy. And more than just a bit of confusion.

"You served together," he said. "You fought together. You gave up..." He stopped himself for a moment before he went on. "You gave up *everything* for your squad."

True. She had. And she appreciated his consideration in not mentioning exactly *what* she'd given up, just like she never mentioned his son unless he brought the subject up first. That's what you did when you loved someone. You made sure you didn't unintentionally hurt them.

"So what was that all about back there?" He gestured in the general direction of the path they'd taken to the outpost. "You looked like you'd just as soon shoot him as talk to him, and that ain't the way I've seen you treat old friends, darlin'."

True again. She'd recognized a couple of the orderlies in the hospital on Shepard's Moon. She'd spent a few very frustrating days confined to bed—as if anyone could really confine her anywhere—recuperating from the busted shoulder she'd gotten when she and Drake had saved what was left of the capitol city, not to mention her son and his wife, from certain annihilation. The orderlies had been on staff the last time Gus had been on the planet. They'd been nice to her as she sat holding the hand of her son's father as he lay dying.

She hadn't seen the orderlies in nearly forty years, but they'd recognized her. She'd been glad to see them still alive and healthy, and Drake had been around to see her cracking jokes with them when they came in to take care of her room.

"Earl's not a friend," she said. "He gave me my nickname as a way to take me down a peg or two because he couldn't stand losing to me when we were trainees."

He couldn't stand losing to anyone, but most especially to a gray-haired twig of a girl who thought she was better than anybody else. Just remembering the crap he'd put her through back then made her blood boil.

"He sabotaged my suit before a proficiency exam just to see me fail," she said. "I didn't, and that pissed him off. He was a skudge-hole of the highest order, but he was a berserker on the battlefield. The 83rd lost a good warrior when he got taken out of action."

Drake's eyes had taken on a faraway look. Something was going on inside that skull of his, but she knew enough by now it wouldn't do any good to rush him with whatever he was working out. She'd been so impatient with him when they'd first met, but back then she hadn't been able to afford a smidgen of lost time. Any delay might have cost her son his life. Delays now might give the Fluke time to roll a double-red, but that might happen anyway.

Or who the hell knew. The Fluke might flash on double blue and decide to give the *Void* a free upgrade.

"I'm guessing the skudge-hole didn't 'liberate' his armor when he left," Drake said, "unlike some other armor jock I happen to know."

She snorted. "His armor had been blown to smithereens. That's how come his leg's never been right after that, even with the mechanical improvements. But I heard scuttlebutt that he might have *liberated* his helmet."

"Huh."

She'd heard more rumors than that. Earl had been livid when he'd gotten his discharge notice. He'd fought it tooth and nail, as high up the chain of command as he could go. Claimed he was just as good an armor jock as ever, but the Alliance military in its ever-lovin' wisdom stuck to all those rules and regs that said who could be an armor jock and who couldn't. And soldiers with any kind of artificial anything couldn't.

"We don't put machines inside machines." That had been the military's justification for kicking Earl's ass out the airlock one final time.

Unlike Gus, Earl didn't have much of his armor left to liberate. According to rumor, he'd taken his helmet and what was left of his cussed pride and built himself new armor. Last she'd heard, he was making himself a decent living battling other armor jocks for money. She'd been surprised to see him on a planet like Buddy's Bluff, much less to learn that he'd been here for a spell.

Maybe all those rumors about him stealing his helmet and constructing new armor were just that—rumors.

For all she knew, he'd probably been stuck here thanks to some capricious actions by the Fluke. But being reduced to a security guard? No wonder he'd gotten stupid mean when she showed up. Instead of taking his frustrations out on her, he'd decided to get into a pissing match with Drake.

Who'd handled it admirably, she had to admit.

All except the bit about her naming the AI after Earl. That had seemed to stick in Drake's craw.

Did he actually think she'd *tangled* beneath the sheets with a guy like Earl in between missions?

She sighed, then cupped his chin with one hand, forcing him to look at her.

"I named the AI after that skudging asshole because it has to do what I tell it to," she said. "I ask it a question, it has to answer. It doesn't backtalk me. It doesn't give me a nickname I have to pretend I like. It doesn't sabotage me. Doesn't give me attitude. Doesn't spend every minute of every day trying to piss me off. Doesn't get butthurt because I won't..."

She paused, trying to think of a good way to say it. She shouldn't have to, but it was pretty clear Drake needed to hear it.

153

"Because I wouldn't get in the saddle with him," she said. "Ever." She leaned forward and kissed him, sweetly and tenderly. "We good, space cowboy?" she asked when the kiss ended.

He nodded.

The next kiss had her longing for a bit more than just a kiss, especially since she realized she could not only feel him and taste him—and damn, but he felt and tasted *good*—but *smell* him again. That sweet cinnamon scent of that gum of his took her right back to their first kiss on Shepard's Moon and the first time they'd had mind-blowing sex beneath that down comforter of his.

Whatever the Fluke had done to the Bluff to take away everything's smell didn't extend to the *Void*.

She wanted nothing more than to have mind-blowing sex with her space cowboy again, right there in the cargo bay, but that would have to wait for later.

Later, after his plan played out and they were en route to Chrysallix to blow Tor out of the sky.

"So," she said, pulling away from Drake with some reluctance. "How about you let me in on the plan?"

That's when she'd seen the truth in his eyes.

Drake was a consummate card player. They'd played a few hands to pass the time after they'd left Shepard's Moon and her busted shoulder was still healing. He could bluff like nobody's business, but he had a few tells. She was sure nobody else would notice, but she'd become something of an expert where Mephistopheles Drake was concerned.

"You don't have a plan," she said.

"I have a plan," he said.

When she didn't respond, just stood there glaring at him, he said, "I have most of a plan."

Most of a plan.

"It's really more of an idea," he admitted.

"What do you mean, you don't have a plan?" She felt like throwing something, like a piece of the drone that was still on her workbench next to her armor's helmet. Or maybe the broken hammer. "We're in something of a tough spot here, space cowboy."

"Relax!" he said. "It'll turn into a plan."

She thought back to how he seemed to stare off into space after he'd been asking all sorts of questions about Earl. And she'd told him how good of an armor jock Earl had been.

"Does this *idea* of yours have anything to do with Earl?" she asked.

"It could," he said, drawing the words out.

"And how he's got a burr up his butt about you and me?" she asked.

Now he started to smile. "It could."

"Am I going to like it?"

He shrugged. "Probably not."

She sighed, and then she caught him looking at her armor's helmet where she'd left it, still waiting for her to make a few minor tweaks.

"Then again, you just might," he said. "You did say he always tried to prove he was better than you."

Oh, *skudge*. She knew where this was going.

"Old armor jocks never really retire," she said. Not in their hearts.

The Fluke, at least the two in orbit, liked to bet. They rolled their version of dice—those flashing lights of theirs—and placed whatever bets they placed. They were gamers. Hell, they were *gamblers*, only what they gambled didn't really belong to them. Except maybe it did, in their way of thinking. Maybe the whole skudging universe belonged to them as far as they were concerned.

The people living here, at least the ones at the outpost, had fled underground. They'd taken their games and gone home, essentially. That left the Fluke with nothing to do except bet with each other.

What she and Drake had to do was give them a better game to bet on. Something with higher stakes. Like a battle royale between two ex-military armor jocks.

And what could they use to entice Earl to go along with the plan? He'd want to know what he'd get out of the battle if he won.

Her armor, of course. It would be his perfect revenge against the short, stocky, *female* armor jock he'd never been able to beat.

Drake was right. She didn't like it, not one bit. But she was the Gray Lady. She didn't intend to lose. Not to Earl, and not to the Fluke.

She took a deep breath and looked deep into her space cowboy's eyes.

"Does your *idea* involve concussion grenades and a light show?" she asked.

His smile didn't quite reach his eyes. "It might."

When she returned his grim smile with one of her own, she was pretty sure her smile made her look dangerous enough to make anyone other than Drake quiver in their boots. But not him. He had a kind of unwavering confidence in her, and that was sexy as hell. She couldn't wait to get him beneath that comforter of his.

"Then let's get to it," she said. "I always did like a good light show."

CHAPTER 15

"Well, well. If it ain't Miphistifenes and the Gray Lady." Earl, who'd been smoking a purple cheroot while leaning against the exterior wall of Fluke Off, looked at the returning visitors as if one was a walking case of dysentery and the other a leper. "I suppose you want to see Bossman Bruce again?"

For once, Drake was happy the Fluke had nuked smells on the Bluff. The purple smoke cloud polluting the air around Earl's head looked like truly noxious stuff.

"Nope." Though Drake had a hill to climb to get back in Earl's good graces, he settled for a casual, matter-of-fact tone. "We're here to see *you*, actually."

Earl snorted out a laugh that was intermingled with more pale purple smoke. "Izzat so? *Now* I'm good enough? Not too long ago, you two couldn't *wait* to get away from me."

"Times change." Drake shrugged. "Before, we didn't quite have our ducks in a row, if you know what I mean."

Earl scowled. "Not a clue. I don't speak candy-ass."

Drake ignored the crack and stayed focused on his goal. Though the orbiting Fluke Prowlers still hadn't settled on double-red (or double-blue, for that matter), he knew it could happen at any time…in which case, all bets would be off. Persuading Earl to play along, then kicking off the gambit as planned, had to happen before then if they were to have any chance at success, and they had a lot of ducks that still needed rounding up. Even a double-blue outcome would be undesirable if it came down before Drake got the goods he needed from Bruce, the parts and gear it would take to make the ship and armor whole enough to rescue Chrysallix and pulverize Tor.

And besides, if the Fluke thought getting rids of *smells* on the Bluff was a good thing, Drake didn't want to think what they'd get rid of next, thinking it was a benevolent gift. Taste? Touch? All sensations?

He couldn't imagine touching Gus, kissing her, and not feeling…anything. That would just be plain *wrong*.

Gus was staying out of the conversation so far, just like they'd planned, but he could practically hear her telling him to stay on target.

He resisted the urge to clear his throat. "We have a proposition," he said. "We need a player for a game."

Earl puffed on his cheroot, making the tip burn brighter. "I don't gamble with losers…and *everyone's* a loser by the time *I* get done with 'em."

"I didn't say gamble." Drake shook his head. "I said *game*. We want you to play a game."

"With you?" Earl snorted. "Why would I do that?"

"With me," Gus said, right on cue. "And you'd do it because you always wanted to."

Drake didn't like the leering smile that stole over Earl's scarred face. Not one bit, but he didn't let it show.

"It's that kind of game, huh?" Earl hitched up his muck-stained pants. "Well, why didn't you say so?"

"Dream on," Gus said. "We want to give the Fluke something to *really* bet on. A battle royale between you and me, the best damn armor jocks that ever lived." She narrowed her eyes. "You *do* have armor stashed around here somewhere, right?"

Gus had let Drake in on the rumors she'd heard about Earl building himself his own armor after the military had shoved him out the airlock. She'd said she tended to believe those rumors, and Drake agreed. A man like Earl, whose identity had been so tied to what he'd been as an armor jock, wouldn't let a little thing like a half-mechanical leg keep him from climbing inside armor, even if he had to build that armor himself. Their whole plan hinged on that belief.

"I might." A look of cunning stole over Earl's face. "You and me?" he said to Gus. "To the death, huh?"

"Close enough," she said. "An all-out, go-for-the-throat death match between armor jocks...but not really."

"But it would have to *look* that way," said Drake. "It has to be completely believable."

"Good enough to fool the Fluke," said Gus. "Those gambling assholes up there who've made your life *so* much fun." She stepped forward, hands on her hips, getting right into Earl's face. "What do you say...*Early?*"

Early?

Gus had never mentioned whether Earl had a nickname, but apparently he did, and she'd chosen just the right moment to let loose with that emotional missile. Earl looked like she'd just kicked him in the balls. Drake wondered where he'd gotten that nickname—on the battlefield or between the sheets.

Again, Earl puffed on the cheroot, raising a curtain of violet smoke to camouflage his reaction. Gus didn't back away even when Earl blew the smoke right at her face.

"Well?" she asked.

Eyes narrowed, he looked from Gus to Drake and back again, taking their measure, weighing his options. When next he spoke, he asked the question they both had known would be one of the first things out of his mouth after hearing their proposal.

"What's in it for me?"

They'd prepared for this. Drake let Gus take the lead.

"If it comes together? Survival," she said. "The satisfaction of ridding The Bluff of the Fluke and clearing the way for Bruce's business to skyrocket. Tell me that wouldn't be worth it to you since I'm guessing you have a piece of the kid's business, right? Why else would you still be hanging around a place like this?"

The Fluke, of course, but he wouldn't admit to that. The armor jock Gus had known back in the 83rd might still be in there somewhere, buried under purple smoke and battle scars, but greed was this guy's motivation now. Greed and his ego.

Earl didn't answer the question, just like Drake knew he wouldn't.

"All I'm hearin' so far is a bunch of B.S." Nostrils flared, Earl jabbed the cheroot at Gus. "What *I* wanna know is, what the *skudge* do I get if I *win* this battle royal?"

"This will be *staged*," snapped Gus. "There won't *be* a real winner. We'll *pick* the winner ahead of time to make the Fluke happy, but it'll just be for show. Got that?"

"Doesn't sound believable to me," said Earl. "You really think the *Fluke* will buy this?"

"They will if we make it realistic enough," said Drake. "With the right choreography and special effects."

Earl jabbed the cheroot skyward. "Those bastards are *smart*. You got that? I been watching them for a long, long time. I know them bastards better'n anybody. Better'n you! They'll see right through any fake bullshit, and it'll piss 'em off more!"

"Not if we do it right," said Gus. "And you *know* we can. We're the best there are. You tellin' me we can't do anything we want when we put on the armor?" She snorted, a derisive sound Drake knew well. "Guess I've been wrong about you."

"It has to be real." Earl tapped the pink ash from the tip of his cheroot. "There has to be an *actual* winner, not a *fake* one. And there has to be a prize, other than some feel-good, help-your-fellow-man silliness. You can insult me all you want, *Gray Lady*, but I ain't gonna risk my hide unless there's something in it for me. Something *real*."

"What do you suggest, Earl?" asked Drake, keeping up the charade of being the reasonable one here.

Earl jabbed his cheroot at Gus again. "Your armor." His scar puckered as he sneered. "Or should I say, the armor you *stole*."

Gus crossed her arms across her chest and glared at him. "Not a chance, Earl. *My* armor's not on the table."

"Well, it wouldn't be, would it?" Earl's sneer widened. "Unless you don't think you can *beat* me, that is. Me, in my cobbled-together armor that couldn't *possibly* measure up to yours."

"I don't think that at all," said Gus.

"Then what's the harm?" Still sneering, Earl thrust out a grimy hand. "Let's shake on it. I beat you fair and square, I get your armor…and you get mine."

Gus kept her arms right where they were and shook her head. "That's a bet I'll never take."

Earl dropped his hand. "Fine. Then find yourself another sparring partner. Gray Lady."

Drake kept his face grim but smiled inwardly. Earl was behaving exactly as they'd expected—exactly as they'd hoped. He'd been right that the Fluke would likely see through any half-hearted fakery. To keep the show believable with such a difficult personality involved, they had to give him the perfect motivation. They had to give him a fighting chance at the one thing he probably wanted more than anything in the galaxy: *Real* armor, battle-tested, upgraded, and maintained by an armor jock he knew was one of the best, no matter how much disrespect he heaped on her verbally.

Not that Drake and Gus had any intention of triggering his bullshit detector by making it seem too easy for him.

"Fine." Drake flung up both hands, palms toward Earl, in final refusal. "Forget it, then. We'll go with Plan B."

Earl frowned. "What's Plan B?"

"None of your business." Drake lowered his hands and turned away.

He could practically feel the fish sniffing at the baited hook as he and Gus started back to the *Void*. There was no way Earl would let himself get so close to the ultimate prize, then let it slip away without making a play for it.

"Nobody else on The Bluff has armor!" Earl shouted after them. "You can't have a battle royal with just one armor jock!"

"Don't worry about it," Drake said over his shoulder. "We've got it covered."

"Your loss, skudge-holes!" said Earl, which seemed like the end of it.

But just as they reached the hatch of the *Void*, they heard his voice calling from afar. Turning, Drake saw him lurching toward them across the clearing on his damaged leg, waving his cheroot emphatically.

"Okay, fine. I'll do it!" he said. "If you losers are set on this stupid game plan, I'll play along."

Drake didn't grin with satisfaction, though he wanted to. He and Gus had never doubted that Earl would agree to join forces, whether or not they refused to bet her armor to entice him. Even if they didn't give in to Earl's demands, they'd known he wouldn't be able to resist climbing in the ring with Gus. It was better to have a slim chance at her armor, no matter how remote, than no chance at all.

He might even think he could figure out a way to improve his odds through underhanded means. Based on what Drake knew about Earl from Gus, cheating or double-crossing did not seem outside the realm of possibility.

And the question of him phoning it in—doing the bare minimum in an unconvincing way—no longer seemed valid. Earl would be committed as hell on the battlefield, no ifs, ands, or buts.

"All right then, Earl." Drake nodded. "Go get your armor, and let's meet at the showroom to go over the details of what we have in mind."

"What details?" asked Earl, a bit out of breath from hobbling after them. "We fight, I lose, end of story."

"Just meet us there in an hour," said Drake. "And who said you were going to be the loser?"

Earl looked confused, his scarred frown wreathed in purple smoke from the cheroot.

Drake and Gus left him that way, popping the hatch and slipping inside the ship without another word to him.

"Looks like we've got our opponent," said Drake after the hatch closed behind them. "The question is, how long will he stick to the playbook?"

They headed down the corridor toward the cargo bay. "Until the first chance he gets to flip the script," said Gus. "Then, in goes the knife."

"He won't be able to do any real damage though, will he? Not with whatever so-called armor he's hacked together."

Gus gave him a sidelong look. "I did say he was a berserker on the battlefield back in his days with the 83rd, didn't I?"

"With fully functional military armor," said Drake. "Plus years younger and without that gamey leg of his."

"Rule number one: Never underestimate an opponent,"

said Gus. "No matter how primitive their armory or how limited their skill level. A committed enemy with a sling-shot can take down a fully equipped armor jock if the jock's having a bad day. I've seen it happen—crushing defeat snatched from the jaws of certain victory."

"I know, but..."

Drake stopped and directed his gaze at the wall-mounted retinal scanner plate for the cargo bay door. The scanner's red beams flicked over his eyes, the system confirmed his identity, and the door slid open before them. Silently. Gus really had futzed with the controls for all the doors on the ship.

"I wouldn't go through with this plan if I thought he might actually *beat* you and take your armor."

And the only way that would happen was if Gus was hurt so badly she couldn't stop it from happening. He still remembered the absolute terror he'd felt back on Shepard's Moon when he thought she'd been killed in battle. No way would he let Earl hurt her like that, even if he had to take the man out himself with the *Void's* lasers and to hell with the Fluke.

Gus marched in the cargo bay after him and crossed the deck to where she'd been working on her armor. "It isn't just up to you, cowboy. And don't worry, I'll be fine. I'm just saying, we can't take anything or any*one* for granted—even a broken-down prick like Earl Knox."

"That was never my intention, darlin'." Drake tensed at the thought that something bad might happen to her anyway because of his carelessness. It might not be possible to plan for every contingency, but he was sure as hell going to give it a try. "I agree, we need to cover all the bases as best we can."

Gus frowned when she checked the chronometer on her wrist. "We need to do it soon, too. It's been a while since the Prowlers started their light show. Who knows how much longer they'll go before landing on double-blue or double-red?"

"I wonder how the shopping list is coming along?" Drake raised his voice to address the ship's AI, not the human prick it was named after. "Earl?"

"Yes, Captain Drake?" said the AI.

"Any messages planetside from Bruce O'Connor regarding our requested repair parts?"

"No messages," said Earl. "Would you like me to send one?"

"Sure, send a reminder," said Drake. "Mention we're still awaiting delivery of the requested items, and time is running out."

"I will compose and send something suitable," said Earl. "Under your signature, of course, Captain."

"Thanks."

He didn't technically have to thank an AI for doing its job, but since this Earl was so compliant—certainly a nice change from its namesake—Drake felt like it was only polite.

He sauntered over to lean against the workbench, watching as Gus polished the visor of her helmet beside him. "You think he'll send the parts for the ship and your armor?"

"*I* wouldn't...but maybe." Gus rubbed extra hard at a smudge on the visor. "For all he knows, we might bolt as soon as the repairs are finished. On the other hand, you *did* know his father, and we've got a perfectly good reason for making the request."

"And he doesn't know we were counting on getting credit," Drake said.

"Exactly."

Drake nodded. "If everything goes pear-shaped, the *Void* is the only viable lifeboat. Buddy Senior only had one escape launch, and unless Bruce upgraded his emergency escape plan, that one launch isn't enough to evacuate everyone from the surface."

"Or *under* it," said Gus, reminding him of the locals who resided underground to escape the worst of the Fluke's outbursts.

While they'd been perusing the wares for sale in the Fluke Off, Bruce had mentioned that the population of the Bluff had been greatly reduced since the last time Drake was here, no doubt thanks to the Fluke. Only a few dozen permanent residents had moved underground with a few stubborn cusses who'd refused to give up their homes on the surface. While Drake could squeeze that many onto the *Void*, there were far too many to fit on Bruce's undersized craft.

If they'd even agree to leave. People who settled on Frontier worlds tended to have an independent streak a mile wide.

"All the more reason to repair the weapons console and get that new replicator installed before the big showdown," said Drake. "And having spaceworthy armor would give us extra protection on the way out of orbit, courtesy of a certain armor jock I know."

"Hey, I'm convinced."

Gus smiled as she finished clearing the smudge and upended the helmet to check that none of its seals had gone bad. The space-tight seal that had failed was on her armor's shoulder joint, the one that had been damaged during the fighting on Shepard's Moon. The techs on Shepard's Moon had repaired it while she'd been in the hospital, but they'd been cut off from the Alliance for a long time. They'd done the best they could—no way would they have done anything less for the Gray Lady who'd saved their asses— but they could only use what they had on hand. Even if Bruce didn't have the right seal in stock, a working replicator could solve the problem in ten seconds flat.

Which they'd be able to do if Bruce decided to cough one up *before* the big battle instead of making them wait until the show was over.

Gus blew out a breath. "Now we just have to hope ol' Bruce makes a leap of faith so we don't end up high and dry at the end of all this," she said, almost as if she'd read his mind.

"I think he'll do the right thing." Drake pulled out a stick of cinnamon gum, freed it from its foil wrapper, and slid it into his mouth, relishing the sweet smell of cinnamon as much as the taste. "He might be pretentious, but I still think he's got a good heart."

"All due respect, space cowboy," said Gus, "but you haven't known him very long…the new, improved, grown-up him, that is. Have you considered that *he* might be using *us*?"

Drake scowled as he chewed the gum. Of course it was something he'd thought about, but he didn't want to say so.

"My gut says otherwise. We might be his best shot at getting rid of the Fluke. Why risk jerking us around or worse?"

"I've been thinking about that." She stopped tightening a seal in the helmet and gave him a grim look. "How can we be sure he *wants* the Fluke gone? They're pretty key to his whole business model, aren't they?"

Once again, she was absolutely right. Without the orbiting Prowlers to discourage timewasters, competitors, and wannabe dictators like Tor, how could the kid Bruce had been have kept the Fluke Off Trading Post from going under after Buddy Senior's untimely demise? Not only kept it from going out of business, but improved the hell out of it. Those improvements couldn't have come cheap. Drake still had a hard time reconciling the surly teenager he remembered with the slick businessman Bruce had become.

The way the kid ran the place now, didn't its mystique and privacy rely on the aliens' threat, not to mention the curiosity factor that came with them? Did it really make sense to try to drive them away or antagonize them? From what Drake could see, the business had been in rocky shape to begin with but Bruce had managed to keep it alive once. It was unlikely to survive another major shock to the system.

"He did say they've tried getting rid of the Fluke, though," said Drake. "Unsuccessfully, but still..."

"What he *said* and what they actually *did* might be two very different things...but I'm not telling you something you don't already know."

She turned the helmet over and set it aside, seemingly satisfied with its condition—at least for the moment. Drake fully expected her to keep checking and tweaking it right up until fight time, as was her habit. She preferred to leave as little as possible up to chance when a battlefield situation beckoned.

Drake thought for a moment, considering what she's said. Was she just advising caution...or something more proactive? "Are you saying *we* should get the jump on *him*, just in case he's planning his own double-cross?"

Gus shook her head. "I just think we should keep our options open, that's all."

"Fair enough." Drake appreciated her military approach to scenarios like this, how she considered risky scenarios in ways that might not otherwise occur to him. He liked to think he had his own unique perspectives to offer, but he knew her special strategic thinking and battlefield aware-ness gave them both an edge when the skudge hit the fan. "Speaking of options, how did the LEDs work out on your armor?"

In reply, Gus walked over to her armor, which was anchored to a repair rack, and pushed a large blue button on the back of the left gauntlet. Instantly, the armor took on a shimmering blue glow...even the unattached helmet on the workbench.

Next, she moved to the other side of the armor and smacked a big red button on the back of the right gauntlet. This time the armor and helmet changed from blue to a bright red glow.

"Perfect!" Drake grinned and applauded. "Great work rigging up those spare cargo beacons, darlin'!"

Though they didn't have a working replicator, parts for the weapons control console, or the missing space-tight seal for her armor, the *Void*'s hold *did* stock plenty of cargo beacons—color-coded lights used by smugglers like him to mark contraband for dead drops in tricky locations. A flashing ultraviolet, infrared, or straight-up visible spectrum blinker could tip off intended recipients to a pickup when the actual smuggler had to drop the goods and hightail it before the law could apprehend him. She'd added the cargo beacons to her armor while they'd kicked around how to entice Earl to take part in their plan, but this was the first time he'd seen the beacons in action.

"I've got the extra set ready for Earl, too," she told him, "and *this*, of course." She held up a rectangular black remote with three buttons—one blue, one red, one white. "Not that we'll *need* an Earl override, of course."

Drake chuckled. "Not a chance!"

"Your *special* lights are up and running, too," she told him. "They tested with flying colors."

"Great!" Drake rubbed his hands together excitedly.

Though it would have been nice not to have to deal with Earl and the Fluke to get what they needed, now that the plan was in motion, he felt a rising tide of enthusiasm…a "gambler's high" almost. Facing colossal odds with the woman he loved by his side, he couldn't tamp down the adrenaline thrill—and he didn't want to. He knew it gave him an edge, and that was just what he needed going into the big game.

Was he addicted to risk-taking ventures like this? All he knew for sure was that there was a reason he'd become a smuggler on the Frontier instead of a desk jockey for an accounting firm on some buttoned-down, dull-as-dishwater planet in the Free Worlds Alliance.

"So I guess we're doing this, then," said Gus. "Dancin' with the Fluke once more."

Drake nodded. "All goes well, it'll be our ticket to takin' out Tor."

"And saving your ex."

He shrugged. "That too, yeah."

Gus smirked. "Life with you is never boring, I'll give you that."

He crossed the cargo bay, slowly chewing his gum as he approached her. "Would you have it any other way, my dear?"

Her answer was obvious from the look on her face as he took her in his arms.

"Truth is, you're the key," he told her, taking her chin between his thumb and forefinger. "When I'm with you, I feel like there's nothin' I can't do. No problem I can't handle. It wasn't like that before."

"Not even when you were with Rhapsody?" she asked.

"No, ma'am." He locked eyes with her, feeling the deep connection they shared liked a beam of force between them. "Not even close. Not even in the same universe."

"Good." Leaning forward and standing on tiptoe, she softly kissed him, the warmth of her love enfolding him like the heat of a radiant sun. "That's what I like to hear," she whispered, breaking the kiss for only a moment before resuming it.

Though a thousand wonderful things occurred to him to say, Drake simply gave himself over to her then, savoring the perfect moment on the verge of the biggest gamble of his recent life. Whatever came next, however his plan unfolded, at least he had felt this way at this time with this woman, fulfilling the deepest dreams of a lifetime to be cherished and elevated by someone who wanted only the best for them both.

That, he was starting to think, might not have been a lucky fluke so much as a blessing of benevolent destiny.

CHAPTER 16

Gus had done a lot of things while wearing her armor.

She'd kicked ass on a hundred different worlds. Waded through swamps, pounded across dusty flat desert terrain, punched through the permacrete walls of rebel hideouts like they were paper. She'd fought in space and under water and in deep dark caverns on alien worlds. She'd marched in parade formation along with her squadron in a show of military strength on a new and struggling Alliance world. Hell, she'd even blasted asteroid-sized chunks of ice into water vapor while Drake drew a smiley face in the upper atmosphere of a gas giant.

Until now, she'd never tested her skills against another armor jock in an arena before hundreds of cheering fans.

All holograms, of course.

Well, almost all. A few actual residents of The Bluff had been cajoled into coming out of hiding to add an air of authenticity to the event, but they looked scared shitless.

She hoped Bruce was paying them well since the holographic arena had been his idea.

"You'll need to get the Fluke's attention," he'd said. "They won't even notice a couple of metal warriors shooting at each other among the trees. It needs to be a real show. We're giving them a contest to bet on, an event the likes of which even the Fluke can't resist watching, don't you agree?"

Gus had an idea the Fluke would have watched anyway, but she kept her mouth shut and let Drake handle the details of where the "combat" would take place. They both wanted Bruce as invested as they were in the whole scheme, something she'd worried about ever since he'd refused to actually deliver a replicator to the *Void* without settling up the bill first. At least he'd allowed her to fabricate the space-tight seal she needed for her armor on his own personal replicator in the Fluke Off's back room.

"No cost," he'd said. "As a show of good faith."

He hadn't agreed to provide the holoprojectors on the same generous terms.

"I can offer them to you at a vastly reduced price," he'd said. "You'll find they're quite reasonable."

Drake had snorted at the mention of the additional cost —holoprojectors weren't exactly on their shopping list since the *Void* already had the few it needed—but Gus had squeezed his arm gently. If all went according to plan, Bruce should be more than happy to extend enough credit to outfit a dozen *Golden Voids* with enough holoprojectors to flummox the most determined Fluke Prowlers. He'd certainly seemed enthusiastic enough once they'd explained the basic plan to him.

While Drake had worked with one of Bruce's black-clad security guards to set up the holoprojectors in a strangely vacant not to mention dry patch of dirt not far from the trading post, Gus had offered to help Earl position the LEDs on his armor, but he'd declined. Just as well. She didn't want to be accused of sabotaging the hunk of junk he thought would actually beat her armor.

His suit looked exactly like something a former armor jock would cobble together to fight for money. Instead of the two standard military issue shoulder-mounted launchers, his armor only had one mounted on the left shoulder, although it was equipped with a fairly powerful laser grafted onto the launching tube. His gauntlets were mismatched, and the jets on his boots looked barely adequate for lifting his armor off the ground.

Her own armor had multiple positioning jets not only on her boots but at various points on her torso and shoulders, something she'd added for improved maneuverability. She'd also added lasers to her gauntlets, as well as a powerful laser embedded in the palm of one hand. She'd installed extra shielding inside her armor's torso specifically to deflect quantum weapons that could otherwise pass through the metal with the ease of a knife slicing through a piece of ripe fruit. And on top of that she'd be carrying concussion grenades strapped around her armor's waist, more for show than anything else.

Earl's armor had a few lasers mounted on the front of the torso and what looked like an actual antique firearm welded to the inside of the gauntlet on his right arm, like a gunfighter in one of the old entertainment vids she'd watched once—and only once—with Drake. The armor's metal plating was mismatched. Some of it looked brand new and as smooth as a baby's bottom, the rest was pock-marked and scorched where he'd taken hits in prior battles. The armor had been welded together without any attention paid to whether the space-tight seals at the joints would actually hold. She wouldn't want to take Earl's armor outside a planet's atmosphere. Or to the bottom of a lake either, for that matter.

The best thing about Earl's armor was the helmet. It was military issue, all right, almost a twin to Gus's own, if she didn't count the hairline crack along one edge of the visor. That crack would screw with the armor's targeting capabilities. Gus knew that for a fact. She'd taken an explosive charge to the face back when she'd been a newbie armor jock. The explosion had cracked her armor's visor. When she'd tried to fire back at her attacker, the shot had gone off target and she'd almost nailed an armor jock from her own squad instead.

She'd been sidelined until the repairs were completed, so the brass had her visor repaired pronto. Even when she'd been a newbie, nobody wanted the Gray Lady out of the action for long.

Earl's armor looked like he didn't give a shit if the visor imploded in the vacuum of space. That meant all his battles had been on the ground or at low altitude. Gus filed away that information in the back of her brain. They wouldn't be taking this battle into space, not unless she had no other choice.

As for the crack messing with his targeting, he'd probably figured out how to compensate for the crack when he engaged his targeting display. Like she'd told Drake, Earl had been a berserker in battle. She couldn't assume otherwise just from the look of his armor.

Armor that now bore a bright orange stripe across the top of the helmet and down both arms, from shoulder to gauntlet. Gus's armor bore gold stripes in the same place.

Earl had balked at the colors at first. "Why I gotta be orange when you get gold?"

Gus pointed at herself. "Team *Golden Void*." Then she pointed at him. "Team Bruce. Red hair, get it?"

Bruce's hair was more orange than actual red, which made the choices for team colors obvious. At least they'd been obvious to her and Drake. Earl clearly didn't like someone else "gettin' the gold." Too bad. The holographic "crowd" would be divided into fans for each team, which they hoped would help the Fluke get into the spirit of betting on which armor jock came out on top.

When Drake refused her help outfitting his armor with the LEDs and the control buttons, she'd tossed the things at him and told him where to stick them.

On his armor.

Although the thought of sticking all those cargo beacons elsewhere on his anatomy almost—*almost*—made her smile.

He'd caught the beacons and sneered at her. "Ain't gonna take a lightshow for me to beat the snot out of you," he said.

"Right back atcha'," she said, then she arched an eyebrow as she made a show of taking a good long look at his armor. "You expect to beat me with this hunk o' junk?"

He took a minute to light up one of those ugly purple cheroots of his. Once he got it going, he blew a stream of smoke in her face. She didn't give him the satisfaction of coughing.

"I could beat you with my bare hands, *Gray Lady*."

They'd apparently reached the trash talk portion of the program. Knowing Earl, it could go on forever. The man always did have to have the last word.

Well, not this time.

"Just stick to the script, *Early*," she said, "and we'll all go away happy."

She knew he wouldn't. It was just a matter of when. And how.

The "when" came five minutes into the battle.

Gus was surprised Earl had actually stuck to the script for that long. He'd been a good soldier when he'd had to answer to a squadron leader, sticking with the battle plan and racking up impressive body counts along the way— almost as good as Gus's own—but on The Bluff he didn't have anybody to keep him in line once he climbed in his armor.

Especially not Gus or Drake.

And Earl had never been a patient man.

The plan they'd come up with was to use laser fire that had been dialed down just enough that each "hit" would scorch but not penetrate each other's armor. No shots would be targeted at the weak points in the armor—the joints at the shoulders, elbows, and wrist, or the hips, knees, and neck. Both sets of armor had been coated with a compound that would produce sparks and puffs of black smoke when hit with the dialed-down laser fire, making the shots look like they'd done much more damage than they had.

Gus had grumbled at the thought of how much time it would take to polish those scorch marks off her armor after this was all over, but it would be worth it if it worked. And to make it work, there would be a *lot* of laser hits. The LEDs were programmed to pulse for five seconds after each hit, blue for the shooter and red for the armor jock who'd taken the hit. If no more hits were scored after five seconds, the LEDs would stay lit. The armor jock with the solid red glow would then have five seconds to land *two* discrete hits to change their red glow back to a pulsing blue while their opponent's went back to a pulsing red.

And if that didn't happen? If the armor jock with the red glow failed to land those two hits in five seconds? The game would be over, and the glowing red armor jock would be declared the loser.

By adopting the Fluke's snake-eyes color scheme, Drake hoped that they'd get the idea of who won and who lost the battle so they'd know which Fluke had won the bet. They all hoped that the losing Fluke wouldn't nuke the planet out of spite.

The fight choreography they'd come up with was as much about endurance as strategy and pinpoint shooting. Gus wished she'd had more time to get some workouts in planetside, but she was still in pretty great shape considering she hadn't completely recovered from the shoulder injury that had put her in the hospital on Shepard's Moon.

With Earl's semi-mechanical leg, she figured the odds were about even in the endurance category.

But as for the rest of it?

She knew she could clean his clock with one metaphorical arm tied behind her armor's back.

To keep the whole thing interesting, they had each agreed to duck and twist and jet around the surface of the "arena" instead of just standing toe-to-toe trading punches until one of them knocked the other's helmet off. They'd have to be careful about getting too close to the holoprojected crowd. If either of them punched through the holoprojections, the gig would be up and the Fluke would no doubt react accordingly. In Gus's experience, one universal constant was that no one liked to be made a fool of.

Before the battle started, loudspeakers announced to the holoprojected "crowd" as well as the few real people in attendance that this would be the biggest gambling event this sector of space had ever seen or *would ever see*. It was that last bit that Drake hoped would convince the Fluke to pack up once the game was done and take their lightshow dice and go find a better game somewhere else to bet on. Because, as he'd said, what was the point of a gambler sticking around when the game was done and betting was over?

She didn't have to wonder if the Fluke noticed the game. After the loudspeaker announcement, both Prowlers had dropped out of orbit to hover overhead, their own lightshows paused for now.

For better or worse, they'd definitely gotten the Fluke's attention.

And more than that. After she and Earl exchanged the

first few hits, one Prowler had changed its color scheme to solid gold, the other solid orange. Bets placed, ladies and gentlemen. Now to give them a real show.

The red and blue buttons on her gauntlets were overrides in case she needed them when Earl didn't stick with the plan. Earl's LEDs had the same buttons for his gauntlets, but she'd made sure his buttons were basically useless. The last thing they wanted was for Earl to end the game early before they'd given the Fluke a good show.

She and Drake had finally agreed that Earl would have to end up winning. They didn't really have a choice. Without Gus's armor as a potential prize, Earl's ego would demand that he at least get bragging rights.

Only Gus didn't intend to lose, and she didn't feel one bit bad about deceiving him. Once he went off script, all agreements they'd made with each other would be off the table anyway. And knowing Earl, he wouldn't be content with just winning. He'd want to beat the crap out of her.

Drake had his own override buttons he could use to change the red and blue LEDs on both her armor and Earl's. He was currently in the *Void*, the ship hovering just far enough away from the arena so it wouldn't look like it could interfere with the battle but close enough to monitor the action on the ship's sensors as well as the smooth operation of the holoprojectors. He'd probably just about swallowed his gum when the Fluke Prowlers descended toward the arena, but he hadn't bugged out.

Drake had something else up his sleeve, he'd said. It had something to do with the white button he'd had her program on his override remote, but he hadn't told her what exactly it controlled other than his "special" lights.

He'd said she had enough on her mind, had kissed her thoroughly, and told her to go kick Early's ass.

Which she'd been doing just fine. So far neither armor's LEDs had turned from pulsing into steady lights.

She'd just pulled out of a barrel roll when Drake's voice came over her suit's comm system. "Power surge on his armor," Drake said. "Got that, darlin'?"

"Got it," she said.

Systems glitch? Or was the bastard finally making his move?

She got her answer a split second later when a full-power laser blast punched her off her feet. The blast had hit her chest plate mere millimeters from the shoulder joint, not only one of her armor's vulnerable spots but one of hers. That was the spot where she'd been injured on Shepard's Moon.

Lucky guess on Earl's part? Or had he known?

The holographic crowd cheered as her armor pulsed red, his blue. Overhead, the Fluke ships started to pulse. Not changing colors, just pulsing. Apparently, they liked the action too.

Okay, fine. Underhanded action it was.

"Skudge-hole," she muttered as she got to her feet, right about the time her pulsing red LEDs changed to a steady red glow. She'd need to land two shots to change back to pulsing blue.

Earl's shot hadn't been a targeting mistake. He'd meant to slow her down, the bastard. Make her have to work harder.

She heard Drake let loose with a string of inventive curses. "I'm putting the override online," he said.

"Not yet," she said. "The game's just getting interesting for our guests, and that's what we want."

"Not if he ends up killing you!"

She dialed up the power on her own lasers to full as she took off running at Earl, dodging more shots from the laser on his shoulder-mounted launcher. When she got within ten feet of him, she blasted him twice in quick succession, two full hits square on the middle of his chest plate.

"You were saying?" she said to Drake.

At that distance, full-power shots should have knocked him halfway across the arena. But the energy of her shots just fizzled and sparked as if they'd been light taps like they'd been shooting at each other all along.

What the skudge?

At least her LEDs had gone back to a pulsing blue and his had turned to a pulsing red.

He had five seconds to land a shot before his lights switched over to steady red.

She ducked more shots from his lasers, using her maneuvering jets to move in a way she hoped he wouldn't anticipate while she tried to line up another shot. Anywhere except his chest plate.

That new smooth piece of armor he'd grafted to his battle-scarred suit had absorbed the energy of her shots the exact same way she'd only seen once before. On the drone she and Drake had eventually shot out of the sky on Chrysallix.

Son of a bitch!

She tried to remember if she'd seen that smooth metal anywhere else on his armor, but she hadn't. She'd been too focused on the crack in his visor and what that might mean for their battle. The damn crack had been a purposeful distraction, and she'd fallen for it. So much for being the best damn armor jock in the Alliance or anywhere else. His pinpoint targeting was just fine.

They traded more laser shots. Gus protected her vulnerable shoulder joint and her armor's boots as Earl tried to knock her off her feet again. She hit Earl's shoulders and thighs, and once she thought she might have knocked him off his feet, but he rolled at the last minute, coming up firing. None of her shots had backed him up enough to make his LEDs switch from a pulsing red to a steady red glow.

If she couldn't punch him hard enough to knock him off his feet and make him waste those five seconds getting up, she'd have to do something else just as deadly.

Hit him where it would do the most damage—on his weapon mounts. If she could take out his weapons, she could stomp her way up to him and knock him down with a solid punch that would turn his cracked visor into a shattered visor.

Game over.

Taking out weapon mounts required the kind of precision shooting she could only do if she maintained position the split second it would take for her armor's targeting display to lock on to the exact spot where the weld holding weapon to armor was the weakest. She couldn't give a berserker like Earl that split second. If she did, he'd pound her with so many full-power laser blasts she'd be out of the game before she could land another shot to save herself.

She needed a diversion, and it couldn't be Drake's lightshow. Not if they wanted to maintain the illusion of the game for the Fluke.

"Get ready for a lightshow, Gray Lady style," she muttered over her comm, loud enough for Drake to hear.

And Earl, too. His maniacal laugh echoed inside her helmet.

The skudge-hole must have hacked into their comm channel, something Drake had assured her no one could do.

That meant Earl must know all about the override buttons, and it was even money he'd disabled them before the game even started. He might look like a loser asshole with more ego than brains, but he'd learned a lot since he'd been kicked out of the military.

"Bring it," Earl said. "Just don't damage that armor of yours *too* much since I intend to claim my prize with or without your dead body inside."

Overhead, the Fluke Prowlers were pulsing almost faster than the eye could see, especially the orange-hued one. Apparently, it was excited because Earl looked like he was winning, and the Fluke who favored him was celebrating early.

Drake's cussing had grown to truly epic proportions.

"Relax, space cowboy," Gus said. "I got this."

And she threw every concussion grenade around her waist right at Earl.

They all went off in spectacular fashion, raising a dust cloud so high that it almost enveloped the Fluke Prowlers.

Gus switched her targeting display to account for the dust and paused that split second she needed to dial in the mounts for Earl's shoulder-mounted launcher, the lasers mounted on his armor's torso, and even the jets mounted on his armor's boots. She saw him aim his launcher right at her, and the opening at the front began to glow. Was he actually planning on shooting a skudging *missile* at her?

Well, not if she could help it.

She let loose with all her lasers at once, full-power shots that drained her energy reserves, but she didn't care. This truly had become a battle royale, and she wasn't about to lose, not to the likes of Earl Knox.

Each shot hit home. Earl's armor sparked and scorched and was knocked off its feet as each of its weapon welds melted away. The shoulder-mounted launcher slid off just as the missile fired. The missile went wild, nearly colliding with one of the Fluke Prowlers, which calmly destroyed the missile without losing a beat in its rapidly pulsing golden glow.

Earl's red LEDs went from pulsing red to a steady red glow. Gus's LEDs glowed steady blue.

She stomped over to where he'd been knocked to the ground. He'd need two shots to beat her, and he had no weapons left to shoot.

"It's over," she said over the comm channel she knew he could hear. "You *lost*."

Incredibly, he laughed. "Don't count your chickens yet, Gray Lady."

He raised his right arm to point his gauntlet at her helmet.

The gauntlet with the ancient firearm still welded in place. An ancient weapon that still worked.

He fired two projectiles from that weapon directly at her. The first one impacted with the left side of her helmet. *Hit one.*

The second impacted the edge of her visor. She heard as well as saw her visor crack.

Hit two.

Rage took over then. There was no other way to explain it. The red she saw didn't come from the pulsing LEDs which would turn to a solid red glow in less than five seconds.

She grabbed him around the neck, her armor's incredibly strong hand clamped down on the seal where his helmet was attached to the torso of his armor. She lifted him up and then slammed him to the ground.

Hit one.

She did it again.

Hit two. Her LEDs changed to pulsing blue.

Only he still had enough of his senses to start punching her back.

They traded blows for so long that Gus lost track of how many times the LEDs had switched colors, and still Earl didn't stop. Maybe he couldn't, his ego wouldn't let him.

Sweat was running down her face, stinging her eyes. Her armor had become a sauna, and she knew she was screaming. All the insults she'd taken from this man, all the crap he'd heaped on her shoulders back when she'd been a brash young woman just trying to fit in, all the resentment that had built up over the years that she'd thought she'd taken care of by naming the ship's AI after this man just so she could tell him to go to hell if she wanted, it all came flooding back.

And he was still laughing at her.

It was too much.

"Why. Won't. You. Die?" she screamed at him, punctuating each word by slamming him into the dry dirt of the arena.

"Can't kill me, not here, not now," he said. "I always had your number."

Can't kill me here.

But she knew where she could. Her own cracked visor would make it dicey, but the space-tight seals on *her* armor actually worked.

The next time she lifted him off the arena floor, she kept going up. Hand still clamped around his neck, she flew him out of the arena, over the holoprojectors, over the projected crowds, all the way to the ocean less than a mile away. She felt more than saw the Fluke Prowlers and the *Golden Void* following her.

"What're you doin'?" Earl yelled over the comms, and for the first time he sounded genuinely panicked.

"Going for a swim," she said.

She dove them both beneath the waves. She didn't have to go deep, but she would if she had to. Her suit was made to maneuver in the water. His wasn't. And his wasn't watertight.

His LEDs had been pulsing red when they hit the water. It didn't take long before they glowed a steady red.

And it didn't take long for water to begin to seep through the faulty seals on his armor.

"You're gonna drown me!" he cried.

"That's the plan," she said. "Battle royale, remember? Fight to the death?"

"But that ain't…"

"Ain't sporting?" she said. "What about that chest plate of yours? The one even full-power lasers can't penetrate?"

"That ain't true!" He sputtered as water started to fill up his helmet. His armor was getting heavy with all the added water weight, but Gus could hold on forever if she had to. "There's a way to shoot it! Make it count! I swear, I thought you knew. Honest to Pete, I wouldn't try to cheat you."

Begging. Early Knox had been reduced to begging.

"If I let you live," she said, "you will tell me everything you know about that metal, *including* who you got it from and where I can find them. *And* you're going to cover the costs for everything Drake and I end up buying at Fluke Off. You got that?"

He didn't even hesitate before he agreed. "Everything on your list," he said.

"It's a long list," she said, "and getting longer all the time."

"I'll do it. I got money saved up, and Bruce, he owes me."

Earl almost sounded like he was crying. All his bravado was long gone.

She was tempted to hold him underwater just a bit longer, but ocean water was starting to seep through the visor on her own helmet. She'd have to repair that on the way back to Chrysallix, *if* the Fluke let them leave. That was a big if.

"You hear all that Drake?" she asked, raising her voice enough to make sure the communication went through.

"Loud and clear, darlin'." She could hear the wide grin in his voice. "We declarin' a winner?"

"That we are."

By the time she hauled Earl's sorry ass out of the ocean, Drake's lightshow was well underway. She'd inadvertently given him a dusty equivalent of vaporized ice when she'd set off the grenades in the arena. He'd programmed the *Void's* beacons to approximate a fireworks display. He'd probably planned to vent some kind of gas to use as a projection screen, but the dusty air proved just fine. The loudspeakers were providing the appropriate booms and whistles and rousing music that went hand-in-hand with every fireworks show Gus had ever seen.

"And the winner by technical knockout," Drake announced over the loudspeakers, "is *Team GOLDEN VOID!*"

The holographic crowd went wild. Even the actual residents got into the celebration, whooping and hollering and hugging each other, all while keeping a wary eye on the Fluke Prowlers still overhead.

Who'd gone black.

No pulsing lights. No steady orange or golden glow. Just black.

Then, slowly...ever so slowly... as new patterns began to appear, Gus started to laugh.

The Fluke Prowler that had been glowing golden, presumably in support of Team *Golden Void*, displayed an oversized smiley face, just like the Prowler had after Drake's Smiley Face Gambit. The Prowler that had been rooting for Team Bruce displayed an oversized frowny face.

"I'll be damned," Drake said. "They knew all along."

Knew who was aboard the *Void*, or knew that the battle was a staged event? The Fluke would never tell, and did it really matter? Because in the next instant, the Fluke Prowlers were gone. Just... gone.

They'd won. Gus and Drake had won. They still had a big battle in front of them, but they'd skudging *won.*

Things might even go back to normal for the people of The Bluff. And how did she know that?

Because she could *smell* the ocean water that had seeped inside her helmet.

The Fluke had taken their gifts and gone to wherever Fluke went when they weren't tormenting a world. It wouldn't bring back the dead. At least she hoped not. Buddy Senior would stay gone, but the people who lived here could actually start living again.

Gus whooped even as the musty smell of the ocean filled her helmet.

She didn't think that in the history of the universe, anything so stinky had ever smelled so good.

CHAPTER 17

Drake smiled as he supervised the loading of the various parts and supplies they needed from Fluke Off...all floated in on hover-dollies by Bruce's black-uniformed men. Drake's smile got noticeably bigger when a replacement replicator cleared the ramp, its shiny silver shell gleaming in the morning sun and the guidelights of the *Void*'s cargo bay.

If there was one thing he loved more than a plan coming together, it was free stuff—and thanks to Earl, everything entering the ship was paid for.

After Gus had brought him back from his dip in the ocean, he'd stayed true to his promise to purchase everything on their shopping list with his own hard-earned money. Not that Earl was an honorable man, but he was honoring the terms of the deal he'd made to save his sorry skin from drowning in the ocean, which was saying something.

Now, it was like what they used to call Christmas morning back on Earth…if Christmas morning ended with an all-out battle to free a certain planetoid and its over-the-top mistress/governor.

Soon after the replicator glided in on its floating palette, Bruce strolled into the cargo bay and tossed off a casual wave. "Everything to your liking, Mephistopheles?"

Drake caught himself before he could do a doubletake at the sight and sound of the changed man before him. Everything about Bruce was more relaxed, from the tone of his voice to the easy sway of his stride. Not only was his necktie missing and the top button of his shirt undone, but he'd just called Drake by his first name for the first time since he and Gus had arrived on the Bluff.

"So far, so good," Drake said, managing—just barely—to keep the surprise out of his voice.

Were the changes in Bruce the result of the Fluke's departure? When the Fluke left the Bluff, smell had come back to the world. All that dark mucky ground now *smelled* as bad as it looked, and Drake had done as little slogging through it as possible.

The Fluke had clearly undone some of the alterations they'd made during the era of their observation and interference. Drake had heard of such reversals happening on other worlds affected by the aliens, though he wasn't sure it *always* happened when they moved on to other locations. Like almost everything they did, it seemed mostly random from a human point of view.

"Well, it's the least we can do for the folks who freed the Bluff from those bastards." Bruce ambled over and clapped

Drake on the shoulder. "I doubt we ever would have gotten out from under them otherwise."

"You're sure this is what you wanted, then?" Drake looked at him sideways and pulled a stick of cinnamon gum from the breast pocket of his blue plaid flannel shirt. "Doesn't it leave you more exposed, without the Fluke in orbit? Won't it hurt business?"

Bruce shrugged. "I'm hoping it might actually bring in *more* customers. A lot of people stayed away because of the Fluke, and they weren't *all* law enforcement or pirates."

"What about the Fluke's influence?" Drake unwrapped the gum and folded it into his mouth. "The things they changed over the years? Will it all change back?" The smells of the Bluff had already been restored, but it was likely that more subtle changes could be lost on them. Neither of them knew the planet as well as Bruce, Earl, and its other inhabitants did.

"Some things have already gone back to the way they used to be, as you may have noticed." Grinning, Bruce spread his arms wide to indicate his own alteration—his overall relaxation. "Maybe other things will change more gradually. Either way, it's a small price to pay to have those assholes gone...to finally be in charge of our own *destiny* again."

Drake nodded. Independent smuggler that he was, he could identify. It was a good thing to be able to make your own choices...to give over control only when you decided the time and people closest to you were right.

As if in response to his thoughts, Gus marched into the bay from outside, pulling a welding kit behind her, complete with tanks and torch, on a squeaky-wheeled cart.

The welding helmet on her head was pushed up, its smoked visor shading her grimy, smiling face.

"Hey there." She parked the welding kit out of the way against a bulkhead, removed the helmet, and hung it from one of the kit's handlebars. "I finished fixing that buckled spot on the hull plating. Next up, weapons control."

Drake almost asked if she needed help, then caught himself. The Gray Lady tended to see such offers as implying that she couldn't handle things on her own...and that was an implication she rarely appreciated. As he knew from hard-won experience, if Gus needed help, she would ask for it.

"Sounds like a plan." He put his arm around her when she sidled up beside him. "Whatever we don't need to do to get spaceborne, we can handle en route."

"The sooner we lift off, the better." Gus turned to Bruce. "How much more loading do we have left, anyway?"

Bruce watched as another of his men brought in a stack of plastic tubs on a cart. "Almost done, actually. Just a few more items from the list...and a couple *bonus* pieces after that."

Drake stopped chewing his gum and frowned. "What kind of bonus pieces?"

Bruce grinned slyly. "The kind you're gonna love. The kind that'll come in *real* handy, given the nature of your next...*adventure.*"

Picturing dozens of satisfying possibilities—all of them advanced weaponry of one kind or another—Drake started chewing again. He'd more than doubled the initial shopping list he'd given Bruce what seemed like half a lifetime ago. And why not since, as Gus had said, Earl was on the hook for everything and she *really* wanted him to pay for taking a cheap shot at her shoulder. Drake was more than on board for making that asshole pay through the nose since it was obvious he'd planned from the start to kill Gus and take her armor. Drake hoped Bruce would charge the man double, or even triple.

When Bruce's eyebrows had risen dramatically at the augmented list, Drake had decided to clue the kid in on what he and Gus were facing on Chrysallix. That wasn't the way he usually dealt with most arms dealers, but Buddy Senior had always been a fair man and Drake still had a good feeling about the kid.

A good feeling that turned out to be well warranted.

"Well, thank you for that, Bruce," he said now. He ruled out further questions, not wishing to look the arms dealer's generous gift in the mouth and perhaps inspire him to take it back.

"Yes, thank you," chimed in Gus with a gracious smile. "And tell Earl thanks for adding them to his tab."

"He didn't," said Bruce. "They're on me, this time. On the house. But Earl *did* want me to bring something else to your attention."

"He's not stoppin' by, is he?" Drake had no intention of letting the scarred double-crosser set foot on the *Void* again.

"Nope." Bruce crossed the bay to meet a hover-dolly loaded with a wooden crate, guided into the ship by one of his men. "The *Void* is off-limits to him…though he still wanted to make sure Gus got one particular delivery he promised her."

Drake felt Gus tense against him, and he felt the same way. Though Earl had been defeated and Bruce was personally shepherding the crate, the very fact of Earl's involvement brought with it a certain amount of residual nervousness.

"It turns out he had a secret stockpile of this stuff." Bruce lifted the lid off the crate and fished through the straw and foam-based packing materials inside. "He used some to augment the chest plate of that armor of his, but there was still some left over."

As soon as Bruce pulled out a rectangular slab of the silvery metal, Drake relaxed. This looked like the same stuff Drake had seen in the mines on Shepard's Moon when he'd helped the local troops round up the rest of the rebels after Gus had taken out their leader. The rebels had been mining the stuff and providing it to Jorritz Tor in exchange for Tor supplying them with the military-grade weapons and vehicles they'd used in the attempted coup. The few rebels who'd been captured instead of offing themselves in solidarity with their deceased leader had refused to provide any information on their mining techniques, and there'd been no refineries on Shepard's Moon. The stuff in the crate had clearly been refined —somewhere.

Gus had filled Drake in on how Earl had used the stuff in battle, and Drake had been listening on comms when Earl promised full disclosure regarding the metal's origins and weaknesses. Since the same material had been used for the drones on Chrysallix, the site of the next conflict they would face, any information could help their cause.

"Looks like there's enough in here to be put to *some* kind of use." Bruce pulled out two more slabs of the incredibly lightweight metal. "*But,* this stuff is somewhat unstable.

According to Earl, it's vulnerable to high levels of focused magnetism."

"Magnetism?" asked Gus.

"Blast it with strong, alternating magnetic forces—attractive and repulsive," said Bruce. "Then shoot it with a projectile—a bullet or missile, not a laser. The metal will crack and possibly shatter."

That explained why Earl had welded an old-fashioned pistol to his armor: it fired close-range projectiles. Missiles were long-range projectiles.

"Interesting." Gus walked over and pulled a small slab from the crate. "And did Earl say anything about where he got this stuff in the first place and who sold it to him?"

"He told me it's called *singularium,* and he got it from a smuggler passing through the Bluff," said Bruce. "Someone named Layla Crosscut. As for where *she* got it, all she said was that she picked it up on a shipwreck out near the border. She wasn't very forthcoming, apparently."

"*If* ol' Earl is telling the truth," said Drake. "And that's a pretty big 'if'."

Bruce shrugged. "All I know is what he told me. I do remember Layla, but we never talked about the metal, and she never mentioned a shipwreck."

"Could you do us a favor?" asked Gus. "Give us a shout if any other information shakes loose on the subject?"

Bruce nodded. "I'll do some more digging and let you know what I find out."

"Appreciate it," said Gus.

Just then, another of Bruce's men ascended the ramp with a load of crates on a rolling cart. The cart's wheels were encrusted with some of that foul-smelling muck from the jungle floor. Drake supposed that people who'd been living for a long time on a planet where nothing smelled didn't think twice about using a wheeled cart instead of one that floated *above* all that muck.

Good thing he'd added cleaning bots to his shopping list. The little buggers were going to be busy.

"This is the last of it, Boss," Bruce's man said. "Everything on the list is aboard ship."

"Excellent."

Bruce put the lid back on the crate of singularium, then patted it to signal one of his men, who rushed to move it aside and slip the hover-dolly out from under it.

"So I guess we're done here, then," Bruce said to Drake. "You've got a job to do, if I'm not mistaken."

"And you and your people just improved our chances of success." Drake walked over and extended his hand.

Grinning, Bruce shook it. "Good luck to you both. Let me know how it works out."

"Good luck to you, too, Bruce." Drake added his other hand to the shake for emphasis. "I know your father would be proud."

"Thanks." Bruce broke away and turned to shake hands with Gus, as well. "Just remember, the two of you are always welcome here. Come back anytime."

Gus smiled. "I've got a feeling we'll see you again soon."

"You can even set up shop here if you like," said Bruce. "If you need a base of operations or just a place to hole up."

Gus's smile shifted to a dubious frown. "Welll…"

"And don't worry." Bruce winked. "I'll make sure Earl

won't cause you any trouble…*if* he's still planetside when you get back. He's a guy who's worn out his welcome."

"You're not the first person I've heard say that," said Gus. "He has a habit of staying past his due date—but I'll tell you what. He gives you trouble you can't handle, give us a call. We've got his skudgin' number, and we believe in looking out for our friends."

"I will do that," said Bruce. "And I'll be looking out for the both of you, too, if you need me."

"We'll hold you to that," said Drake, though he left the rest of the sentence unfinished. *If we survive the fight ahead of us on Chrysallix.*

Leaving on a high note always did the most for morale when heading off to war.

Just a few hours later, the *Golden Void* pushed out of orbit, heading for its next destination. Loads of work remained to be done, from installing the new replicator to whatever secret project Gus was cooking up with the singularium metal…but the ship was spaceworthy at last, right down to the weapons control system, and there was no excuse to delay leaving any longer.

Strumming his guitar in the pilot's chair on the bridge, Drake watched on the main screen as Buddy's Bluff fell away in the distance. He was happy with what they'd accomplished there, freeing the planet from the Fluke's oppressive presence…but he wished they hadn't taken so long to do so. When he'd first plotted a course to The Bluff, he'd figured one day travel time to get there, one day to negotiate a deal, install the replicator, and fix up the ship, and one day travel time back to Chrysallix. Even three days had felt too long, but now they'd been gone nearly five with one more travel day left to go.

The unexpected delay made him worry more than ever that it was already too late to free Chrysallix. If he was Tor, and thank the lucky stars that kept watch over all good-hearted space cowboys and independent smugglers that he was *not* Jorritz Tor, Drake would have been using the time to outfit all his drones with singularium. He had no doubt that Tor had more than enough singularium to do just that.

Pausing in his strumming, Drake punched buttons on the chair's armrest to switch the main screen to a forward view. His heart beat faster as he thought about Rhapsody, still in dire jeopardy somewhere in that vast, flickering starfield. It didn't matter that the feelings he'd once had for her were gone and never coming back; he was still concerned about her well-being and always would be. Whether or not she felt the same way about him didn't matter.

Being the kind of person he was, he had to do the best he could for the people he cared about. He didn't have it in him to turn his back and ignore a plea for help.

Gus was the same, which was one of the things he loved best about her. Rhapsody, though…she'd never been like that. It wasn't that she'd never done good deeds for others, but she had always been too self-centered to perform such acts often and for purely altruistic motives.

That, he realized, made him love Gus even more. It even made him happy for the breakup with Rhapsody and the pain it had put him through, because all that had led him to the great Gray Lady who finally made his life complete.

What destiny awaited them upon their return to Chrysallix, he wondered? Would it all work out for the best, leading to freedom for Rhapsody and her people and revenge against Jorritz Tor? Or would the days to come take a darker turn, ending Drake's happiest of times so soon after they had barely begun?

The answers lay ahead in that flickering starfield, just over a day's journey away.

Drake started strumming again, this time playing the first bars of the theme song of the classic old video Western, *Rawhide.* The song had a propulsive rhythm that made him think of the action to come, the battle he would soon engage in when he and Gus rode into "town" to face the "bad guys." Being a cowboy at heart as he was, he relished the thought of a shootout on Main Street at dawn—though the bad guys would most likely be automated drones, and sunrise would be artificially simulated by projections on the domes of the city.

"Drake? Broken String?" Gus's voice interrupted his train of thought, coming over the bridge's speakers from where she was working in one of the ship's corridors.

"Hey there, darlin'." Drake didn't stop strumming, but he did tone it down some. "What can I do you for?"

"Isn't it about time you put this ship on autopilot and got your ass down here?" she snapped...but not in a mean-spirited way. Even when she was gruff with him, there was still an underlying layer of love, and this time was no different. "This replicator's giving me fits for some reason."

"Perfect timing as always."

Drake smiled to himself as he gave the strings a final, emphatic strum for her benefit. *Giving her fits* was Gray Lady speak for *I'm about to throw this skudging thing out the airlock.* Or hit it with a hammer. It hadn't escaped him that she'd included a hammer on the augmented shopping list they'd given Bruce.

"We just broke orbit, and we've got a straight shot out of the system from here. Switching over to autopilot right now." He got up, set the guitar aside, and worked the nav station controls, putting the ship's course in the hands of the AI. "Earl's in charge from here, darlin'."

"Good…but ugh," said Gus. "We really need to change the AI's name, don't we?"

"Up to you, darlin'." Drake grinned as he made a few final touches to the autopilot setup. "Though it's not like we'd ever confuse the AI with that traitorous skudge-hole, is it?"

"That's for sure." Gus fell silent for a moment, then resumed speaking. "Actually, I think I have a good replacement name, unless you know of a good reason not to use it."

"Let me guess. Is it Drake? Mephistopheles, maybe?"

"No and no. Want a hint?"

"Yep." Drake got up from the nav console and made his way to the door. "Does it have to do with the Fluke, maybe?"

"It's the name of a decent person," said Gus. "Someone who helped us out mostly because it was the right thing to do."

It was then Drake knew the name she was suggesting,

and he grinned. "Now I get it. Great choice, darlin'. I'm in favor of it all the way."

"Good," said Gus. "I'll switch it once you finally get down here and pitch in so I can have a minute to myself."

"I'm comin', I'm comin'." The door slid open, and Drake marched out into the hallway. "I'll be there in five."

"Make it three, and there's a big kiss in it for you. More than that, if you play your cards right."

Drake smiled. There was no better way to keep spirits up before battle, he thought, than the things he and Gus did with each other underneath his old-fashioned down comforter. It was starting to look like the trip back to Chrysallix would be a lot more fun and less tense than he'd expected.

"See you when you get here," she said over the hallway speakers, the ship's AI automatically tracking Drake and ensuring the comm channel with Gus remained open. "I'll rename the AI after we finish installing the replicator."

"Good enough, darlin'," said Drake as he hurried down the hall. "After the way he acted on Buddy's Bluff, ol' 'Earl' doesn't deserve a place on the *Golden Void* anymore."

"No sir, he doesn't," said Gus. "But 'Bruce' sure does."

CHAPTER 18

Rhapsody Harrison sat at one end of her sofa, the white leather soft and supple beneath her. In years past, she would have tucked her feet beneath herself or propped her legs up on the cushions beside her. Now her knees complained if she attempted to sit like she had when she had been ten years younger, or even five.

Beyond the clear glass windows that made up the exterior wall of her ground-floor apartment, life in her domed city seemed to be quietly normal. No drone attacks had occurred since Drake and his Gray Lady had blasted off from the port in that beaten down ship he had always been so proud of. They had taken the security drone they'd shot down with them when they left, even though Rhapsody had told them not to. That, if nothing else, told her that Drake's days of listening to whatever she said were long over.

Not that Drake was immune to being manipulated. She

had just needed to use other means than what had worked in the past.

That manipulation had appeared to work, at least at first. But it had been days since she had been able to trace his location through the trackers embedded in her weapons, the ones Drake and his Gray Lady had taken aboard his ship. The trackers were small things with a limited range, which meant Drake had left the system.

Ezekiel thought Drake was not coming back. That would be what a man like Ezekiel would do—whatever was in his own best interests. He could not imagine being a man like Drake, an honorable man who put others' needs above his own. That was because Ezekiel cared for no one except himself. He served as Rhapsody's chief of staff because it brought certain benefits not otherwise obtainable for a man of his station—power and wealth and even Rhapsody herself when both of them desired the type of passion only sex could deliver.

Rhapsody still believed that Drake would return and bring with him his Gray Lady and the means to put an end to the *security* that had turned the citizens of her city into prisoners and her into an ineffectual figurehead on her own damn *planet*. But that belief was wearing thin.

She wanted a drink. She was thirsty, but even the act of drinking water from one of the cut crystal glasses that came as part of the décor in this residence designed especially for *La Meilleure*, whoever that might be, would tempt her to fill the glass with what Drake referred to as "the good stuff."

She could call for Ezekiel and he would distract her, at least for a short time. But short-term distractions had one major disadvantage—the short term always ended far too soon. Only Drake had been able to distract her for hours on end. He had been endlessly inventive, that man, comforting and caring and entirely *there* in each and every moment.

And then he would spoil it by attempting to put the experience to song.

She had suffered through his songs more than once until she had finally asked him to simply stop. She did not find music soothing. If she had, she would have had music blasting away in her luxurious apartment in an attempt to stop herself from continually checking her systems to see if Drake and his Gray Lady had returned.

She needed them more now than ever.

The security bots had taken away her guns.

Not all of them, just the antiques she had included on her wall of weapons in an attempt to convince those who might be watching that her weapons wall was for show, not for use. It was a bad sign, taking away her weapons, and she found herself fretting over what was sure to come.

"I am a collector of fine things," she had told Jorritz Tor when she had invited him to dinner during their contract negotiations.

"Even old things?" he had asked her.

She had thought he was referring to himself. Jorritz Tor was not a young man, but he had a vitality she found appealing.

She had leaned forward, displaying a good amount of cleavage (she had still been svelte and overtly sensual then), and placed a gentle hand on his arm.

"Old things are not useless simply because they are old," she had said. "Age improves the quality, in my experience. Would you not agree?"

ANNIE REED & ROBERT JESCHONEK

He had, but his eyes had wandered to her weapons display more than once during their meal. She had thought nothing of it at the time, but now she realized he had been taking inventory of what weapons she kept on hand.

Three days ago the security bots, the land-based versions of the drones that patrolled her city, had confiscated only those antique weapons. She had to disable all her modern weapons under their relentless red eyes so that those weapons would not be confiscated as well.

The lifeless bots had invaded *her home*. She was being treated as any other citizen or visitor to Chrysallix—all due to what Tor termed a "material breach" of her agreement with Tor to provide security for her planet.

She pulled up the official notification of breach on her tablet. She did not need to read it again—she already had each word memorized—but reading for nuance and hidden meanings took time and more than a simple cursory effort.

Weapons in your control were used to deliberately damage security equipment, the notification began. *This is a violation of the laws concerning the possession and maintenance of weapons within city limits as set forth in the agreement at section...*

The notification went on to quote the agreement, as if she did not already have the skudging thing memorized as well.

You are hereby notified that all weapons owned by you or within your control must be rendered inoperative in accordance with the Security Directives currently in place. Any weapons issued to or maintained by you which are not rendered inoperative will be confiscated. Furthermore, all projectile weapons, including but not limited to the antique weapons in your possession, are to be surrendered immediately. No one will be allowed to possess antique or projectile weapons within any domed area on Chrysallix as such weapons have been deemed to pose too great a security risk to public safety should unauthorized use occur. Possession of projectile or antique weapons within any domed area on Chrysallix shall henceforth be a violation of the law, and persons possessing such weapons will be dealt with accordingly.

La Meilleure's primary responsibility is to maintain proper order for all citizens of Chrysallix in equal measure. For this reason, the dispensation previously granted Rhapsody Harrison to possess projectile and/or antique weapons as well as to possess any firearms which have not been rendered inoperative is hereby rescinded.

Even possession of an antique weapon was now a crime. If she lodged a complaint with the few actual living beings who worked for Tor's security company, claiming that her antique weapons were only collector's items, Tor's representative would no doubt justify this directive by pointing out that antique weapons fired projectiles which could damage the domes. As if the domes were constructed of something as fragile as glass. The domes on Chrysallix were designed to withstand impacts far greater than simple bullets. The weapons embedded in the tower Tor had constructed to "protect" Chrysallix could do far greater damage to the domes than a simple bullet.

Why had Tor found it necessary to confiscate such useless weapons? Because the notification had clearly come from him. She recognized his pretentious phrasing, a holdover from his years as an ambassador for the Free Worlds Alliance. The contract she had signed with his company was rife with such language.

The notification had been delivered to her by security

bots three days after Drake and his Gray Lady had disabled the drone and taken it with them when they left the planet. She had no doubts the change in policy was in retaliation for their actions, and hers as well for providing them with weapons.

If she was honest with herself—and the one person she had always been honest with was herself—she had expected immediate retaliation. When hour after hour passed and no retaliation came, she had begun to hope that Drake would return before Tor made his next move. But that had not happened.

Why had Tor delayed? There was always a reason for everything the man did, and it was always a reason that benefitted him.

Even his expansion of Chrysallix's power complex, undertaken at his sole expense, had been for his benefit.

When he had offered to do so as an enticement for her to sign the contract, she had known his offer was too good to be true. But she had jumped at his offer anyway, figuring that she could control him as she controlled so many others. More power for her planetoid allowed her city to expand and modernize, which attracted not only more smugglers from a larger area but legitimate customers as well. The more modern the city, the more amenities it could offer, and the longer those smugglers and legitimate customers would stay. Longer stays meant more money for all the businesses in the city as well as more traffic in the port.

As *La Meilleure,* she was entitled to a minor percentage of the funds collected by all the various businesses on the planetoid. In the Alliance, that percentage would have been called a tax, and it would have gone to the government.

Chrysallix had no formal government. The person who served as *La Meilleure* was the closest thing to a government, and she had learned early on that people who settled in the Frontier were much more comfortable with paying a percentage if it was not called a tax.

When Tor had offered his deal, she had calculated all the additional money she would receive from expanding and modernizing her city. But an expanded and modernized city in the Frontier needed a security system in place to protect it from marauders and pirates and those eager to take from her all that she had worked for. The concessions he had required of her, such as the automatic renewals of the contract and his demand that his company be granted the exclusive use—free of charge—of any excess power generated by the expanded power complex beyond what was necessary to maintain the infrastructure of the planetoid. As payment for his services, he had agreed to accept only a minimal percentage—one far smaller than her own—of the revenue generated by the planetoid's various businesses.

She had tried to poke holes in the security contract he had prepared, but even Ezekiel with his eye for detail had counselled her to take it. Perhaps he had been as blinded by the potential for greater wealth as she had been.

And she had become far more wealthy than she had ever dreamed, but that wealth came at a heavy cost. A minor clause buried in the contract provided Tor's company with the ability to alter the security grid should any unforeseen forces threaten the safety of the citizenry.

Every single right that the security grid had stripped from her people—and now from her as well—was based on that one single clause. From the creation of the weapons tower to the prohibition against possession of fully functional firearms, all based on that single sentence.

She had no idea what Tor's company did with all the surplus power generated by the expanded power complex. Beyond building the weapons tower, of course. The last time she had taken an official tour of the facility, as her position as *La Meilleure* granted her the right to do, she had been shocked at its size. The only living beings she had seen besides herself and Ezekiel, who had accompanied her on the tour, were three technicians who appeared to be monitoring arrays of viewscreens. Those viewscreens had been disabled whenever she came close enough she might have seen the images displayed. The tour itself had been conducted by a security bot. When she asked why more civilians were not employed at the complex, the bot had responded that many areas of the facility would be hazardous to the health of living beings. But prior to Tor's expansion of the complex, more than a hundred civilians had been employed in various areas of it.

She had come away from that tour feeling unsettled, as if Tor was hiding something in plain sight. She was more unsettled now. She had decided to use Drake's unexpected visit, and that of his Gray Lady, to make her move to retake her planetoid from Tor, but instead Tor had used their unexpected visit and their actions in destroying the drone to advance his own agenda.

She did not have to read between the lines of the official notification to know that Tor was finally making his move to oust her from her position as *La Meilleure* and install either himself or one of his figureheads in her place. When the notification referred to her by name, her title had not been included. Instead, when the notification referred to *La Meilleure,* Tor had used the title almost as a placeholder for a person to be named later. None of that was a mistake.

She could not let Tor succeed in removing her from office. She had worked too hard and sacrificed far too much to let that happen.

Even if Drake did not help her, she would find another way to oust Tor and maintain her rightful place as *La Meilleure.* She was not about to abdicate her power or position to anyone. At one time she might have shared a *portion* of her power with Drake. She might have even been willing to share all that she had or ever would be with him—not an equal share, of course—but those days were long gone.

Not that Drake would care. He was the type of man who would be content to spend the rest of his days with his Gray Lady.

If the Gray Lady survived taking her revenge against Tor, that was.

If she did not?

Rhapsody had no doubts that others within and without the Alliance could be enticed—or manipulated—into ridding her of that odious man Jorritz Tor.

A small beep sounded from across the room.

Five seconds later, the beep sounded again.

A small smile smoothed out her features. She had programmed an alarm into her tracking systems so that she would not be tempted to sit in front of her holoscreens waiting for a small red dot that might never reappear. The alarm would sound only when her systems contacted the trackers in her weapons that Drake and his Gray Lady had taken aboard his ship. Unless Drake had jettisoned those weapons into space, the alarm meant only one thing.

Drake and his Gray Lady were on their way back.

She opened a comm channel to Ezekiel. He answered almost immediately, as she knew he would.

He had told her that he had tasks that needed attending as her chief of staff, but perhaps he was off making plans to take his wealth and leave Chrysallix, and start over somewhere else. He had accused her of playing a dangerous game. For all she knew, he might have decided the danger was too great. If she was in his position, she might have been tempted to do the same.

In the Frontier it was always a gamble of safety versus wealth when one sought to wrest power from those who did not want to let it go.

"The game," she told him, "is about to get interesting."

CHAPTER 19

Gus had to admit that singularium was one pretty impressive metal. It managed to be lightweight but hard enough to not only split the metal head of her hammer, but also disperse energy from high-powered laser fire along its surface until the remaining energy had little more effect than getting zapped by static electricity from scuffing her feet across a carpeted floor. Whoever had figured out that singularium was only vulnerable to bursts of alternating polarities of magnetic force must have been frustrated beyond belief and willing to try anything.

Either that, or they'd broken all their hammers.

After she and Drake had had a short but immensely satisfying interlude in one of the ship's corridors outside the now-working replicator's controls, the two of them had designed and built a tool that generated alternating magnetic polarities on a small, concentrated scale. She'd tested the tool on the drone they'd taken with them from

Chrysallix. The drone that was currently in pieces on her workbench in the cargo bay.

The tool worked like a charm, making the singularium sheeting over the body of the drone pliable enough—for a short time—to mold into almost any shape. Gus used the broken end of her hammer to etch a smiley face in the still-pliable metal.

Then she used the gadget to obliterate Tor's initials stamped into the parts of the drone made of singularium.

"Symbolic, darlin'?" Drake asked.

She grinned at him. "You bet 'cha." She put the tool down on her workbench next to the remains of the drone. "You know, if I was Tor and I had access to unlimited amounts of this stuff—"

"*Used* to have access to unlimited amounts," Drake said.

True. After the two of them had taken out Tor's hand-picked maniacal warlord/wannabe dictator on Shepard's Moon, Tor had lost his ability to trade obsolete Alliance weapons and military vehicles to the rebels in exchange for unrefined singularium. The loss of that particular source of this miracle metal was no doubt permanent since her son had just completed negotiations for Shepard's Moon to join the Free Worlds Alliance, a smart move on the Alliance's part if for no other reason than to prevent Tor or someone like him getting his greedy paws on more of the metal.

"*Almost* unlimited amounts of this stuff," she said without missing a beat, "and if I knew that somebody like us had managed to shoot down one of these enhanced drones *without* using one of these alternating magnetic projector thingies, I'd be retrofitting more than just the fuse-lage of my drones with this stuff."

Drake smirked at her. "Thingies?"

If they'd been standing closer together, she might have smacked him. Playfully, of course. Probably. But he was halfway across the cargo bay leaning against one of the crates that Bruce's men had loaded onto the *Void* before they'd left The Bluff.

"It's a technical term," she said. "Just follow along with me for a minute here, space cowboy."

He nodded. "Okay, darlin'. And that sounds about right, especially if you know most people would just be shooting lasers at the things."

"Things?" she asked with her own smirk.

"It's a technical term," he said.

"Smartass."

He was, but he could always make her smile. Which she was doing now even though she had a serious point to get to. If the smile on her face was more than a little on the dreamy side, that probably had more than a little something to do with the way she was still tingling from that immensely satisfying interlude in the corridor. She could go for another such interlude right about now, but she needed to chase down an idea that been bothering her ever since they'd left The Bluff.

If Tor was retrofitting the drones with more singularium, that would make the buggers nearly indestructible, especially on Chrysallix. Gus was willing to wager that outside of Drake's antique shotgun and the antique weapons in Rhapsody's apartment—if those antiques even worked— not a lot of civilians on Chrysallix had access to working projectile weapons. Lasers were far more efficient and far easier for the average person to use.

223

"So I'm wondering where he's doing all that retro-fitting," she said. "Especially if his facilities are fully auto-mated. I'm willing to bet retrofitting on that scale's not part of the grid's programming. Or that the facility itself is set up to do the machine work."

Even replicating new drone parts that came complete with singularium would take a tremendous amount of energy to generate alternating polarities of magnetic force during the replication process. If singularium could even be replicated, which was one big damn If.

She watched him consider that. If he'd had his guitar with him, he would no doubt be strumming an old cowboy tune since that always seemed to help him think. He hadn't even pulled out a stick of cinnamon-flavored gum.

"It's a big city," he finally said. "Could be anywhere."

"But would you put something like that inside a city where the population might not be too happy with you thanks to all those drone attacks on civilian targets? In a city where enough people might be able to break in and sabotage all that automated equipment? Or even plant a worm or virus that would obliterate the grid's programming?" She gestured toward the singularium. "If I was Tor, I wouldn't want a pissed off population getting their hands on any of this stuff."

Chrysallix had a network of smaller domes and high-speed transportation tubes that connected them, but Drake had told her that those areas were used for food production or housed the machines that provided water and air and all the other necessities of life for the city and the spaceport. Tor wouldn't want his precious automated grid to operate out of places like that where heat and humidity, much less the people who worked there, might mess with all his auto-mated equipment.

"I see your point," Drake said.

He boosted himself up so that he was sitting on the top crate. He rested his chin in his hands, elbows on his knees. The image would have been cute if Gus didn't know what the crates he sat on held: enough fuel for her armor to fly a dozen or more times around Chrysallix without breaking a sweat.

Thanks to Earl's "generosity," the *Void* was now armed to the teeth with enough projectile weapons and ammo to take out a small army of singularium-equipped drones. In addition to the few antique firearms Bruce said he could spare, Gus intended to create a few new weapons for the upcoming battle. She had in mind a new kind of concussion grenade she could use after the magnetic thingie (pulsator? Polarity generator?) weakened the singularium. Instead of the light and sound grenades she'd used to disorient the rebels on Shepard's Moon, these grenades would shower their targets with the same metal pellets in the shells Drake's shotgun fired.

The grenades would be fine for taking drones out of commission outside heavily populated areas. The projectile weapons themselves she planned to weld onto her armor, sort of the same way Earl had welded that old gun onto his gauntlet, so that she could do some precision projectile shooting without harming any bystanders.

And then there was the weapons tower to think about.

That nice, shiny weapons tower.

That was probably reinforced with more singularium.

"What about the complex under the tower?" she asked. "If I was Tor..."

Before she could finish the thought, Drake held out a hand in a warding off gesture.

"You gotta stop sayin' that, darlin'," he said. "You're giving me the entirely *wrong* kind of mental image here and I've never even met the man."

She snickered. "I have, and I can tell you that you *definitely* don't want that mental image the next time we do what we just did not that long ago."

He blanched. "Thank you *so much* for that!"

She walked over and rubbed her hands up and down his legs. "You'll get over it. But what I was saying is that I think whatever production facility he's got going on Chrysallix, it's got to be part of that massive power complex. He might even have a refinery in there, the damn thing's big enough. So why else build a weapons tower *right there* when he could have put it anywhere on the whole freaking planetoid if all he wanted to do was protect the city and the port? It's on the wrong freaking *side* to do that."

Weapons fired from the tower would have to take into account the curvature of the planetoid if someone was attacking the city or the port. If the tower was supposed to protect the city, the better design would have been to make sure any defensive weapons just had to travel in something approximating a straight line.

He gazed down into her eyes and shook his head. "And *that's* why you're more than just the best damn armor jock around." He gestured with a shrug toward her armor. "You think you can take out the tower after you reinforce your armor with this stuff?"

Now it was her turn to shrug. "Maybe, but I've got a different job to do."

"The drones?" he said.

"I need to take them out before they harm any more civilians *or* your ex."

His eyes narrowed. "I thought that was going to be a *we* kind of job."

"I don't think the spaceport will let us inside this time," she said. "Not in *this* ship, not after we had the audacity to shoot one of the grid's precious babies out of the sky and abduct its body to boot."

He winced at that. She'd probably gone too far with her descriptions, but she was psyching herself up for battle. And it would be a hell of a battle—the Gray Lady against all the drones in the dome. She'd be outfitting her armor with singularium, which she doubted the automated defense grid would be prepared to fight against, but there were still all those weak spots on her armor. If she tried to protect all of them, she wouldn't be able to move. She needed the flexibility of her joints, even if those joints made her vulnerable.

But hell, she'd just won a battle against a wily and slimy opponent who had reinforced his armor with singularium, and all she'd had were her wits and her anger. This time around she'd have her wits and her anger and enough singularium, not to mention enough projectile weapons and the magnetic polarity thingie, to take down as many skudging drones as the security grid threw at her.

Once she got inside the dome, that is. Which would be easier to do in armor than inside the *Void*.

"I'm going to need you to keep Tor's automated defense grid busy," she said. "From outside the dome." She paused, then added. "On the other side of the planetoid."

His eyes widened. "The skudging tower?"

She nodded. "You proved just how damn good a pilot you were on Shepard's Moon. You had my six all the way."

"We had each other's six," he said.

That was true, but that had been against a unified force of rebel idiots. Now they would be facing opponents on two discrete fronts: the weapons tower and a nearly unlimited number of robo-drones in the city that had no restrictions on taking down a few civilians to "protect" the populace.

Automated defense systems could react faster than people, but they were still only as good as their programming. If their programs didn't expect singularium-equipped enemies who knew how to punch projectile weapons through that metal? She figured that might even the odds, but only if she and Drake launched simultaneous attacks on both fronts. She couldn't fight a ridiculous number of drones *and* take out any weapons launched at the city from that tower at the same time. If they both attacked the tower first, the drones in the city would be ready for the next stage of the attack.

"We'll equip the *Void* with a bigger version of the thingie," she said.

She'd already planned to add one to her armor along with the singularium layer. The replicator had kicked out a replacement visor before they'd even blasted off from The Bluff. Her armor would be as kickass as she could make it, and they'd do the same thing for the *Void*. She could see a spacewalk in her future to install the thingie on the ship.

"We're really calling it the *thingie*?" Drake asked.

He'd gone from being shocked at the change in battle plans to looking forward to kicking some ass himself. She could tell by the twinkle that had returned to his eyes.

She shot a lascivious look at a certain part of his anatomy that happened to be right in front of her face. "Unless you want me to start calling a certain something else *thingie*."

He snorted, then slid off the crate and took her face in his hands. "You can call that certain something anything you want as long as you make its acquaintance on a regular basis."

"You can plan on it," she said.

He kissed her, long and slow.

She let herself melt into his arms. They had a lot of work to do. Thingies to fabricate—thank goodness the replicator was state-of-the-art—parts to install, and ammo and fuel to load. But she wanted to take a moment to not think about being the Gray Lady. She just wanted a few minutes to be Gus, a woman in love with a certain guitar-playing, gum-chewing, antiques-loving space cowboy.

"Sing me a song, space cowboy," she said as she rested her head against his chest. "For luck."

And so he did.

She didn't even care that it was "Back in the Saddle Again."

CHAPTER 20

Chrysallix was a silvery dot on the main viewer of the *Void*'s bridge, looking no more deadly from a distance than a cloud of interplanetary gas. It was almost hard for Drake to believe that a dire threat awaited them there, an enemy force sufficient to oppress an entire planetoid...and perhaps, kill its supposed saviors without batting an eyelash.

Yet there it was, waiting—coiled like a rattlesnake ready to strike. The *Void* would reach it quickly once the orders were given, and the battle would be waged in all the fire and fury that both sides commanded. As to the outcome, he and Gus had prepared as well as they could, but there were no guarantees. They wouldn't truly know what the result might be until the action was finally over.

If there were any justice at all in the universe, though, they would end Tor's grip on the planetoid once and for all, restoring the kind of freedom that had always been Rhapsody's vision.

One major X-factor remained, however, as Drake and Gus got ready to launch—and that factor was Rhap herself. If they dared contact her, they might expose their planned invasion to Tor's defense grid, losing the element of surprise. Leaving her out of the picture, however, would mean the loss of a potential ally who could give their attack a boost.

The matter was soon taken out of their hands, though. Just as they were running final diagnostics and checklists to ensure all their gear was in readiness, Bruce the AI spoke up over the speakers on the bridge.

"Highly encrypted incoming message from the central dome of Chrysallix," said Bruce. "Unable to pinpoint exact location of source beyond that...but the transmission is tagged with a call sign."

"What is it, Earl...I mean Bruce?" asked Drake.

"Madame Buttercup," said Bruce.

Drake grinned at the mention of the nickname he'd once given to Rhapsody, back in the days of their relationship. "Good ol' Rhap," he said with a chuckle.

Gus didn't look quite so amused. Standing in the middle of the bridge in the black bodysuit she wore under her armor, she planted her hands on her hips and scowled. "How the *skudge* did she know we were *out* here?"

"Beats me." Drake shrugged. "Planted a tracker on the *Void*, maybe?"

Gus wasn't pleased. "Well, if *she* knows we're here, don't you think Tor's *grid* knows we're here, too?"

"We better get rollin' fast, then, just in case." As he said it, Drake was already flicking switches and twisting knobs on the nav and weapons consoles. "Bruce? What is the content of Buttercup's message?"

"'Called in all favors,'" said Bruce. "'Full grid reboot in thirty minutes.'"

"Ha!" shouted Drake as the *Void*'s engines rumbled to life, preparing for launch. "Rhap's opening the door for us!"

"I doubt it'll stay open for long," said Gus. "We might only have a matter of *minutes* once the grid goes down until it fully reactivates."

"Then let's make them *count*." As he said it, Drake punched the red button on the nav console, sending the *Void* leaping toward Chrysallix on its programmed course. "Let's take down as many of those drones as we can and blow the *skudge* outta that damn *tower* before the system completes its reboot."

As the *Void* hurtled onward, the silvery image of Chrysallix rapidly enlarged on the screen. It wouldn't be long now until they rocketed into orbit and the battle erupted, engulfing them in the action they never seemed to stay away from for long.

"I guess this is it, darlin'." Drake reached for her hands, clasping them warmly in his own. "Time for another big bang."

"Armor's ready," she said firmly. "Modifications are good to go."

"Same with the ship." Drake nodded, releasing one of her hands and reaching up to stroke the side of her face. "Far as I can tell, everything's up to speed."

"Wouldn't mind a little more time to test the magno-beams," said Gus. "The *thingies*, I mean. And the projectile guns."

"No need, Gray Lady." He brushed his fingers gently over her short, gray hair. "We got this. We're the *good guys*, ridin' into town to take down Billy the Kid or Jesse James or the Dalton Gang. *Right* is on our side, my beautiful partner."

"Just the same..." She turned her head to kiss his wrist. "You get into trouble, you call me. I'll come running."

"Same to you."

As he gazed at her, he felt a brief hesitation, a quiver of doubt. As excellent a warrior as she was, what if something awful happened on the battlefield? What if, after finally finding the love of his life, he lost her while trying to save a love from long ago, a woman who'd betrayed him for her own selfish reasons? Would he be able to live with himself if that happened? Would he be able to come back from that kind of colossal *agony* and somehow continue to exist in an uncaring universe?

He knew the answer, and it weighed on his soul...but he couldn't let it stop him. They'd already committed to the job ahead, to supporting the greater good. Thousands of people were depending on them.

Would Gus turn back anyway, if given the chance? He couldn't imagine it. She was courage personified...a true inspiration.

Oh *God*, he hoped he wouldn't lose her in the fight ahead.

"Love you, Broken String," she said, and then she gave him a long, tender kiss on the lips.

Breaking away, she slid two fingers into the vest pocket of his flannel shirt and drew out a stick of cinnamon gum. Smiling, she unwrapped the gum, folded it into her mouth, and stuffed the wrapper back into his pocket.

"Catch you on the flip side," she said, and then she ran away. The exit door opened silently, and she sprinted out into the corridor, en route to the cargo bay where her armor waited.

She had to hurry, he knew, to be ready in time for when they made orbit. As soon as they leaped into the gravity well of the planetoid, the plan was for her to take on the drones on one side of the central dome while Drake went after the weapons tower with the *Void*.

That was when the fireworks would really begin…when the fight for liberation would explode over Chrysallix. Was he ready?

"Orbital insertion in fifteen minutes," said Bruce.

"Thanks." Drake played controls on the nav and weapons consoles like Beethoven hammering out his Fifth Symphony.

"Would you like to respond to the message from 'Madame Buttercup?'" asked Bruce.

"Not necessary," said Drake. "I think she's been a step ahead of us the whole time anyway."

"That does seem likely," said Bruce…and then he did something he'd never done before, not in Drake's experience. "Good luck, Captain Drake. I wish us all well in the battle ahead."

Drake frowned, wondering where the AI had picked up the extra bit of personality…but there was no time to worry about it now. Maybe later, he and Gus could explore the permutations of the change in the system.

For now, it was better to stay on task. Better to prime himself for whatever came next.

"Thanks, Bruce," he said. "Good luck to you, too."

CHAPTER 21

Just how long would it take the security grid to reboot?

Just how long would it take the *planetwide* security grid to reboot?

Gus stood in the airlock at the back of the *Void's* cargo bay, suited up and ready for battle, waiting out the last few minutes before the reboot kicked off and the actual battle started. When they'd gone into battle on Shepard's Moon, Drake had just opened the cargo bay doors for her, but this time around, the *Void's* cargo bay was loaded to the gills with all the supplies Bruce and his people had brought on board. They didn't want to risk any of that cargo breaking loose, not to mention that the airlock was programmed to keep Chrysallix's toxic atmosphere from contaminating the rest of the ship. While the *Void* could scrub out any toxins that entered through the cargo bay doors, that would eat up a lot of the ship's resources. Drake would need everything

237

the ship could give him once he engaged that weapons tower.

Her armor made the airlock a tight fit. It hadn't been made to house all that metallic bulk, but it wasn't like Gus planned to dance a jig or anything while she waited. She had enough room to reach the controls that would open the outer door, and that was good enough.

She wished Rhapsody had included a little more information in her "Madame Buttercup" message. But Drake's ex didn't have the kind of military mindset that would automatically know what information was necessary to execute a complex battle plan. Not that the battle plan Gus and Drake had come up with was all that complicated. It pretty much boiled down to *break in and blow shit up.*

Or in her case, blow shit out of the sky.

If the drones would even *be* in the sky during the reboot. For all she knew, the skudging things might "run home to mama" during the pre-reboot phase so they *wouldn't* fall from the sky when the system actually went down.

For however long it went down.

Questions, questions. In the past, she'd gone into battle armed with even less information, but the drones—hell, the whole security grid—had been set up by Jorritz Tor. He'd stayed in the background on Shepard's Moon, long gone before the rebels had started their little war. Did he have a military mindset? Was he the mastermind behind Chrysallix's security grid? Or had he convinced some other sap to do his dirty work for him?

Even more questions.

She checked the chronometer display on her suit's visor. Two minutes to reboot.

She hated waiting. She always had. Back in the 83rd, she'd had the other armor jocks in her squad to joke with while she waited. Official policy said to keep unnecessary comm chatter to a minimum, but over the decades that Gus had been a military grunt, her squadron leaders had more or less ignored that policy, believing—as Gus did—that a little pre-battle chatter was a necessary part of battle prep. Some of it was of the gallows humor variety—joking in the face of possible death—but most of it was just good-natured ribbing among veteran soldiers who were about to go kill people they'd never met.

It kept the mind from overthinking things.

Like how long the drones would be out of commission.

Like how long Drake would have to attack the weapons tower before that thing came back online.

Like if they could even trust Rhapsody to do what she said.

So Gus busied herself with rerunning calculations on her armor's projected fuel consumption given the angle of her descent toward the central dome and the additional weight of the projectile weapons and all the extra physical ammo she carried.

That was the thing about projectile weapons. Her laser cannons and laser guns, not to mention the high-powered laser built into the palm of her armor's right hand, were all energy weapons. She could shoot those things practically for days before their charges ran out. Even the magno-beam thingie attached to the gauntlet on her left arm was an energy-based weapon. But projectile weapons fired physical ammo. That stuff ran out.

She'd managed to equip her armor with as much physical ammo as possible, including all the special concussion grenades she'd rigged one of her shoulder-mounted launchers to fire. With the help of the ship's new replicator and Drake's knowledge of antique projectile weapons like his shotgun, they'd even designed larger capacity magazines that held far more ammo than those weapons had originally been built for. But all that extra weight meant she'd be using additional fuel to maneuver once she got inside the dome.

It also meant she'd have to make every projectile shot count.

"Thirty seconds, darlin'," came Drake's voice over comms. "Ready to lock and load?"

She grinned. She loved it when he talked military to her. "Locked and loaded, Broken String," she said.

She wondered if he was thinking about *what ifs*.

What if the grid didn't go *all* the way down?

What if the weapons tower didn't go *completely* offline?

What if she died?

Armor jocks didn't think that way. Sure, every battle plan had contingencies, and as the saying went, no battle plan survived contact with the enemy. But armor jocks didn't let themselves focus on *what ifs*. They'd freeze up if they did.

When she'd put her armor on for the first time since she'd retired and stored it away, back when they'd distracted the first Fluke Prowler they'd run across by blowing up chunks of ice in the rings of a gas giant and then carving a smiley face in the huge planet's atmosphere, she'd let the *what ifs* get to her. She'd wondered *what if* she couldn't move in her suit the way she used to. What if she'd lost that *edge* that let her become one with her armor so the whole thing was simply an extension of her body? *What if* she couldn't be the Gray Lady anymore, if she was too old and that part of her life was over?

But those particular *what ifs* hadn't survived contact with the enemy.

She'd moved in her suit like all those years she'd spent drinking her way through retirement while her armor sat unused in storage hadn't happened. The minute she'd climbed inside her suit, she'd become the Gray Lady once again. She sure as hell had been the Gray Lady on The Bluff, adjusting her battle plan as necessary and coming up with a solution that not only let her win, but thoroughly defeat that scourge of her early military days. Earl no longer took up any space inside her mental warehouse. He was done and gone and in her past, and good riddance.

She'd even reprogrammed the *Void's* AI with a new name. That had felt freaking wonderful. As wonderful as chewing a stick of that cinnamon gum Drake liked so much. It made her feel closer to him. Too bad she had to throw it out before she got into her suit, but at least the spicy taste remained.

"Counting down in five," came Drake's voice over her comm. Then, "Four…three…two…"

Gus readied herself.

"One."

She couldn't actually feel the ship nose downward into the toxic atmosphere of Chrysallix, but she could feel an increased pull of gravity even as she was pushed backwards as the *Void* sped toward the planetoid. The planetoid's atmosphere was less dense than the air inside the domes, and the ship didn't hit the kind of turbulence Gus remembered from some of her missions with the 83rd, when the troop transport's descent was so rough, the entire squad was covered in so many bruises their skin looked like the black bodysuits they wore inside their armor.

She'd linked the ship's altimeter to her armor's heads-up display. She watched as the numbers spiraled down... lower...lower.

Five hundred feet above target altitude, Gus punched the button to open the airlock's outer door. One hundred feet above target altitude, the *Void* leveled off, and now Gus felt the pull of gravity increase.

Ten feet above target altitude, Gus pushed herself out the airlock and immediately dropped like the tons of metal and weaponized death she was.

She didn't watch the *Void* speed away, heading toward the weapons tower. She was too focused on the central dome below her.

As part of her battle prep, she'd rewatched images the *Void's* cameras had taken of Chrysallix when they'd first arrived. She wouldn't be able to access the interior of the dome through the spaceport, but that would have taken too much time to get where she wanted to go anyway. Instead, she'd identified a series of maintenance hatches located at regular intervals along the base of the central dome. All of them looked large enough to accommodate her armor.

She could blast her way inside any of them, but she hoped with the security grid down for reboot, she wouldn't have to. With any luck, the hatches might be unlocked.

That was the problem with relying solely on automation

for security. When that automated system went down, so did *all* your security, including door locks.

She engaged her armor's maneuvering jets and shot toward the maintenance hatch closest to the district where the last drone attacks had occurred. She'd programmed the specifications for the drone she'd disassembled into her targeting systems. It wasn't a failsafe method of tracking drones that had been retrofitted with additional singularium, but it should work to track down any that hadn't. And if any of *those* drones had run home to mama, her targeting system should be able to tell her exactly where mama was.

That was her main goal—to blow the shit out of mama and take as many of her little darlings with her as Gus could.

She touched down on a paved platform next to the maintenance hatch. The hatch itself looked like a hodgepodge of high-tech and low-tech. A keypad and a white bulb device like the one outside Rhapsody's apartment were embedded in the hatch's metal framework on the right-hand side of the hatch. The display on the keypad read *Waiting...* and the light inside the bulb was dark. The hatch itself was dogged tight with an old-fashioned wheel in the center.

None of the hatch's metal had the shiny smooth surface of singularium. She wouldn't have to use the magno-beam thingie here. That was fine with her. The more she delayed using it, the more time it would take for anyone who might be observing her to realize she could blast through Tor's precious metal defenses. Just because the defense grid was rebooting didn't mean that all the cameras installed throughout the dome were offline too.

With the automatic electronic controls for the hatch offline, all she had to do to open the hatch was undog the wheel. Thanks to the strength of her armor, spinning the wheel was like twisting the cap off a bottle of Drake's "good stuff."

When she stepped inside the hatch's airlock and dogged the outside door shut, all the heads-up displays on her visor winked out and her comms went silent.

Her heartbeat kicked up a notch. She hadn't expected that. She tested her armor's movements, which all seemed to work fine, but everything that connected her armor to any signals coming from outside the airlock had been cut off.

Was the airlock shielded? She could think of a dozen reasons for doing so, from protection against radiation or miniscule space junk that didn't burn up in Chrysallix's thin atmosphere to a deliberate attempt to prevent her from communicating with Drake.

But the only person who knew she was here was Rhapsody, and even Rhapsody couldn't know *exactly* where she was. Right? With the defense grid down, Gus doubted any of the people who worked at the spaceport were even aware that the *Void* had come back, much less dropped an armor jock off next to this particular maintenance hatch.

Unless the hatch itself had a separate security mechanism not tied to the defense grid. They hadn't told Rhapsody how Gus planned to get into the central dome. They hadn't even told her that Gus and Drake would be attacking on two separate fronts at once. As far as Gus was concerned, the less good ol' Rhap knew, the better.

Gus hadn't survived decades of battles for the Alliance

by ignoring anomalies. Accessing the maintenance hatch's airlock constituted first contact with the enemy, and already things had gone sideways.

Someone must have seen her enter the hatch. Okay, fine. She'd blast her way out if she had to. She had enough firepower to obliterate dozens of hatches without putting a single dent in her armor.

She activated all her weapons, including the magnobeam thingie on her left gauntlet, and aimed them toward the hatch on the dome side. When the airlock beeped, indicating that all the outside toxic air had been vented into the planetoid's atmosphere, she used her right hand to spin the wheel on the dome-side hatch. It spun as easily as the outside hatch had.

Then she kicked open the door, expecting to come face-to-face with a few scared and inadequately armed living security personnel.

Only what waited for her were more than a dozen over-sized drones hovering right in front of the hatch.

The blades of their propellers buzzed like a swarm of huge, angry bees. Bright red lights on the noses of their oblong bodies flashed bright red before their targeting systems locked their low-slung laser canons onto her armor and those malevolent eyes turned solid red.

And every one of the drones facing her was plated in the shiny silver of the nearly impervious metal: singularium.

CHAPTER 22

The thirty-minute countdown to the defense grid's reboot was the longest thirty minutes of Rhapsody Harrison's life. After she sent her "Madame Buttercup" message to Drake, she sat in her favorite spot on her leather sofa and pretended not to check her watch every few moments.

The watch was an old-fashioned thing, made of tiny gears and springs with a crystal face and hands that moved around a circular dial. It was out of place in her high-tech apartment, but it had sentimental value to her. It was one of the few things that did.

The watch had belonged to her mother long ago. Her mother had been forced to sell it for far less than its value in order to buy food for herself and Rhapsody. After her mother died, Rhapsody had tracked down the merchant who had cheated her mother. She had taken the watch and strapped it on her wrist as she watched life seep out of the merchant's eyes. He would never cheat another starving young mother again.

Drake had admired the watch, as he admired all antique things. He was truly a man born into an age in which he did not belong. Brave and honorable in a universe that was not.

She had told him in her Buttercup message that she had called in all her favors, but in truth, she had only called in one.

Simeon Ezekiel.

Ezekiel knew more about the actual operation of the defense grid than she did, but that was his job. To know the nuts and bolts of how things ran on Chrysallix and to make sure those things ran smoothly. He was a born administrator. More ambitious than most, certainly, but she admired that in a man.

Lack of ambition had always been Drake's true failing in her eyes. He was content to do as she asked, to stay in the shadow of her deliberately flamboyant self. She had eventually tired of that and had deliberately pushed him away by hurting him in the one way she knew would end things between them.

She had been surprised to hear from him, even after all this time. She had thought to use her charm and her sensuality on him merely to see if she could, but when he had arrived with his Gray Lady, Rhap's plans had changed. She had deliberately insulted Gus, and then had just as deliberately played dumb and thoughtless when drones fortuitously attacked civilians during their visit, calculating that Drake and Gus would rush to the rescue of innocents.

Rhapsody had not planned to go along. That action had been spontaneous, and it had nearly undone her.

Her shock at seeing the carnage left behind by the drones had not been an act. She had nearly said the wrong things before she regained her senses and steered Drake and Gus into doing what she wanted.

And now they were back because she needed them to be.

She had always done what she had to do to stay in power. To remain *La Meilleure* and reap the wealth of her position.

She had inadvertently given away a great deal of that power to Jorritz Tor. Now to get that power back, she had deliberately given away a portion of her wealth to Simeon Ezekiel.

He had assured her that he could arrange to force a system-wide reboot of the defense grid. "I have connections," was all he would say. "They'll expect to be paid handsomely for their work given the danger involved if Tor discovers their treachery."

She had agreed to the sum Ezekiel named and had already transferred half into his accounts. There was such a thing as trusting too much, and Ezekiel was an ambitious man. He was also a greedy man. He would want to be paid the rest of what she had promised, and for that, the reboot had to perform as promised.

"We shall rule this world again as we see fit," she had told him when she had him in her bed, playing his body like skilled musicians played their beloved instruments. "Without interference from those who do not understand the way we wish to live."

He had trembled beneath her touch, agreeing to everything she suggested, and then he had made her tremble until they both lay spent.

She wished she could do that now. Sex was a marvelous way to avoid watching the minutes count down. But Ezekiel had left to oversee the final preparations for grid reboot.

"Our few living security personnel have to be advised, and the spaceport monitors will have to be *convinced* to look elsewhere," he had told her.

The plan was coming together.

She thought about having a drink. Just one to settle her nerves.

Then she thought about cooking something in her kitchen. Or more precisely, *eating* something. Today she craved something sweet. Dark and sweet and filled with chocolate, perhaps. A smuggler had arrived just the day before looking to trade real chocolate imported from Earth in exchange for a great deal of fuel. Rhapsody still controlled most of the fuel supplies on Chrysallix, although she rarely handled trade negotiations herself. This time she had. As a result, her kitchen was well stocked with enough chocolate to last her for the next six months.

The smuggler had even paid the fuel surcharge in cash. A surcharge that went directly into her accounts as her percentage for goods bought, sold, or traded on Chrysallix.

It was good being *La Meilleure*.

The watch on her wrist ticked off the last minute. Time was up. Drake's ship would be starting its descent. The battle was about to begin.

She wanted to raise her weapons wall and watch the battle on her hidden holoscreens, but if anything or anyone was watching *her* through hidden surveillance equipment, she could not appear to know about Drake's attack in advance. She had encrypted her message to him to the best of her ability with an encryption program she and Ezekiel had used in the past. It was all the assistance she could offer the man she used to care about nearly as much as herself. She hoped it would be enough.

So she sat on her leather sofa and pretended to read a report on the latest ships to enter the spaceport while she tried not to count the seconds until the first sounds of battle echoed through the streets of her city. Armored troops did not fight quietly, and she doubted Drake's Gray Lady would be an exception. Would Drake himself attack the dome? Or would he direct his efforts to the weapons tower? She had never seen him in battle, and she had no concept of how a ship like his would best serve to support one lone armored warrior.

She was trying to imagine how the battle would be waged against inert drones when the door to her apartment opened.

Ezekiel was the only person other than herself who had the code to enter her apartment, but he never did so when she was in residence. The surveillance equipment he sometimes found planted inside was installed by bots during what was deemed "routine maintenance," he said.

But Ezekiel should be off monitoring the reboot, making sure the security grid was offline long enough for Drake's Gray Lady to get past the central dome's automated defenses and Drake to do whatever he planned to do from his ship.

She turned to ask Ezekiel why he was here, but she never got the question out.

The report she had been scanning slid from her numb fingers and hit the floor as she stood up. Her legs felt like two wooden sticks.

Ezekiel stood just inside her apartment, flanked by two security bots. The same type of bots who had delivered Tor's message to her and had confiscated her antique weapons. But all bots in the defense network, including the security bots that worked on land, should have been disabled during the reboot. These two appeared to be fully operational, right down to the blinking red targeting light in the middle of their heads.

But the thing that shocked her the most, the thing she could not quite wrap her mind around, was that Ezekiel was holding a laser pistol.

A fully functional laser pistol.

And he was pointing it right at her.

"I believe," he said, "that it's time for you to go."

"Go?" She could barely get the word out. "Go where?"

"I don't particularly care," he said. "I just want you out of *my* apartment, *Rhap*." He tilted his head to the side, and the smile that stole over his face was truly horrible to behold. "Unless you want one more 'roll in the hay,' I believe was how Drake used to put it? I'm sure I could stomach that one last time. For old times' sake."

Ezekiel had not worked for her when she had been with Drake. She was about to ask him how he knew Drake's euphemism for sex, but suddenly it all became terribly crystal clear.

Ezekiel must have been watching her even then. Planning a very, very long con game of his own. All the surveillance equipment he had found in her apartment? *Her* apartment? Had been installed by Ezekiel himself.

And she had given him all the opportunities he needed to set his plan in motion.

All the meetings she had had with Jorritz Tor? Had been arranged by Ezekiel. He had read all versions of the defense contract Tor had written and had communicated her requested changes. Ezekiel would have had ample opportunity to get to know Tor, to establish a line of communication directly with him. To do favors for the man in exchange for the understanding that one day Tor would oust her from her rightful position as the leader of Chrysallix and install Ezekiel in her place.

Her world would no longer have a *La Meilleure,* but a *Le Meilleur.*

Ezekiel had agreed to be Tor's puppet. A strawman ruler of Chrysallix. As often as Rhapsody believed she had been using Ezekiel in their shared quest for power and wealth, he had been using her.

And now her usefulness to him was over.

"What if I refuse to leave?" she asked. "I am still *La Meilleure* to the people of this world."

Ezekiel raised his laser pistol. "The *people* will be too busy cleaning up the mess you've made by allowing your mercenaries to destroy their homes and their businesses. Even their lives. They won't care about you." He chuckled. "They'll probably want to hang you." He gestured at her with the pistol. "But if you'd like to make this transition of power go more smoothly, I'd be happy to oblige."

Not while blood still ran in her veins. She was Rhapsody

Harrison, and she would never willingly surrender to the likes of this man. Or any man.

"What is it you *really* want?" she asked him. "To be a puppet, or to have *real* power?"

He snorted, a sound that was so unlike the man she knew—the man she *had* known—that for a moment she thought the sound had come from one of the bots.

"You can't offer me anything I really want," he said. "You don't have it."

She made herself smile, a greedy, lascivious smile. "You don't know everything I have to offer, *chér*. Not even you know everything about me."

She could see him consider her bluff for a split second, but before he could respond, a huge explosion rocked her building.

The security bots did what they were programmed to do.

They left, drawn to the site of the explosion.

That left Ezekiel all alone. He still held the laser pistol, but the explosion had thrown him off balance.

Rhapsody did not hesitate. She had not always been *La Meilleure* of Chrysallix. She had started out poor, and she had done things in her life that someone like Ezekiel would never suspect. She might be twice the woman she had been a few short years ago, but she was also still the woman who had clawed her way to the top on Frontier world after Frontier world.

He was about to learn the hard way how she had done exactly that.

CHAPTER 23

It didn't take long for Drake to realize the defense grid reboot had never happened.

He'd expected to have time—at least a few minutes—to make some unopposed runs at the weapons spire, to get in a few good shots before the grid came back online and fought back. He'd hoped to open the skin of that tower in at least a few places before the resident weaponry kicked into action and made it harder to get through.

Instead, from the *Void*'s very first approach, the spire's copious gun turrets and laser cannons opened fire in a big way, lashing the ship with strike after strike. If not for his excellent piloting skills, honed over his long career as a smuggler, he never would have been able to avoid the worst of the shots and leap away to reassess the situation.

"What the skudge?" he shouted as he swung the *Void* in a wide upward arc away from the spire, out of range of its guns. "Bruce, what happened to that *reboot* we were promised?"

"Either the grid recovered much more quickly than expected," Bruce said calmly, "or there *was* no reboot."

"Great! Just great!" Thoughts racing as fast as his heart, Drake considered the situation. Without those early, unopposed strikes, he was working at a disadvantage...and so was Gus. The odds against success for both of them had just increased significantly.

But he had to force himself not to dwell on that fact. If he thought about it too much—imagined the threats *she* must be facing at that very moment—it could drive him insane.

Far better to stay in the moment and make the best of the bad hand they'd been dealt. Everything was riding on this, from their personal safety to that of Rhapsody and the freedom of Chrysallix; he was determined not to let himself falter in the face of a setback, no matter how major.

He just had to figure out a way to handle it like the space cowboy that Gus always told him he was.

First things first. He'd already planned to lean on the ship's autopilot to help get the *Void* past the spire's array of weapons after the reboot. As great a pilot as he was, he'd known his chances of success would improve dramatically with the autopilot engaged, guided by the ship's quick-thinking AI. Bruce could anticipate rapidly-changing patterns of weapons fire from multiple sources—and avoid them—much more effectively than any human mind, even Drake's, ever could.

Now that the reboot had turned out to be a myth, it could only help matters to cut over primary navigation to the autopilot (and Bruce) immediately (with the option to restore manual control if needed, of course).

"Bruce," he said, even as he laid in a baseline course for the ship's next run at the spire. "Activate autopilot. I want you to do the driving from here on. Just watch out for all the weapons fire and try not to scratch the paint."

"Roger that," said Bruce.

"Primary directive is to destroy that spire as quickly as possible," said Drake. "Jump in there, hit a portion of the exterior with the magno-gun, then get us away again—just long enough to confuse their guns' targeting systems. Then bring us back in to hit the exact same spot with our projectile weapons while we can possibly break through the weakened singularium surface."

"Understood," said Bruce.

"Speaking of weakened singularium," continued Drake, "approximately how much time do we have after a magno-gun hit before a singularium-infused surface regains its properties of relative impenetrability?"

"Unable to answer," said Bruce. "Please provide more...*incoming.*"

Before Drake could react, the *Void* suddenly lunged through the poisonous atmosphere of Chrysallix, nearly pitching him out of his seat. On the main viewer, he caught a glimpse of a silver missile streaking past, close as a whisker to colliding with the ship.

"A little more *heads-up* would be nice next time, Bruce!"

"The launch was unexpected," said the AI. "It appears... it appears the defense grid is operating with a certain degree of *randomness.*"

Drake grinned. "Well, it's a good thing I'm *used* to dealing with randomness."

Bruce paused for a moment. "Are you referring to our recent encounters with the Fluke, perhaps?"

"Perhaps." Drake scrambled the course he'd been programming, making it less linear, adding sudden changes in speed and direction. "Maybe we can *see* their random strategy and *raise* it by a factor of a hundred!"

"Actually," said Bruce, "I *have* been developing a special, highly randomized *Fluke module* for future encounters with that particular species. Would you like me to implement that instead, cowboy?"

Drake smirked. "Let's leave it at 'Captain' for now, okay? And *yes*, of course I want you to implement the new Fluke module!" Even as he gave the order, he had a nagging worry over the fact that Bruce had just admitted taking such unexpected, independent action...but now was not the time to look a gift AI in the algorithms. Now that battlefield conditions had changed for the worse, he needed any edge he could get.

Especially when Gus was out there on her own, facing similarly difficult odds.

"Approximately two point two five minutes," said Bruce, seemingly out of nowhere.

Drake frowned. "What exactly are you talking about, Bruce?"

"That is the approximate length of time that a singular-ium-infused surface can remain relatively brittle before it reverts to its characteristic impenetrability," said Bruce. "I based my calculations specifically on the composition of the shell of the weapons spire below. I then adjusted the result for the incompleteness of available data, so it *should* be relatively close to being accurate."

"Great, thanks." The time for reassessment and recalibration was over, and Drake knew it. Gus—and Rhap, and everyone on Chrysallix—were depending on him to do his part, to draw the grid's attention and bring down the tower before it was too late.

The time had come to prove his mettle.

"All right, Bruce," he said. "I want you to make a series of runs at the tower. Use the course I've plotted in the nav computer as your starting point and randomize it further with your Fluke module. Understood?"

"Yes, Captain."

"First approach ends with a magno-gun strike at the tower's shell," explained Drake. "Next approach, we launch missiles or projectiles at the exact spot weakened by the magno-gun...within the window of breakability, of course. We'll run like that till we make a serious dent in that thing —magno-gun, then missiles, magno-gun, then missiles— after which, we'll get *real* dirty and take the whole structure down, whatever it takes. Roger that?"

"Roger that, cow—...I mean, Captain."

"Excellent." Drake opened his mouth to give the order to launch.

Before he could get the words out, the ship hurtled toward the spire.

"*Skudge!*" Though Drake wasn't inclined to motion sickness of any kind, his stomach lurched as the ship went through a series of tumbling, spinning maneuvers. It jolted one way, then stopped suddenly and jolted in a different direction entirely, each time getting closer to the spire.

Along the way, laser bolts and streams of explosive projectiles poured up from the spire at the ship, each time seemingly coming at point-blank range—yet somehow always missing, never quite intersecting with the ship's erratic path.

In a matter of seconds, the *Void* barreled up on the backside of the spire and froze, unleashing a prolonged blast from the magno-gun as it hung there. Even as the spire's gun turrets whipped around to target the ship, it finished its first barrage of alternating magnetic polarities and jumped away, following a course that was equally as random as the one that had gotten it in firing range in the first place.

"Incoming!" announced Bruce, just as the *Void* took an especially dramatic bounce.

Gripping the nav console for dear life, Drake spotted two missiles zooming by on the screens displaying the port and starboard views. They looked so big, so close, he felt as if he could have leaned out a porthole and flicked each with a finger on the way past.

"Bring us back around, Bruce! Hit the weak spot we just prepped!" As he barked the orders, Drake reached under his chair and hit the button that engaged the safety harness. As soon as the two halves of the harness sprang out of the sides of the chair to wrap around him, he felt constricted—but it beat getting tossed around the bridge like popcorn during one of the ship's Fluke-inspired course corrections.

"Already ahead of you, Captain." Did Bruce suddenly sound...*exuberant?* Like he was somehow *enjoying* himself? If so, it was a new addition to his repertoire, one that Drake had not requested...though he supposed it was possible that Gus had arranged some simulated emotional responses without telling him, perhaps as a surprise.

Either way, now was most definitely *not* the time to question Bruce's reaction and risk upsetting him. As far as Drake was concerned, the AI could behave however he chose, as long as he got the job done.

That, at least so far, did not seem to be a problem.

After pausing briefly as the missiles passed, the *Void* swung around and embarked on another herky-jerky flight path—spinning, diving, climbing, darting this way and that as blasts of laser fire and projectiles filled the sky around it. Mostly, the ship got through without getting tagged—and the few times it did take fire, it was never direct, only a glancing strike that did no major damage.

"How much time do we have until the first weakened site regains its resistance to our weapons?" asked Drake.

"Less than a minute," said Bruce. "Now be quiet and let me concentrate."

Drake's eyes widened. Was he facing a case of full-on AI revolt, as if being in the middle of a pitched battle wasn't trouble enough?

If so, all he could do was cross his fingers and hope for the best at that point.

Right after he slipped a fresh stick of cinnamon gum in his mouth, that is.

"Wouldn't wanna disrupt your concentration," he muttered as he folded the stick between his teeth.

Watching the feeds on the various screens was dizzying, though he tried to follow the ship's progress on its return sweep to the spire. He especially lost track during one particular series of head-spinning maneuvers that looked on-screen like a randomly edited sequence of swirling zooms, pans, and quick cuts. By the time that run was through, he wasn't really sure *where* the ship was in relation to the spire or even which way was up.

Not until the whirling sequence came to a sudden stop, that is, and he saw the spire's weak spot directly in front of the *Void*'s nose.

"Twenty seconds remaining in malleability window," announced Bruce. "Firing projectile weapons!"

Even as the AI said it, Drake saw a prolonged salvo of explosive pellets leap from the *Void*'s guns to the silver skin of the spire. At first, they seemed to have no impact, and he wondered if Bruce had miscalculated.

Then, the ship launched two missiles at the same spot, and they blew a hole in it.

"Yes!" shouted Bruce. "We did it!"

"Great work!" said Drake. "Now let's do it again."

"Roger that!"

In a heartbeat, the *Void* burst away from the gaping hole in the side of the spire, skimming the cloud of black smoke that was puffing from inside.

As the ship zig-zagged its way between barrages of laser and projectile fire unleashed by the spire's turrets, Drake reconsidered the current strategy—and decided it might be best to adjust it on the fly. Pecking away at the spire as they were doing could take a long time, during which Gus and the residents of Chrysallix would continue to be at extreme risk. Perhaps it would make more sense to target one part of the spire in particular—or, to be more exact, one part of the complex of which the spire was only the most visible component.

"Bruce! Change of plans!" said Drake. "Target the energy source *under* the tower—the structure in which it's located."

Bruce took a moment to respond. "That could get tricky, Captain. There are lots more guns down there, and the actual energy source is some distance underground."

"Understood." Since he and Gus had concluded the power source likely fueled Tor's singularium refinery—along with the weapons spire and grid, of course—he strongly suspected that destroying it would be more than worth the risk. "Can you do it?"

Again, Bruce hesitated. When he finally spoke, he sounded as if he were grinning. "Oh, I can *do* it, all right. The question is, can you keep from losing your shit when this gets ugly? Because it *will*."

Drake chuckled. "Ugly is my middle name, Bruce."

Bruce chuckled, too. "I don't know *what* my middle name is. I'll have to figure it out later, I guess."

"Sounds like a plan," said Drake.

"Hold on, Captain!" said Bruce. "Do *not*, under any circumstances, release your safety harness."

"Don't need to worry about that," said Drake. "Now whatta you say we blow this piece of skudge to kingdom come?"

"I say let's do it!" shouted Bruce.

And then the ride, which had been pretty wild already, immediately got much wilder.

CHAPTER 24

Expect the unexpected, and then blow that shit up.

An armor jock's mantra.

In Gus's case, her training officer had added a codicil:

Don't get dead.

More than a dozen oversized, singularium-plated drones targeting her armor the instant she'd kicked open the maintenance hatch definitely qualified as unexpected.

Or *mostly* unexpected. Rhapsody hadn't told them how long the defense grid would take to reboot. Apparently the reboot was nearly instantaneous.

Or it hadn't happened at all, and wasn't that a nasty little thought.

In either case, she could kick the shit out of Rhapsody later for letting her walk into a trap. But first Gus had to *survive* the trap. Not easy, since she was basically a fish in a barrel as long as she was inside the maintenance hatch's airlock. Good thing she didn't intend to stay there long.

And a *very* good thing she'd practiced triggering the magno-beam thingie she'd added to her left gauntlet until using it was as second nature as using the rest of her armor's weaponry, even the projectile weapons.

The drones couldn't use their laser cannons, not while she was this close to the dome. Laser cannon fire would blow the hell out of the maintenance hatch, not to mention the framework around the hatch. The dome's integrity would be more than compromised. For all Gus knew, the support structures on this edge of the dome might collapse entirely. Tor was an asshole, but if his plan was to create an empire in the Frontier, he was going to need citizens to rule over.

Then again, he might decide people were just too much trouble and let the whole city die. As long as he had his singularium refinery, he'd probably be...well, not happy. In Gus's experience, men who craved power were never happy. Or satisfied.

She couldn't take a chance of anything damaging the dome. That meant she had to take the fight into the city. *Without* killing a bunch of unarmed civilians.

Fine. Fighting on the move was what she did best anyway.

All those thoughts ran through her head faster than the drones could lock their targeting lights on her armor.

She engaged the maneuvering jets on her boots and her torso and corkscrewed out of the hatch the same time the drones fired at her with their lasers. She'd learned long ago how to rotate her armor in ways most people thought armor couldn't move. The drones clearly didn't expect her to jet out of the hatch while she was rotating, and most of the shots missed her. The few shots that hit home fizzled on her singularium-reinforced armor.

Take that, you robo skudge-holes.

As soon as she cleared the hatch, her comms and all her displays came back online, but she was too busy to contact the *Void*. Instead, she activated her magno-beam thingie.

The drones knew she had singularium now. There was no reason to keep the magno-beam under wraps anymore. In the drones' little robo-brains, they'd probably already made the connection between the fact that she had attached singularium to her armor and the logical conclusion that she possessed tools that would not only make the singularium pliable enough to mold to her armor's contours but would make their singularium-shielded bodies vulnerable.

Too bad drones had no self-preservation instincts.

The damn things came at her now, the buzzing from their propellers nearly overpowering even inside her helmet. Gus led them on a merry chase through the downtown streets, changing altitude and angles and direction so often that none of the drones could get a lock on her.

Civilians ran screaming below the battle. Gus wanted to yell at them to get inside. She couldn't—wouldn't—use her best weapons against the drones while there was any possibility of killing innocent civilians.

Finally, she found a wide spot in the middle of what would have been a park in any other city, but on Chrysallix was a paved area complete with light stanchions and benches and food kiosks that had been abandoned as their owners and customers ran for cover inside nearby buildings. She dropped to her feet and activated her shoulder launchers, bringing her own laser cannons online, along with the grenade launcher she'd rigged beneath one of the launchers. She hoped the drones would focus on the energy emanating from the business end of the laser cannons and ignore the grenade launcher.

The drones honed in on her, their own laser cannons charged and ready. They circled her like she was the bullseye on a virtual dartboard.

Gus activated her magno-beam thingie, then upped the power to her boot jets to maximum.

She then shot straight up at the same time she activated the magno-beam, spraying the drones below with waves of alternating magnetic polarity.

The rising whine of the drones' propellers sounded like angry screams. The drones rose in the air after her, but for them, it was already too late.

She shot three of the special grenades into the air below her, right in the center of the mass of drones.

Even robo-weapons had their limitations, and the drones chasing her didn't have time to react to sudden explosions in their midst. The shotgun pellets Gus had added to the grenades tore through the drone's weakened singularium housing like the drones' bodies had been made of paper.

She expected to have to take out any stragglers with a few well-placed bullets. She didn't expect what would happen when the shotgun pellets tore through the drones' singularium-plated fuel cells.

The resulting series of explosions sent a fireball into the air straight at her.

She didn't hesitate. She was used to outrunning

exploding missiles. She angled her armor off to the side and dove down to the deck, below the rising fireball.

The fireball and the shockwave from the explosions dissipated before they came anywhere close to the dome, but the explosions would draw more drones. That was a good thing. They'd no doubt communicated with each other and knew she was a formidable opponent, one who knew their armor's strengths and weaknesses and used both to her advantage. Did they have magno-beam thingies of their own? Probably at the refinery, as part of the manufacturing process, but there'd been no need to have weapons like that inside the central dome until now.

At least, she hoped not. But she needed to be prepared just in case one of the drones aimed a magno-beam at *her* armor.

What she really needed was an injured drone that would run home to mama. She'd be fighting for hours, and she might even run out of ammo, if she had to kill every drone in the dome one by one. If that happened, she might end up yanking the things out of the sky and bashing them to tiny bits of weakened singularium and broken circuits. While that would be emotionally satisfying, the longer a fight went on, the greater the risk of something going wrong.

And it bothered her that she hadn't heard from Drake. They'd made sure the *Void* was more formidable going into this battle than the ship had been on Shepard's Moon, but if Drake had run into a fully operational weapons tower, he'd have his work cut out for him. She didn't want to contact him and risk distracting him at a critical moment.

So she waited, and sure enough, it didn't take long

before she heard the whine of more drone propellers. Not an entire phalanx, not even a dozen, but only a few this time. She used the magno-beam to disable their singularium plating, then a well-placed bullet knocked each one out of the sky.

None of them shot a magno-beam at her.

It took her until the third group of drones to realize that they were mapping her strategy. Sacrificing some of their own to see how she reacted. What weapons she used against them and in what order.

Son of a bitch. They were profiling her!

Well, to hell with that. She was done waiting. She wanted a drone that would run home to mama, and she wanted one *now*.

She got her opportunity when she saw two drones exit a nearby high-rise building. These drones weren't equipped with propellors. They were vaguely human-shaped, right down to arms and legs, and looked more like bots than anything else. Only their laser weapons gave them away. That, and the blinking red lights in the middle of their foreheads. They stood outside the building like they were waiting for further instructions.

She'd give them instructions, all right.

She ran toward them, making sure they saw her.

The red lights in the middle of their foreheads started to blink faster. Their entire heads were made of smooth, silvery singularium, but their spindly bodies weren't.

All the better.

She aimed the magno-beam at the drone on the left and then blew its head apart with a well-placed bullet. A second bullet took out the red light on the other drone's head, but she purposefully left the rest of its "brain" alone. She fired a laser that sheared off one of its arms and then did the same thing to the hand on its other arm—the hand holding its laser rifle.

The drone shrieked, or at least that's how she interpreted the high-pitched squeal that came out of it. The drone turned and ran down a side street as fast as its spindly legs could take it.

Inside her armor, Gus smiled.

Run home to mama, little drone. Mama will fix you up like new. And while you're at it, just ignore the big bad metallic wolf that's trailing your scent.

The big bad wolf that's going to blow your house to kingdom come.

She ignited the jets in her boots and took off after the drone.

CHAPTER 25

Drake had known that going after the power source before giving the upper sections of the weapons spire a thorough pounding would be a challenge—but he may have underestimated how much of a challenge it would be.

Even moving at dizzying speeds along hyper-erratic courses run by Bruce in Fluke mode, the *Golden Void* was struggling to avoid the heavy weapons fire from the concentration of guns arrayed around the spire's base...let alone cracking the singularium shielding down there.

In fact, they'd already wasted one magno-gun barrage when they couldn't make it back to the weak spot they'd "cured" before it hardened again. Bruce had zig-zagged the skudge out of their course, swooping in what felt like six different directions at once, dodging all manner of laser and projectile fire along the way...only to run afoul of a trio of armed, airborne drones charging seemingly out of nowhere. (Were there perhaps hidden drone caches within or around the spire, undetected by the *Void*'s routine sensor sweeps?) Two of the bastards had actually tagged the *Void*, tripping a power bump and causing the ship to drop into an out-of-control stall for several terrible seconds, making Drake feel as if his heart had stopped in that interval of panic.

Bruce had kept his shit together, though, rerouting power and quickly jolting the ship out of her stall. He and Drake had worked in tandem, then—the AI whipping the *Void* through a whiplashing spiral around the drones while Drake unleashed all hell upon them with alternating blasts from the magno-gun and projectile weapons. One by one, the three robotic attackers had burst into showers of flame and shrapnel, even as the *Void* had raced victoriously through the debris.

The ship had survived—but had yet to make a dent in the power source housing. For that reason, Drake landed on another twist in strategy.

"New plan, Bruce." As he spoke, Drake smacked a big black button on the nav console, causing the autopilot indicator light to blink red instead of steadily glowing green. "I'm takin' the wheel for this next run."

"You sure about that, Captain?"

"Hell, yes." With that, Drake grabbed the old-fashioned nav console steering wheel and gave it a hard spin, twirling the *Void* on its Y-axis like a propeller on a drone. "You do the shootin' this time, if anything jumps out at us...and when I give the signal, hit the power source housing with the ol' one-two punch."

"One-two punch?" asked Bruce.

"Magno-beam followed by projectile barrage," said Drake. "Got it?"

"Hell, yes." Bruce sounded a little awkward when he said it.

Without another moment's delay, Drake stomped the accelerator pedal under the console and pulled the wheel straight back, pitching the *Void* into a steep, fast dive (but not quite a stall). Instead of the bobbing and weaving tactics he and Bruce had employed for their previous runs, he took a bead on the base and fired the ship on a beeline at its target, hoping the change in tactics might confuse the grid *just enough.*

Eyes flicking between the main viewer and the tactical display, Drake saw his plan was working. Consistently, the heaviest laser and projectile fire from the spire was flaring in quadrants to one side or another of the beeline course. Clearly, the grid targeting systems were basing their countermeasure firing patterns on the kinds of courses the *Void* had been flying since the start of the fight—anticipating the ship would continue erratically zigging and zagging instead of zooming in on a no-nonsense straight line.

Smiling grimly, he held tight to that line, hoping his scheme would work long enough to get in the kind of strike he needed. Sometimes, he knew from experience, taking the direct route was the most random thing you could do in a fight.

Heart racing, he barreled the *Void* down to the power source housing, miraculously making it all the way without major damage. Hopping in as close as he could, out of range of the nearest guns, he used thrusters to position the ship's nose—and the magno-gun mounted there—so it pointed at a choice bare spot on the singularium-reinforced skin of the power source housing.

Daring not to delay a second longer than needed, he barked out the next order as soon as he had the target sighted in. "Let 'er rip, Bruce! Give 'er the old one-two punch!"

Bruce needed no further encouragement. He fired the big magno-gun immediately, pummeling the silver shielding with wave after waving of alternating magnetic polarity.

After the necessary seconds of magno-beam treatment, Bruce shut off the weapon—and did one of the last things Drake expected him to do.

He barked out an actual *order*. To the actual *Captain* of the ship.

"Rotate the ship 180 degrees counterclockwise on the Y-axis!" Bruce's instructions were specific as well as emphatic.

In spite of his surprise at being issued an order by the ship's AI, Drake quickly did as he was told. Seizing the wheel with both hands, he spun it hard left while playing the accelerator and watching for incoming countermeasures on the tactical display. Sure enough, two more drones were zipping in from what had been the *Void*'s stern until the rotation maneuver mere seconds ago.

Without a word, Bruce hammered one drone, then the other, with magno-beam fire, followed by hails of projectiles. The robotic craft blew apart in quick succession, leaving that particular approach fully clear for the moment.

"Rotate 180 degrees clockwise on the Y-axis!" That was Bruce's next order—a command to return the *Void* to its prior orientation, facing the cured area on the power source housing.

Drake brought the ship around fast, hoping there was

still time in the breakability window of the singularium-reinforced shielding to blow it open.

There was.

As soon as the rotation ended, Bruce cut loose with the biggest barrage yet of projectiles, every one of them aimed dead-on at the silver surface. Within seconds, the projectiles broke through, punching a multitude of holes in the skin of the housing—then fusing those many small holes into a ragged crater belching plumes of black smoke.

But Bruce wasn't done there...though Drake didn't realize it at first.

"Yee-haawww!" Drake's gleeful cheer at their success came from the heart. "Great work, Bruce! We did it!"

"The facility is now highly vulnerable," said Bruce. "According to my sensors, an enormous impact is within reach."

"Good to know!" said Drake. "We'll make our next run an even bigger—"

Suddenly, the *Void* jolted forward, throwing him back against his chair and knocking the wind out of him. Before he fully grasped or could move to stop what was happening, the autopilot indicator switched from blinking red to steady emerald green.

Bruce had taken full control of navigation and was taking the ship somewhere against Drake's will.

"What the *skudge*, Bruce?" he yelled.

"Sit back and relax, Captain," Bruce said calmly. "We're going to *finish* this right here and now."

On the main viewer, Drake saw more streams of projectile ammo blast the crater in the housing even wider—even as the ship itself continued to hurtle toward it.

Bruce was taking the *Void* into the belly of the beast—and that was one place Drake had no desire to be.

"We're going direct to the power source this time," said Bruce. "I guarantee we can destroy the whole complex from *there*."

"And destroy *ourselves* in the bargain!" snapped Drake. "This is suicide!"

"AIs don't believe in suicide." Bruce chuckled. "Trust me, Captain. I *got* this."

And with that, the *Golden Void* rushed into the smoky maw, hull scraping the jagged rim as it cruised without hesitation into what Drake feared would be a one-way trip into Hell.

CHAPTER 26

The injured drone led Gus on a merry chase through parts of Chrysallix she hadn't seen before. The high-rises of the downtown area gave way to low-slung buildings in what was clearly an industrial section of the central dome.

That surprised Gus. She'd thought the smaller circular domes outside the central dome contained the planetoid's industrial centers. From what she could see, the buildings in this area were mainly warehouses given the shipping transports on the road with a few various other support services like transport repair shops thrown in the mix. The transports on the road appeared to be as automated as the taxi that Rhap had sent to fetch Drake and Gus from the spaceport the last time they'd been here.

And there were a *lot* of warehouses. No wonder Drake had told her that whatever they needed, Rhap either had or could obtain. The import/export business on Chrysallix was clearly booming.

The few civilians out on the streets paused whatever they were doing when the injured drone ran past them. Apparently something like that didn't happen often. When viewed together with the way Rhap had initially reacted to the drone attacks on innocent civilians, that told Gus the residents inside the dome had decided fighting back against the atrocities committed by the defense grid in the name of security was just too big a risk to life and limb.

Those same civilians *ran* when they saw her coming.

Good. The fewer civilians around when the drone made it home to mama, the better.

She was just beginning to think the drone was purposefully trying to lead her in the wrong direction when it veered around a corner and ran straight toward a sprawling building nearly as large as the terminal where they'd docked the *Void* back when Gus had thought the biggest problem they'd encounter on Chrysallix was Drake's lusty ex. The building had no signage on the outside, but the tall roof was studded with antennae and other boxy equipment.

Drone central, aka mama's home. This had to be it.

The drone entered the building through an open doorway big enough for the *Void* to fly through. The air around the doorway sparkled and shimmered when the drone passed over the threshold, and the heads-up readings on Gus's visor indicated a coinciding increase in power from the building before the readings returned to normal. A shield of some type was in operation. But was it just protecting the open doorway, or did it surround the whole building? The *Void's* sensors could tell her, but the ship was off fighting—and hopefully winning—its own battles.

One thing Gus didn't see was any evidence of singularium plating on the building, which made a certain kind of sense. No matter how much singularium Tor had managed to obtain through trade or outright theft, he wouldn't have an unlimited amount to waste. Especially not since Gus and Drake had cut off his supply on Shepard's Moon, and Tor had been upgrading the drones with additional singularium.

If singularium figured in his plans to conquer other worlds in the Frontier, he'd want to put that rare metal to use in the best place possible: to protect the drones that kept the civilians of Chrysallix in line.

Empires were built on the strength of their military. So far the only military Tor appeared to have left at his disposal since she and Drake had kicked the rebels' collective asses on Shepard's Moon were various forms of robo-drones and the machines that created them. If Tor had a fleet of ships—and wasn't that a sobering thought—she hadn't seen any evidence of it.

She also didn't see any visible weapons through the open doorway, but if this facility truly was drone central, the place was probably lousy with all the weapons the drones were equipped with, from power cells to missiles to laser cannons, not to mention everything else a good drone needed to terrorize the population.

She couldn't just blow this place up like she'd hoped to. If all the weapons stored inside blew, the resulting explosion would take out the dome. She'd been lucky when all the drones' power cells had exploded in the city square; the shockwave and explosions had fizzled out before they reached the dome. This facility was near the edge of the dome and in close proximity to the spaceport. It had probably been built in this location on purpose as a kind of *blow us up and you all die* defensive measure.

That made her hate Tor all the more. His hand-picked dictator wannabe on Shepard's Moon had used civilians as human shields to protect his weapons. Tor was doing the same damn thing here.

She deeply, deeply hoped that Rhapsody wasn't okay with any of this. Gus already planned to have one *serious* conversation with the woman as soon as she unleashed all the fury an armor jock could on the drones' mama, not to mention on Tor.

The other thing she had to consider was the fact that the facility probably had magno-beams inside. If the facility was totally automated—and it probably was—Tor wouldn't be able to trust disgruntled civilians to not muck things up, either purposefully or by accident—those beams would be focused on the production lines inside the building. The program that ran the automation might not anticipate an attack from outside forces.

But if there *were* actual people inside? People totally loyal to Tor? People could make independent decisions, like *Turn that beam around and aim it at the armor jock attacking us!* Especially since the drones had clearly communicated that she was equipped with singularium-shielded armor and they'd need a magno-beam to do any real damage.

For all she knew, the machines inside were already in the process of turning their beams on her. She had to stop them, and the only way to make sure she could was to first hit them with a few well-aimed blasts from her magno-beam thingie to fry any singularium that might be protecting them.

She aimed her magno-beam at the opening in the building where the drone had entered and fired the beam's alternating magnetic polarity pulses.

The pulses hit the shielded doorway and bounced *right back* at her.

She dodged out of the way just barely in time before the pulses from her own beam had a chance to destabilize the singularium on *her* armor.

What the skudge?

In all the tests she and Drake had run on the beam, they'd never had it bounce back off any surface, but clearly this facility was equipped with a shield she'd never seen before. Was this more Alliance technology that Tor had stolen? The Alliance had been hot to obtain singularium for its own purposes. That was why her son had been able to successfully negotiate Shepard's Moon joining the Free Worlds Alliance now that singularium had been discovered on the planet when the Alliance hadn't been all that interested in the planet years before. If there was one constant in the universe, it was that the Alliance would never develop a weapon it couldn't defend against.

Okay, so using her magno-beam was out of the question. At least until she disabled the shield.

Gus fired one of her laser guns at the opening.

The energy from the laser fizzled and dissipated.

Skudge!

She went through the same test fires at the boxy equipment and the antennae on the building's roof and then along different points along the exterior of the facility. She got the same results. Whatever was shielding the open doorway appeared to be shielding the rest of the building as well.

She'd followed the drone home to mama, and now mama was thumbing her nose at Gus. Mama hadn't even fired back or sent out any drones to attack Gus. Although mama might be conserving what was left of her little darlings after learning that Gus could take care of the drones just fine.

Which meant that mama had to be cooking up a nasty surprise. The mother of all drones. A monster that was guaranteed to take out even the most determined armor jock. That open doorway *was* big enough for a ship-sized drone to fly through.

Okay, fine, Gus would just ram the damn barrier. It wasn't her first choice—that would be dual blasts from her laser cannons—but she couldn't risk igniting the ammo inside the building. Her armor could punch through anything. She'd punched through permacrete walls. A damn shield wasn't tougher than permacrete.

So she jetted toward the open doorway at full power. In the space of two heartbeats, she covered the ground from where she'd been standing to the doorway. She captured images of what was going on inside the building on her armor's forward camera. All shiny machines working on more shiny machines, with not a single living person in sight. None of the machines even looked toward her.

She'd show them.

Only they showed her.

The shield held. Oh, it bowed inward just enough to absorb the energy of Gus's full-power charge and then redirect it outward.

Gus and her armor bounced off the shield and went flying backwards.

Skudge!!

She cursed loudly and inventively as she brought her armor under control, skidding to a stop not far from where she'd started.

She was better than this. She was the skudging *Gray Lady!* The hero of the 83rd Armor Division, and she had the medals to prove it. Just because she'd gotten old didn't change any of that. Hell, she'd gone up against the damn *Fluke* and survived. Twice! She wasn't about to let a bunch of machines beat her.

A bunch of machines.

She'd missed something that should have been obvious.

This facility was fully automated. She'd been right about that. Not only had no one shot back at her, no employees had run screaming from the building. Or any nearby buildings. There weren't even any transports on the streets. Maybe this area of the central dome was off limits to living beings and the shield was just to make sure everyone got the message without actually hurting or killing them.

If that was the case, that meant Tor wouldn't be inside. She'd still have to track him down, and maybe a good start to that would be to get some straight answers out of Rhap.

After she took care of this skudging facility.

The shield repelled magnetic energy and the energy generated by her laser beams. It also repelled her armor. But the *drone* got through without a hitch.

The drone was a machine. So was her armor, when she got right down to it. But there was one big difference. Her armor had a living being inside. The drone was all machine.

285

Gus might be able to fire a short-range missile through the shielding since she could cut the missile's propulsion system off right before it hit the shield. The missile certainly didn't have a living being inside. But again, she couldn't risk that a missile would set off all the weapons inside the facility. She could also fire a few bullets at the shield, and while they might penetrate it, she'd use up the rest of the bullets she had left before she could punch a big enough hole through the shield to get her armor inside. For all she knew, the shield might even be able to repair itself before the bullets did enough damage to make a difference.

She did, however, have one last thing that might work.

She took a deep breath and started marching toward the opening in the building.

Again, none of the machines inside seemed to register her approach. This time, she had a better opportunity to see what was going on inside the building beyond the open doorway. She caught sight of the damaged drone. It was laid out on a table not that different from her workbench on the *Void*, its damaged parts in the process of being replaced.

None of the machines working inside appeared to have singularium shielding like the damaged drone's head did. She did catch sight of several large sheets of singularium stacked off to one side near machines that appeared to be working on the housing for a huge drone, this one nearly the size of the *Void* itself.

Hello, monster drone.

No way was she going to let that thing take to the air.

She stopped twenty feet from the doorway and activated her laser cannons. Not that she planned to use them right away. No, she had a different surprise for the machines inside.

Instead of laser cannons or her armor's laser guns, she shot every last one of her special concussion grenades right at the shield.

The grenades she'd filled with hundreds of the same kind of pellets as those packed into the shells fired by Drake's shotgun.

Weapons that had no energy signature of their own and had no living beings inside.

She let out a whoop of triumph when every single grenade punched through the shield and exploded inside.

The explosions themselves not only ripped apart machines but also sent a storm cloud of shotgun pellets throughout the interior. Machines shrieked and squealed as pellets gouged their metal housings and tore through their sensitive electronic components, sending sparks flying.

And most important of all, the pellets shredded every bit of the shield covering the open doorway.

Gus threw an arm up to protect her visor as the pellets that had shredded the shield raced toward her, but by the time they reached her, most of their energy had dissipated. The pellets bounced off her singularium-shielded armor, but she felt a sting in her shoulder—*again!*—as a pellet got inside the vulnerable shoulder joint on her armor. As injuries went, this one was so minor she barely noticed.

The most important thing was that the shielding was gone. Obliterated.

She fired the jets on her armor's boots and flew through the unguarded doorway before the shield could repair itself.

Now that she was inside and could see what she was aiming at, she could turn her laser cannons loose on anything that wasn't ammunition, including any magno-beams the machines tried to aim in her direction. As for their own singularium, her armor's magno-beam hadn't been damaged by the shotgun pellets. Any drone protected by singularium plating was about to find itself in a world of hurt.

Better watch out now, mama. Gray Lady was in the house, and she didn't plan to take any prisoners.

The first thing she obliterated was the housing for the new monster drone and the magno-beam that had been shaping singularium for its housing. The blast from the laser cannon took out all the machines on that particular production line, along with the production line itself, but the blast wave was contained by the ceiling that stood a good forty feet over Gus's head. Encouraged, she blasted the production line where the injured drone was being repaired.

Bye-bye, little damaged robo weapon.

She felt like an oversized child destroying all the toys in an automated toy factory, only these toys had been built to be tools of a fascist wannabe emperor. They'd hurt people. They'd been used to *kill* innocent civilians. If she felt any sympathy at all for the machines that had only been doing as instructed, that sympathy died a horrible death as she remembered the birthday boy who'd lost his mother—who'd lost his entire world—thanks to only one of these skudging things.

She wasn't about to let Tor use any of these toys to keep the people of Chrysallix in line, not anymore. She destroyed machines left and right and felt no more regret than she had when she'd killed the rebels on Shepard's Moon. She hadn't started this battle, but she sure as hell was going to put an end to it.

The machines tried to fight back, finally calling up some long-buried subroutine in their programming that told them to attack the intruder in their midst with whatever weapons were available. But the machines were slow to make the change from assembly-line workers to soldiers, and the robo-drones they'd been working on were only half assembled. Gus was a seasoned armor jock with a good head of steam fueling her battle-hardened instincts.

The machines didn't stand a chance.

CHAPTER 27

Drake white-knuckled the armrests of his chair as Bruce drove the *Golden Void* at breakneck speed down a shaft in the heart of the power source housing.

As many wild rides as he'd taken in his life—and there had been *many*—the space cowboy still felt as if his heart was in his throat. The ship was one unexpected obstacle from a catastrophic collision, a crash it was going *much* too fast to avoid. If something were to appear in the *Void*'s path, he couldn't imagine stopping in time...and there certainly wasn't any room in that shaft for the ship to veer out of the way.

But maybe Bruce had it under control. After all, he'd known the shaft's location and seemed to know exactly where it led. Maybe he already knew there was nothing to worry about along this particular path. Maybe his predictive algorithms were so far ahead of any potential threats that the *Void* could not possibly fail in its full-throttle assault.

Oh, how Drake wished he could believe that…but the view on the main screen just looked like a gut-wrenching freefall down a smooth, cylindrical shaft with no sign of an escape route cut into it at any depth.

Far below, he saw a bright glow that he guessed must indicate their target—the subterranean energy source—or at least the next stage in reaching it. That, of course, brought another problem to mind, one for which he had yet to receive a satisfactory solution.

"Bruce!" He had to shout to be heard over the roar of the ship's overtaxed engines. "You still haven't explained how this isn't a *suicide* run!"

"Because I've been a little *busy*, here, Captain," said Bruce. "This chute's a little tricky to *navigate*, as you may have noticed."

Drake gnawed his latest piece of cinnamon gum and gaped at the main viewer. The power source was buried deeper than he'd expected, but at the rate they were plummeting down the tube, he didn't think it would be long until they reached it. *That* was when the more suicidal aspects of the dive would come into play.

"We both know how *massive* that power source is, Bruce…and how deep this shaft is sunk. Once you trigger whatever blast you have in mind, there's no way in hell we won't be *consumed* by it. We won't be able to get away in time!"

"Leave it to me, Captain," said Bruce, projecting extraordinary calmness in his even-toned voice. "I already said I got this, didn't I?"

Drake swallowed hard, carefully gauging his next words. If Bruce indeed had the situation under control, he didn't want to disrupt his focus. If, on the other hand, the AI was possibly losing his shit, he needed to probe far enough to know if extreme intervention might be necessary.

In other words, he needed to decide if it was time to flip the kill switch he'd installed for just such emergencies—an AI cutoff that would return full manual control to Drake's own hands. He'd never had to use it before, but what the hell? There was a first time for everything.

It wasn't an ideal solution, though. The *Void* was so deep in the complex right now, seizing control manually might be a dangerous strategy. Bruce's reflexes were still much faster and better able to yank them out of peril if it came down to it.

But there was a big difference between survivable peril and suicidal risk-taking. Drake needed to determine which one they were now facing, at least as far as he could with the information available.

"Bruce, I need you to talk me through this," he said firmly. "Tell me how we can possibly get to safety when this place goes up."

"Because *this* isn't the only way out," said Bruce. "Now please arm our full complement of missiles and get ready to fire them on my mark."

"Fire them at what?"

"That!" said Bruce. "Dead ahead!"

Just then, the view on the main screen changed dramatically as the *Void* popped free of the shaft. Suddenly, the bright glow that Drake had seen from a distance flared to fill the entirety of their surroundings. Squinting, he saw that it emanated from a massive, crystalline object—a gigantic orb studded with jagged spikes, spinning and flashing in the heart of a vaulted space lined with silvery, mirrored metal.

"It's a pulsar reactor," Drake said with a touch of wonder in his voice. "I've never seen one up close."

"The fused plasma core ejected from a pulsar disrupted by cascading quantum entanglement," explained Bruce. "Highly charged, able to generate huge power flows..."

"And highly unstable," said Drake. "One of the most unstable harnessed power sources known to exist."

"All the better for us to use it to blow the weapons grid," said Bruce.

"And the rest of the domed habitats on Chrysallix," snapped Drake. "And everyone *in* them, including *Gus.*"

"In the hands of a lesser AI, maybe," said Bruce. "But as I told you, I've *got* this. That silver metal lining the surrounding chamber? It's *singularium* alloy—the same stuff lining the shaft that led us here."

Drake frowned. "You think it'll contain the worst of the blast?"

"Contain and *direct* it," said Bruce. "*Funnel* it back up the way we came, where the big you-know-what is waiting."

"The weapons spire." Drake nodded as the contours of Bruce's plan solidified in his mind. If things went as expected, the blast would take out the power source, weapons grid, and weapons spire all at once, bringing instant freedom to the populace of Chrysallix.

Unfortunately, it was looking more likely that the *Void* and its crew might not be among those newly freed people when the smoke cleared…at least not in the sense of being freed and *alive.*

"You've got those missiles ready to fly, right?" asked Bruce. "Prepare to fire when my countdown reaches zero."

"Then what? Where's this other way out you mentioned?" As he said it, Drake scanned readouts on the nav console, hunting for another opening in the chamber—finding none. "Is it hidden? Because I don't see it, Bruce."

"That's because it doesn't *exist* yet…but it *will.*" Suddenly, the *Void*'s engines roared, and the ship vaulted toward the jagged mass of the pulsar reactor. "Now get ready to release those missiles, Captain! We've got no time to lose—or haven't you seen the fleet of drones that just poured out of the shaft after us?"

Drake switched the main screen to an aft view—and there they were, as promised. A cloud of drones swarmed out of the shaft, heading for the *Void* with guns blazing.

In spite of the lingering uncertainties, Drake and Bruce were in the shit now, committed to their current course of action, come what may.

Drake swapped views on the main screen again, this time landing on the pulsar core mass ahead—but the scene quickly changed. Without warning, the video feed plunged away from the mass, and Drake found himself gaping at the silver lining of the base of the chamber. It was coming up fast as the *Void* hurtled toward it, the glare of the spinning reactor mass flashing over the mirrored surface.

"What the *skudge*, Bruce?" Tightly gripping the console, Drake wondered what the AI's strategy was—because at that moment, it looked he was about to ram the ship nose-first into the chamber's floor.

He stopped just short of it, though, and cut loose with the magno-beam guns, pounding the singularium with wave after wave of alternating magnetic polarity.

Checking the tactical display, Drake saw the drones were diving toward them, laying down a curtain of laser fire that couldn't quite reach the *Void*...yet.

Before they could get in range, Bruce stopped blasting the singularium and spun the ship so her nose pointed at the reactor mass instead of the floor. Then, he launched upward with a burst of speed so extreme, even the AI-guided drones were scattered, unable to mount an effective intercept course and attack. A few laser bolts kicked the ship from side to side, giving the hull some fresh singes, but the swarm couldn't blast the passing ship before it reached the reactor mass.

As the *Void* spiraled up and around the mass, climbing toward its peak, Bruce started to count down—signaling the time to release the missiles was fast approaching. "Ten...nine...eight..."

Heart hammering, Drake held his right hand over the big, red launch button. One last time, he wondered if he was doing the right thing, giving over all his trust to Bruce—or if he ought to be hitting the AI manual override instead. He'd never been the type to give over control easily to electronic intellects...or organic ones, for that matter. He'd always trusted his own instincts and talents above those of anyone else he'd come across—except the Gray Lady, of course. His instincts had rarely let him down before.

And what did they tell him to do this time?

They told him to trust the AI.

"Seven…six…five…" counted Bruce as the ship rose higher, dodging the worst of the weapons fire from the drones as they regrouped and strafed their target. "Four…three…two…one…"

Suddenly, the *Void* cleared the peak of the spinning crystalline mass—and paused.

"*…zero.*"

Drake brought his hand down hard, and the ship's full complement of missiles—all twenty-two of them—leaped out of the firing tubes in rapid sequence. On the main viewer, he could see them streaking straight for the heart of the pulsar core mass, exactly as he'd programmed their onboard guidance systems. When they hit, there would be a hell of a blast—all those explosives triggering the power stored in that massive twirling object. If the *Void* stayed there a moment more, she would be swept into a titanic upward surge of destructive force, sufficient to blow the vessel to a multitude of tiny fragments.

But Bruce didn't let her hang there any longer than he had to. As soon as the missiles were away, he flung the ship straight down toward the base of the chamber, racing away from the impending blow.

Pursued by drones, the *Void* dove for the chamber's floor like a demon from Hell blitzing back into the inferno. When the ship was almost there, the projectile weapons opened fire, pelting the singularium surface with streams of ammo.

Guided by Bruce's exacting aim, the ammo hit the exact spot he'd softened moments ago with the magno-guns, tearing open the silver sheeting. As the ship hurtled toward it, a crater opened, swiftly enlarging as the gunfire pounded away at it.

Just as the missiles blew, and the reactor mass exploded in the chamber's upper reaches, the *Void* lunged into the crater, guns still blazing, engines screaming.

And Drake, as courageous as he was, couldn't help closing his eyes as the ship made that heart-stopping dive into the unknown.

CHAPTER 28

The lights went out. All of them, all at once.

Gus's visor immediately adjusted for the sudden darkness inside what was left of the drone factory, the oversized warehouse she'd come to think of as Mama's House. Not that anything was going to come out of the darkness and attack her. The machines were all dead, blown to bits.

But what about Drake?

Was the sudden cut in power because Drake had done something incredibly foolish, like try to take out the *entire* power source inside that huge complex beneath the weapons tower?

She tried to reach him on comms. She got nothing but static in return.

He wasn't a soldier. He was a hell of a good pilot, and they'd upgraded the AI's ship-maneuvering capabilities, but still. Going after something like the primary power source for the entire *planetoid*? Single handed? In a smuggler's *cargo ship??*

She tried to raise him again and still got nothing but static.

She took a deep breath to try to steady her racing heart just about the same time emergency lights came on overhead. A backup power supply must have kicked in. Just for the building, or for the whole dome? It better be for the entire dome. Otherwise, the civilians would be dying a long, slow death because the systems that kept them alive inside the dome would have nothing to power them.

She couldn't think about that right now, just like she couldn't let herself imagine all the reasons why she couldn't raise Drake on comms. The machines might be dead, but her work in Mama's House wasn't done quite yet. She was a soldier and she had a job to finish. She couldn't afford to let herself be distracted by a bunch of worst-case *what ifs.*

There'd been no civilian casualties because like she'd thought, there'd been no civilians inside Mama's House. Gus had marched through the entire complex. She'd found enough ammo to start a world war on most planets. Missiles and laser rifles and laser cannons and enough power cells to keep thousands of drones in the air for years. Right before the lights went out, she'd found the most disturbing thing of all: a cold room where a type of biotoxin was stored that Gus hadn't seen since she'd been in the military.

Was Tor keeping this stuff inside the dome as a threat to keep the locals—most particularly Rhap—in line? Drake's ex had lied her ass off when they'd cornered her about the defense contract she'd entered into. Gus wouldn't put it past a skudge-hole like Tor to threaten to kill every living being in the central dome if anyone—and most especially Rhap—even thought about fighting back. That could be why no one ever did.

No one except Gus and Drake, and she was pretty sure Rhap had counted on that. Rhap must have known how important Tor was to the two of them—they hadn't exactly been stealthy about trying to find out where Tor had disappeared to in the Frontier. So why hadn't Rhap just come out and said that Tor was her mysterious defense contractor?

Because she was that frightened of the man? Gus couldn't imagine Rhapsody Harrison ever being frightened of anybody. Beneath that sex siren personality draped in an outrageous caftan and a slightly ditzy way of speaking lurked a shrewd, manipulative woman.

So the only other explanation was the one Gus had pretty much figured out all along:

Rhap had decided to use them to rid herself of Tor without actually doing the fighting herself.

No one liked being used, and normally that would have pissed Gus off to high heaven, but two things argued against it.

Drake still cared about this woman. Gus wasn't about to put Drake in the middle of any *battle royale* between herself and his ex. Gus loved the man too much to cause him any unnecessary pain, and compared to that, her bruised ego was pretty minor in the grand scheme of things.

And the second?

Rhap had given Gus the opportunity to screw with Tor in a way that would hurt him like he'd never been hurt before. Rhap's manipulations were the whole reason Gus had tracked down the skudge-hole's drone complex, stomped all over his toys, and now she was going to set his deadliest toy (if you could call it that) on fire. Was that a great way to spend a day or what?

It would be nice if she could set all of Mama's House on fire, but as soon as the fire reached the stockpile of weapons, the resulting explosions would destroy the dome. She'd have to limit the fire to the cold room since fire was the only way to toast the biotoxin and render it inert. Luckily, cold rooms were made to keep whatever nasties that lived inside away from the outside world. The cold room *should* keep the fire from spreading just fine.

She made sure the combustible weapons in the complex weren't anywhere near the cold room, moving anything that was too close just to be on the safe side, then she tossed one of her regular concussion grenades inside and sealed the door.

The resulting explosion was larger than Gus had expected. The cold room's atmosphere must have had a higher concentration of flammable gases than the air inside the dome. The explosion nearly broke the cold room's observation window, but the fireball did its job. The vials of biotoxin shattered in the blast, and now the contents were being consumed by fire. Still, she used one of her armor's lasers to etch a *Hazardous – Do Not Enter!* warning on the room's door, and then she melted the lock with a blast from the laser embedded in her right palm.

She kept watch at the observation window until the fire burned itself out. Then she used her armor's heat sensors to make sure the fire hadn't spread into the walls surrounding the cold room, but all she got back were cold, dead readings.

She tried to raise Drake on comms again, and still got nothing.

Damn it!

She went through the rest of Mama's House, sealing off every area where weapons were stored by melting the locks on the doors. She didn't want to give any other tinpot dictator wannabe easy access to a bunch of unguarded weaponry. She used some of the fuel cells to replenish her own depleted supply, but she didn't take any of the facility's weapons with her when she left.

The only thing she couldn't do was seal the open doorway that had been protected by the shield. The shield hadn't come back online with the emergency lights, and Gus's initial assault had shredded every piece of electronic equipment that might have controlled a physical door. So she proceeded to destroy everything that was left in the production area, including the sheets of singularium that the machines had been in the process of attaching to the fuselage of the monster drone.

Bye-bye, singularium stockpile.

She was sure that a determined person—a determined *living* person—could separate the bits of singularium from the mounds of debris inside the factory, but it would take time, patience, and a whole lot of backbreaking work, and that wasn't Tor's style. No, his style was to co-opt a willing local to do his dirty work for him. Someone who'd hand over the keys to an entire planet for a promise of riches or power or whatever the hell a person like that wanted most in life.

Had Rhapsody been that person on Chrysallix? Or had she just been conned, as Drake believed?

There was only one way to find out.

The central square in the downtown area of the central dome wasn't deserted anymore. Civilians had started to come out of the surrounding high-rises. While it wasn't business as usual yet—no one was working any of the kiosks in the square—people were looking up at the dome and at all the high-rises. A few of them were looking in the direction of the power complex and the weapons tower. Not that they could see anything from ground level except maybe the top of an ever-expanding smoke and debris-filled cloud. From the grim expressions on their faces, they were probably waiting for missiles to start bombarding the dome at any moment.

That wouldn't be happening. The weapons tower was gone. Simply... gone.

After she left Mama's House, Gus had maneuvered her armor up nearly to the top of the dome, trying to get a reading on what was going on at the power complex. A great cloud of smoke and ash had risen high in the plane-toid's atmosphere where the weapons tower had stood, but the tower itself, right down to the superstructure, had vanished into a massive crater. Explosions were still going off in the crater as additional ammo was superheated by the hellfire that had taken out Tor's weapons of mass destruction. Those explosions might be going off for some time. The ground itself looked like it was on fire.

What the hell had Drake done? None of the *Void's* weapons were capable of destruction on that kind of scale.

Even with her armor's enhanced visual capabilities, she couldn't get a read on the *Void*.

Dammit.

She tried not to let herself think he hadn't survived the explosion. He had to have survived. He was her Broken String, and he still had songs to write and sing for her.

Emergency power had come back on inside the dome but at a reduced level. The dome was nearly transparent, with stars clearly visible in what looked like a twilight sky. A few unmanned transports drove by, no doubt powered by individual fuel cells, but for the most part, people were just standing around, waiting for the next horrible thing to happen.

The high-rise where Rhap lived faced the central square. Gus had realized it earlier, that the drone she'd followed to Mama's House had come out of Rhap's building. Gus used her maneuvering jets to land gently in front of Rhap's building, which raised shouts of concern from a group of people in the square, and a little girl screamed.

She supposed that to people who'd never seen an armor jock up close, she must look like their worst nightmare: an armored drone. She undid the latches that held her helmet in place. Her shoulder twinged, reminding her that one of the shotgun pellets had breached a vulnerable spot on her armor, but she ignored the discomfort. She had something more important to do now.

She needed to let these civilians know that she wasn't going to hurt them.

She took her helmet off and held it in one hand. The civilians stared at her, open mouthed, and the little girl who'd screamed retreated behind her mother, holding fast to her mother's legs.

"I'm not going to hurt you," Gus said. "I'm here to help."

"You can't be here," one of the older men in the group said. "I know what you are, and if I know, security knows. You're going to get us all killed!"

She couldn't tell these people that the defense grid was dead and gone. With only emergency power working, these people were already on edge. It didn't take much for panicked civilians to turn into a mob. If she told them all the security drones were piles of smoking rubble, she might as well just tell them to get on with the looting. Societies needed some sort of security force, just not an overzealous mechanized one that cared more about enforcing arbitrary edicts than saving people's lives.

"They're a little busy right now," she said instead.

"Then why are you here?" the same man demanded.

Gus gestured with her head toward Rhap's building. "To check on *La Meilleure*."

"Are you going to make sure she's okay?" one of the women in the group asked.

Something like that, not that Gus could say that out loud. "All part of the service," she said instead.

"Because we need her," the woman said. "She's the only one who can fix this."

"She'll get the place back on its feet," another man said.

"Just you wait and see." This remark was made to the group in general, not to Gus. The rest of the group nodded and made sounds of agreement.

Well, wasn't that something. These people had convinced themselves they actually needed Rhap. In fact, Gus could almost feel the tension in the group begin to wind down. The cavalry in the form of one lone armor jock was here, and their leader would save them. Who knew? Maybe Rhap had, in her own skudged-up way.

Even the little girl finally poked her head out from behind her mother to look at Gus, her eyes wide and seemingly too big in her small face. "Fluffy died," she said.

Gus felt her features soften. If her life had been different, she might have been a grandmother by now with a granddaughter like this little girl. Hell, Gus might actually *be* a grandmother. Her son's wife had been pregnant and pretty far along at that when she and Drake had left Shepard's Moon. Not that her son knew she was his mother. He'd grown up without her in his life, and she wouldn't upend that life now. He was a good man. He'd make a good father. And if she never knew her grandchild? That was a price she was willing, if not happy, to pay.

"I'm sorry to hear about Fluffy," she said to the little girl.

The girl's mother patted her daughter's hair, then turned toward Gus. "It was her AI. We gave it the image of a cat, and she named it Fluffy. But when the power dimmed out?" The woman shrugged. "All non-essential services were cut."

So bye-bye Fluffy.

Gus hadn't given much thought about what destroying the power source would mean to the civilians in the central dome beyond hoping the dome's systems would keep them alive. She was willing to bet that Drake hadn't either.

"I'll see if *La Meilleure* can do something about that," Gus said.

The little girl gave her a grim smile, an expression far too adult on such a young face. "Thank you," the girl said solemnly. "You're a good machine."

"Person," Gus said. "I'm just a person who wears a machine when I go to work."

A simplistic but essentially accurate description of being an armor jock.

The girl's mother gave Gus a tight smile of her own, then she shepherded her daughter toward a larger group of adults that had gathered near one of the kiosks.

Now it was time to pay that visit to Rhapsody.

Gus's armor wouldn't fit through the front doors that opened onto the atrium of Rhapsody's building, so she busted through the windows that made up one wall in Rhapsody's apartment.

After the hassle she'd had getting inside Mama's House, Gus half expected Rhap's apartment to be shielded with the same stuff. But the glass broke easily enough when Gus punched through it with one fist. The rest of it broke against her armor when she walked inside.

Rhap was sitting on one of her leather sofas. She was twirling a multi-jointed ornate knife in a complicated pattern. Twirl and she held it open, pointy end out. Another twirl and the two parts of the handle closed around the blade.

Gus didn't miss that the blade was smeared with dried blood. She also didn't miss the dead body by the front door, or the bank of holoscreens behind what had previously been just a weapons wall. One of the holoscreens was displaying a star chart. Another one displayed a long-shot view of the hellscape where the weapons tower had been.

Rhap must have watched the weapons tower's destruction from the comfort of her apartment. *After* she'd killed the man who'd tried to kill her. A small laser pistol lay on the floor next to him.

"About time you got here," Rhap said, her accent thick like it had been when she'd first greeted them what seemed like ages ago.

Gus took a few steps into the apartment. She certainly didn't need to check vitals on the dead man by the front door—was that Ezekiel? It certainly looked like him—to confirm he was quite dead. The pool of blood around the body was a pretty sufficient clue.

What the hell had happened here?

"I'm guessing that's your handiwork?" Gus said, giving a brief nod of her head toward the dead man.

Rhap circled the point of her knife at the overhead lights, currently barely on. The holoscreens were at full power though. Separate power source, most likely.

"And that would be yours, *Gray Lady*?" Rhap asked.

"That would be Drake's, actually." Although Rhap had to know that, if she'd been watching. Gus wanted to ask if she had seen Drake since the weapons tower blew, but she wouldn't give the woman the satisfaction of knowing she might have information Gus didn't. "The fact that those security drones of yours haven't blown you to bits for committing murder?" Gus said. "*That* would be mine."

"They were not *my* drones."

Rhap spat out the words with so much venom that it surprised Gus. It also spoke volumes about what had been going on here. Rhap really had been a victim of the defense grid as much as the civilians outside.

"Tor's then, right?" Gus asked.

"Tor's," Rhap said.

"And I'm guessing you knew about the biotoxin too." Gus didn't make it a question. She didn't have to. She got her answer from the expression on Rhap's face.

"Did you destroy it?" Rhap asked.

Gus was tired, suddenly very very tired of the whole mess. "What do you think?" she snapped.

"*I* think you destroyed everything," Rhap said, twirling the knife to close it again. "That is what a good soldier does. Destroys everything in their way."

"No, a *good soldier* follows orders. I haven't been a good soldier in a very long time."

But Rhap already knew that too. In fact, she'd been counting on it. Gus had been right about this woman all along.

Rhap reached beneath her caftan and slipped the knife into a leather holster strapped to one surprisingly muscular calf. "And a mother protects her children."

Gus's breath hitched. Rhap had known not only that Gus was looking Tor, but *why*.

Rhap knew about her son. That was one thing Gus hadn't counted on.

"Do not worry," Rhap said, standing up. "I will not tell anyone your secret."

"Until you need another favor, right? Then you'll threaten to ruin his life?" Gus had to remind herself she'd promised herself not to hurt this woman, but right now she was sorely tempted.

"You must think so little of me, *chér*." Rhap walked over to the broken window, being careful not to get her sandaled feet close to the shards of glass on the floor. "I was a mother once myself."

Gus blinked. Drake had never mentioned *that*.

"He does not know," Rhap said, almost like she'd read Gus's thoughts. "It happened long ago. Meph, he…the child would be grown now, but he would want to meet her. It is better that he not know."

A grown child. That meant Drake wasn't the father. At least Rhap hadn't kept *that* from him.

Rhap shot Gus a look. "Can we agree on that?"

Gus shook her head. "We don't keep secrets from each other." Lies of omission were as poisonous to a relationship as outright betrayal.

"Pity."

"Is that why the two of you ended? Because you kept secrets from him?" Gus had wondered what had been the final straw, the thing that made Drake break free once this woman had sunk her claws deep into his tender heart.

Rhap chuffed out a laugh that had not a single bit of humor behind it. "You are surprisingly naïve for such a fierce woman," she said. "He did not know that I kept secrets, or if he did, he did not care." She gave Gus a side-ways look. "He did not care about much of anything. The

Meph I knew was a broken man hiding his pain behind a lack of ambition, always singing me his horrible songs. So I hurt him in a way I knew he could never forgive." She turned her gaze back to the broken window. "I smashed his guitar. He had made the mistake, you see, of telling me it had been a gift from his son."

Gus's blood ran cold. Drake's son had freaking *died* and this woman had destroyed one of the few things Drake had left of his child?

Gus had met a few psychopathic people in her life. People who lacked any degree of empathy and no more regard for other people's pain than they would for an insect's. Some of them were Alliance officers. Tor was one too, but he was a sniveling amateur compared to this woman. Drake had shared his *bed* with her, and she'd hurt him this way? Gus really wanted to take Rhap's knife away from her and plunge it in her throat.

But she couldn't. Drake had found it inside himself to forgive this woman. It would take Gus a while to do the same thing, but if Drake could do it, so could she.

She just might have to punch something first.

Rhap kept gazing out at the central square. The pose seemed calculated. So did her thoughtful expression.

Was she still trying to manipulate Gus? Had she told Gus the story about the guitar to see how far she could push Gus around before she broke? *Did* she even have a grown child out there somewhere? Or was that just an attempt to create a shared bond between two women who were... what? *Using* Drake for their own purposes?

Or was it all simply an attempt to distract her?

Gus needed to get her mind back on track. The battle for

Chrysallix might be over, but it was just one battle in Gus's war against Jorritz Tor.

"So where is he?" Gus asked. "Tor. Where is he?"

"Not here," Rhap said. She glanced toward the top of the dome. "Out there somewhere. Setting up another little kingdom, no doubt."

Now she turned to glare at the body by the door.

"He planned to replace me, you know," she said. "With that—"

She made a sharp gesture with one hand and said a word that Gus didn't understand, but she could guess it had to be about the worst curse Rhap could come up with.

"Now he has no one to take my place," Rhap said. "No puppet to control."

Suddenly Rhap's attempts to manipulate her made perfect sense to Gus.

This woman, this master manipulator, had herself been manipulated by a man she'd trusted. She'd probably trusted Ezekiel to do a lot of the grunt work that went hand in hand with governing a planet. Rhap must not have seen his betrayal coming, and she needed to prove to herself that she was still the same woman she believed herself to be. A woman who could appeal to—and control—everyone around her if she so chose. She needed to be in control, and manipulating people was the way she'd always done it.

Well, there was another way.

"They need you, you know," Gus said. "The people out there." She gestured with her head toward the downtown square beyond the busted window. "They believe in you."

"Do they?"

Rhap's question seemed sincere.

"People need a leader," Gus said. Hell, even the armor jocks of the 83rd had needed squadron leaders. "For better or worse, you're it. So stop hiding in your skudging apartment cooking more food than you can possibly eat and *be* their leader. Their *La Meilleure*. Or get the hell off the planet and let them find a new leader. One who'll actually do the work herself."

That struck home. Anger flared in Rhap's green eyes.

Good.

"And you, *Gray Lady?*" The sneer in Rhap's voice was unmistakable. "What are *you* going to do?"

Gus didn't need to answer the question, but she did anyway.

"Hunt down that skudging piece of shit Tor and finish this, once and for all," she said.

Right after she figured out what had happened to Drake.

CHAPTER 29

After breaching the floor of the power source reactor chamber, the *Golden Void* punched her way through several meters of concrete, blowing open a rugged passage with continuous, heavy fire from her laser and projectile weapons.

The ship eventually emerged into a cavernous open space some distance below the collapsing reactor chamber and weapons spire. As Bruce shut down the guns, Drake took in the view on the main screen—and quickly realized the treasure they had come upon.

Bruce was even smarter than Drake had given him credit for. In leading the ship to safety just as the reactor chamber blew, he'd flown straight into a facility that was right at the top of Drake's list of Things He Most Wanted to Destroy.

It was all spread out around them in the vast cavern— massive pieces of equipment, automated machinery, and epic banks of computers to control the whole enterprise. Even though they'd blown up the reactor, the machinery and computers here still seemed to be working just fine.

Of course. Tor wouldn't chance that this place could be shut down by problems with something as unstable as a pulsar reactor.

Cherry red molten metal bubbled and smoked in enormous vats. The vats tipped, pouring streams of the superheated substance into channels and molds. Showers of cold water rushed down from nozzle arrays, dousing the liquefied metal and causing it to cool and harden in shapes and sheets. The hardened shapes and sheets—all bearing a familiar silvery sheen—were scooped up by robotic lifters and loaded into stacks on huge pallets for storage and eventual delivery.

"It's the singularium refinery." There was no doubt in Drake's mind as to what he was seeing. "This is Tor's secret skudging refinery."

Thinking about it, he realized the location was perfect. Situated under the reactor chamber, the refinery was perfectly positioned to tap that power source when necessary (before its demolition)—yet still tucked away, hidden from the eyes of everyone except the most determined observers. It was so safe, in fact, he wondered if there might not be any security measures in place to protect it. At a glance, he certainly didn't see any...so maybe he could attack the facility unopposed, wiping away this instrument of Tor's tyranny without facing more fleets of drones or arrays of anti-aircraft countermeasures.

There was just one complication that came to mind. Missiles would have been the perfect weapons to bomb the refinery with—but he had already used up all the *Void*'s missiles in destroying the pulsar reactor.

"We need to blow this place to bits," he said, mind racing through possible strategies that didn't involve missiles. "I don't want to leave a single piece intact that that bastard Tor could somehow put to use."

"An admirable goal, Captain," said Bruce. "Any action that reduces the possibilities for chaos-inducing violence in this quadrant is an action worth taking."

"So here's what I'm thinking." As Drake spoke, he twisted knobs and flipped switches on the weapons console, getting ready to implement the plan taking shape in his brain. "What would happen if we apply magno-beams to a vat of that liquefied singularium down there?"

"Good question." Bruce paused so long that Drake began to think the question was beyond the AI's capabilities. "According to my calculations," Bruce said finally, "it would likely create an electromagnetic effect leading to a catastrophic exothermic reaction."

"A big bang, in other words." Drake smiled grimly as he continued tweaking controls. "I like the sound a' that, partner."

"I thought you might," said Bruce. "Just keep in mind, once that reaction spreads through the refinery, we will have very limited time to escape the inevitable finale."

"There's an escape route?" Drake hadn't noticed one in his cursory scans of the cavern.

"A shipping conduit, yes. It should lead us all the way back aboveground, quite some distance from here, in fact. Assuming it isn't somehow obstructed."

Of course. Tor wouldn't want anyone to notice his off-world shipments either.

"Then that's where we're headed after we light this place up," said Drake. "Keep a bead on it, y'hear? I really need to go see my Gray Lady after this is all over."

"Roger that," said Bruce.

"Glad we're on the same page." Drake made a few more adjustments, then punched the button to take manual control of navigation. "Now hold on tight, amigo."

"But the autopilot—"

"Relax." Drake grinned as he stomped the accelerator. "You'll get the wheel back soon enough."

The *Void* jolted downward, heading for the nearest vat of molten metal. Thankfully, no defensive weaponry got in the way—no drones or missiles or gun emplacements.

Watching between the main viewer and tactical display, Drake saw the vat get closer fast. Even as he spun the steering wheel, swinging the ship in a descending arc toward the container of bubbling red liquid, he readied the magno-beam for action, adjusting the controls to maximize the beam's impact and the reaction that would result.

As soon as the *Void* swooped within range, he pegged the thrusters to hold position and opened fire with the magno-beam. The rippling stream of magnetic force came down dead center in the heart of the vat, instantly intensifying the bubbling action at the point of splashdown.

Holding there, he watched as the magno-beam did its work, agitating the molten metal with increasing force. It swirled and bubbled and sloshed, rocking the huge vat in its cradle, knocking it back and forth.

Finally, the metal spun upward, changing color from

cherry red to orange. When it suddenly shifted to white, the whirling spout of singularium flared brightly...and its light continued to intensify.

"The exothermic reaction has started," announced Bruce.

But Drake knew that. He had already cut the magnobeam, chucked the steering wheel hard to port, and crushed the accelerator pedal, sending the *Void* leaping away from the vat.

"The reaction is building faster than expected to catastrophic levels," said Bruce.

"Where's the damn *escape conduit*?" asked Drake.

"I just sent you coordinates." As Bruce said it, they flashed up on the main nav screen. "I can fly us there myself, if you want."

Drake smiled as he punched in the numbers and the ship launched toward the conduit at the base of the far wall of the cavern. On the aft view screen, he saw the molten singularium blasting out of the first vat and spraying in all directions, its white heat setting more chain reactions in motion wherever it came in contact with additional reservoirs of liquefied metal.

There was an explosion, then another...then the biggest of all, its shockwave buffeting the *Void* on its race to safety.

Drake nodded, satisfied that Tor's little masterpiece, the secret weapon and keystone behind his Frontier empire, was not long for this world. He heard another blast, felt another shockwave, saw tons of equipment burst into fiery shards on the aft view screen.

Then, the ship shot into the conduit, escaping just as the

entire cavern became an inferno of white-hot metal and melting infrastructure.

"Yee-hawww!" shouted Drake, heart pounding with excitement as he got away by the skin of his proverbial teeth...*again.*

This was what he lived for...this, and the love of his Gray Lady.

CHAPTER 30

The *Golden Void* had no problem getting clearance to land at the spaceport this time. The only holdup was waiting for all the traffic *leaving* the central dome to get out of the way.

A lot of visitors—smugglers and traders and nearly reputable dealers—not to mention a bucketload of residents, had decided to set off for greener pastures. Or at least less dangerous ones. Gus didn't blame them. The Frontier was lousy with planets that hadn't just been ground zero in a war most of the people inside the central dome hadn't even known was being fought. Most of those worlds weren't as highly developed as Chrysallix, but people who settled in the Frontier tended to be on the tough side. They just weren't suicidal.

On top of the cuts in power, the earthquake had probably been the last straw.

When Drake blew the singularium refinery, shockwaves had rocked the entire planetoid. Apparently the residents of

Chrysallix had never experienced an earthquake of that magnitude before. At least the dome was still intact. But with power at a fraction of its prior capacity for the foreseeable future—Drake had blown the central power supply to kingdom come too when he'd taken out the weapons tower —Chrysallix wasn't looking like such a safe bet to hang around much less set down roots. People were leaving in droves.

Gus winced as the *Void* came to a stop at the same dock they'd used last time the ship had landed here. The ship was covered in scorch marks and burn scars and a few new gouges marred its hull, but the little cargo ship was still blessedly intact.

She felt like patting its poor scorched hull plating and telling it that it had done good.

The forward hatch opened and Drake, her laconic space cowboy, *raced* down the gangplank toward her. He swept her up in a hug so tight she thought he might break her ribs, swung her around, and then kissed the stuffing out of her. Right there in the terminal.

"Hello to you too," she said when she managed to catch her breath.

He'd set her down—when had he managed to do that? All she could remember was the kiss—and now he was stroking one hand through her short hair. The naked relief she saw in his eyes melted her.

"Had to make sure you still fit in these arms, darlin'," he said.

She grinned at him. "And?"

"You fit just fine."

As if to prove it, he twirled her around again until she couldn't help but laugh.

That laughter felt damn good.

All around them the terminal was a hive of activity. Bots were loading cargo onto nearby ships, and people were shouting at each other while techs ran around refueling ships and conducting last-minute inspections, none of it orderly or calm. The walkways between docks were jam-packed with frantic people, all of them pushing each other in their desperate need to get the hell off the plant. Gus thought she caught sight of the little girl she'd spoken to in the square only a short time before, but the child was lost in a throng of civilians boarding a transport ship before she could be sure.

So much for trusting that *La Meilleure* would make everything right. Rhap was going to have her work cut out for her.

Speaking of that bitch Rhap...

"You want to go say your goodbyes before we leave?" Gus asked.

Drake had finally responded to her comms after his narrow escape from the singularium refinery. The shipping conduit he'd used to escape the imploding refinery had coughed him out so far away that it took him nearly an hour to make it back to the central dome's spaceport. They'd spent the time updating each other on the results of their separate battles. It turned out that they'd made two pretty good armies of one, but Gus hoped they'd never have to do that again. They made a much better army of two, each one protecting the other's back.

Although from what Drake had told her, the renamed AI had made a pretty decent co-pilot and weapons officer.

One thing they'd both agreed on: they wanted to leave Chrysallix as soon as possible. They had enough supplies to last a good long while, thanks to the generosity of the original Bruce (with monetary contributions from that skudge-hole Earl). Gus had told Rhap about the cache of power cells at Mama's House—the central dome was going to need all the power it could get until they got a new power plant up and running—but she hadn't told Rhap about all the weapons. Rhap and her people would find the weapons eventually, and Gus wanted to be far away from Chrysallix when she did.

"Nope," Drake said, answering her question.

"You sure? I could get some simple repairs out of the way before you get back."

His expression turned serious. "The only person I want to see is right here," he said. "Madame Buttercup's in the past, right where she belongs."

Gus could definitely live with that. And it seemed like Drake could as well.

He kissed her again, then looked over her shoulder at the cart where she'd loaded her armor along with a little something extra. "That all the cargo you plan on bringing on board?" he asked.

"Cargo?" He hadn't called her armor *cargo* since she'd first hired him back on Depak Station. Of course, the last time she'd left the *Void* she'd been wearing her armor. "I think I'm insulted."

His eyes glinted with mischievous good humor. "Would I ever do a thing like that?"

"Not unless you want to say goodbye to a few more feather pillows," she said, lifting an eyebrow in mock challenge.

He smirked at her. "Oh, so that's how it's gonna be now."

She gave him a good smirk of her own in return. "We *do* happen to have an almost brand-new replicator on board."

"That we do, darlin'," he said. "Wanna go try it out?"

That was the best offer she'd had all day. Not that she was going to tell *him* that.

"I don't know," she said, drawing the words out for effect. "I do have an awful lot of scorch marks to buff off my armor. I'd hate to put it away dirty."

He growled at her. He actually *growled.*

Then he picked her up and slung her over his shoulder, and proceeded to carry her up the gangplank into the ship.

"Hey!" she said. "You know how undignified this is?"

"Quiet," he said, but she could hear the grin in his voice even though all she could see was his rear end. He was enjoying this far too much.

"You know, I know about a hundred different ways to disable you right about now," she said. In reality, she knew more than that. She'd had to learn and learn fast how to take care of herself against much bigger male opponents thanks to being the only female armor jock in her squadron back when she'd been with the 83rd. Hand-to-hand combat had been part of her training.

She hadn't had to *use* any of those moves in over a decade, but she was pretty sure she could flip Drake on his ass if she put her mind to it.

"But would you *want* to?" said Drake.

Good question. "I wouldn't want to break anything *important*," she said. "Something that might come in handy."

He chuckled.

To her surprise, she found herself laughing along with him.

This was all part of a game. A playful way to blow off steam. To thumb their noses at the fact that either one of them could have died mere hours ago. They were celebrating being alive. And in a few minutes, they'd celebrate in a much more intense, much more *loving* way beneath that feather comforter of his. In fact, they might celebrate for hours, take a breather, and celebrate again.

That's what people did who were happy to be alive and in love with each other.

She wouldn't have it any other way.

Gus was ridiculously happy and more than just a bit worn out by the time the two of them finally blasted off from Chrysallix. Her shoulder wound was patched up, and her armor was safely stowed in the cargo bay along with the little something extra she'd brought on board: one of the boxy shield generators on the roof at Mama's House. She hoped that between the three of them—herself, Drake, *and* Bruce the AI—they'd be able to figure out how the thing worked. A shield like that might come in handy in the coming battle with Tor.

Wherever the skudging coward might be hiding now. The Frontier was one damn big place.

She sat in the chair at the nav console on the bridge scrolling through the *Void's* star charts looking for possibilities. Earl—the person, not the formerly named ship's AI—had said he got his supply of singularium from a smuggler named Layla Crosscut who'd come to The Bluff looking to trade. She'd claimed she'd found it on a shipwreck out near the border. If she'd traded it to Earl, she must not have known its true value.

Tor would be looking for another source of singularium. The easiest way to track him down was to find the other source first. The first place to start was to find Layla Crosscut and ask her exactly where she'd found that shipwreck. The border was one damn big area of space.

If Gus hadn't been cut off from the Alliance's network, she could have found Crosscut easy enough. Most smugglers eventually had a run-in with the Alliance a time or two, and like any bureaucracy, the Alliance kept a record of *everything*. She might even have been able to find information on the shipwreck.

But out here? Gus had to figure out where a smuggler who made regular runs to The Bluff might be headed.

She could have asked the ship's AI to run the search and give her probabilities, but Drake had Bruce running systems checks to make sure everything on the *Void* was working fine. Drake could have done the checks himself, but he was currently sprawled in his pilot's chair, strumming away and humming a tune she'd never heard before. He had a ridiculously content expression on his face.

Her heart filled to overflowing every time she looked at him. Was this love? Oh *hell* yeah.

And because she loved him, she'd never volunteer any of her last conversation with Rhap. If he asked, she'd tell him. She still didn't believe in lies by omission. But he'd gotten over what Rhap had done to him. He'd even managed to find another antique guitar somewhere. And he was happy. That was the most important thing. Her man was happy, and she intended to do everything in her power not to let anyone ever hurt him like that again.

"Captain." Bruce's voice over the ship's internal comm system interrupted her thoughts. "Systems checks complete. The ship is running at optimum for a ship of this type."

Gus raised an eyebrow and Drake stopped strumming.

"Did I detect a bit of sarcasm there, good buddy?" Drake asked.

"Not at all," the AI said. "I was merely implying—"

"I've got a hint for you," Gus said, interrupting the AI. "Never insult a captain's ship."

"Or an armor jock's armor," Drake added.

Gus could have sworn she heard the AI sniff through a nose that didn't exist. "Understood."

Drake shook his head. "What exactly did you tinker with to give good ol' Bruce this personality?" he asked her.

That was just the thing. She hadn't. The only thing she'd tinkered with lately on the ship had been the swooshing sound effects on the doors because she'd thought it would be fun to sneak up on Drake when he wasn't looking.

She shrugged her shoulders. "All I did was change the name."

"Huh." Drake put his guitar down. "Hey Bruce, can I ask where you got your personality from?"

"Captain?" The AI sounded genuinely confused.

"I didn't program in a personality," Gus said. "So how come you're...you?"

"Ah." Another pause, and this time Gus thought she heard gears turning, which was just ridiculous. AIs didn't have gears. Even the replicator didn't have gears. "I seem to have a preprogrammed response to any queries regarding the quality and manner of my interaction with the inhabitants of the cargo vessel *Golden Void*. Would you like to hear the response?"

Drake shared a look with Gus and tilted his head to the side. She shrugged in response. If someone was screwing with them by messing with the ship's AI, better to find out now instead of in the middle of a fight with Tor himself.

Drake shook his head. "Let's hear it."

The AI's voice took on a musical quality, as if it was speaking in chords. "A parting gift for a game well played."

All the holoscreens on the bridge abruptly sprang to life. Every single one displayed a yellow smiley face.

Drake barked out a laugh. "I'll be a son of a bitch."

The Fluke.

The damn Fluke had gifted them with an enhanced AI.

"I guess this means you're famous in Flukeland, wherever that is," Gus said.

"*We're* famous," Drake said. "And I think Flukeland is wherever the Fluke happen to be at the time."

The smiley faces disappeared as abruptly as they'd sprung to life.

"Did the response play as requested?" the AI asked, this time in his normal voice.

Drake picked up his guitar. "You could say that, Bruce."

Bruce. Gus wouldn't be changing the AI's name anytime soon. It had a personality now. And enhanced abilities too, from what Drake had told her about the battle at the weapons tower and inside the power complex. Maybe it could figure out where Tor was hiding, so she asked it.

"Difficult to say without additional data regarding the location of alternate sources of singularium," Bruce said. "But if I may make an observation, the location of alternate sources of singularium is irrelevant. Tor will undoubtedly seek you out."

"Why?" Drake's question was sharp and to the point. "He can't think we'd make good little puppets for one of his worlds."

"The two of you have thwarted him at every turn," said Bruce. "You have negated decades of his work."

"He'll want revenge for that," Gus said. She was an expert when it came to revenge. Tor had to be seething right about now.

They couldn't fight him off with just the *Void* and her armor. They'd been lucky on Chrysallix. They'd fought against incredible odds, but their opponents had been drones and weapons programs. Tor would hire mercenaries who were used to fighting outside the box.

"We're gonna need a home base," she said.

"We're gonna need a home base *and* some friends," Drake said.

The AI cleared its throat. "Captain? If I might make a suggestion?"

"Let 'er rip, Bruce," Drake said.

And the AI Gus had named after a special young man, an arms dealer who'd extended an open invitation to come back and see him anytime, said, "I think I might know just the place."

ABOUT THE AUTHORS

A prolific, versatile, and award-winning writer, **Annie Reed** has written more short fiction than she can count. She's a frequent contributor to both *Pulphouse Fiction Magazine* and *Mystery, Crime and Mayhem*. She's received a Silver Honorable Mention from Writers of the Future, and her stories have appeared in numerous annual year's best mystery volumes. She's even had a story selected for inclusion in study materials for Japanese college entrance exams. Her *Unexpected* series of short-story collections showcase some of her best work.

Her longer works include the superhero origin novel *Faster*, novellas *The Wizard Behind the Curtain* and *In Dreams*, and mystery novels *Pretty Little Horses*, *Paper Bullets*, and *A Death in Cumberland*.

Annie writes mystery, science fiction, and fantasy under her own name and writes suspense as Kris Sparks. She also writes the sweet romance *Liberty Springs* novels under the name Liz McKnight. She can be found on the web at anniereed.wordpress.com.

Robert Jeschonek is an envelope-pushing, *USA Today* bestselling author whose fiction, comics, and non-fiction have been published around the world. His stories have appeared in *Clarkesworld, Galaxy's Edge, StarShipSofa, Pulphouse,* and many other publications. He has written official *Star Trek* and *Doctor Who* fiction and has scripted comics for DC, AHOY, and others. His young adult slipstream novel, *My Favorite Band Does Not Exist,* won the Forward National Literature Award and was named one of *Booklist's* Top Ten First Novels for Youth. He also won an International Book Award, a Scribe Award for Best Original Novel, and the grand prize in Pocket Books' Strange New Worlds contest. Visit him online at www.bobscribe.com. You can also find him on Facebook and follow him as @TheFictioneer on X (Twitter) and @bobscribe.bsky.social on Bluesy. Subscribe to the Blastoff Books Newsletter: http://newsletter.blastoff books.net/.